THE END OF LIBERTY

WAR ETERNAL, BOOK TWO

M.R. FORBES

Quirky
Algorithms

Published by Quirky Algorithms
Seattle, Washington

Cover illustrations by Tom Edwards
tomedwardsdesign.com

XENO-1

Where did it come from? Damned if anyone knew. Space, sure. That much was never in doubt. Alien? Of course. The whole time the world was fighting over it, the scientists were wondering. Asking questions. Trying to work it out. If an alien craft had crashed on planet Earth, it meant that us humans weren't alone, and that there was something out there that was more advanced, more evolved, and maybe more intelligent. Definitely more intelligent, if television those days was any judge.

How many times did they call for the fighting to stop? How many times did they ask the right questions, and worry about what the tech could do for humankind, instead of what it could do for this or that nation? How many times did they wonder, loud and in public, if the aliens who lost the ship would ever come along, trying to find it?

The fighting did end, of course. Those very same scientists did get their crack at the wreckage. It didn't take long for them to begin to unravel the secrets. It was all there in ones and zeroes. In the simple, glorious, holy and universal language of math.

It was as if God had sent the ship Himself and spoke unto the masses, "thou shalt discover the stars."

- Paul Frelmund, "XENO-1"

[1]

Major Christine Arapo crouched against the inner wall of the building, holding her M97 carbine tight against her chest. Her hair was disheveled, her forehead was sweating, her arms were bare and dirty. Almost every inch of her was covered in some measure of blood and grime.

None of it was hers.

A tight beam of clean light pierced the darkness of the space where she was hiding. They were searching for her, and getting closer.

She sniffled out softly to clear a bit of dust that was lodged in her nose, lifting the carbine a little higher so she could see the readout on the left side. She was down to fifty rounds. She knew the enemy had more than fifty soldiers.

A lot more than fifty.

She still wasn't completely sure what had happened. Every event from the moment she had rescued Mitchell from being outed as a fraud by Tamara King, to assisting him in escaping the reach of the UPA military police seemed almost like a dream to her, a waking dream where she could observe her actions in a strange, millisecond delayed hindsight. She was only able to question them once it was too late to do anything about it.

She knew it was still her. Her decisions. Her control. She didn't regret what she had done. When the MPs had come for her to take her in for questioning, she hadn't offered excuses. She had let them bind her hands and take her back to base, past the blown-out entrance to the hotel's basement where a number of Liberty's finest had died.

At Mitchell's hand.

Because she had helped him get away. Because she had to.

There was nothing random about what Mitchell had done or what she had done. It wasn't an isolated incident, a beginning and an end.

It was only the beginning.

They had brought her back to the Space Marine base in York. They had placed her under guard. General Cornelius had come to her a few hours later, begging her for answers. Why had she, with the spotless record and the multiple commendations, with all of the trust and respect and power of UPA Command ready to back her up, helped a suspected rapist and proven fraud escape justice?

She risked a smile at the thought. Justice? There was none. Not here. Not now.

Christine watched the beam of light sweep across the floor in front of her. It was made of polished stone, and the light made too many shadows and reflections against it. She was motionless, breathless, her eyes shifting back and forth, searching for any sign that she might be revealed in it.

She could hear the boots now, the slightly off step of soldiers in light exo casing the area in tight formation. She shifted her arms, bringing the muzzle of the coilgun down and aiming it towards the sounds. Her finger eased onto the trigger. She was at enough of a disadvantage to be without the mechanical musculature that enhanced their strength and speed. She was also without her p-rat, having disabled it during her escape from the York barracks. She didn't know how she knew which tools to grab from Medical, or how to use them on herself to break the link between the small computer and the secondary implant in her brain. She just did.

There hadn't been any time to wonder about it since.

Once she had gotten away from the base, it had been easy to blend in with the crowd. Disappearing was one of her simpler skills in a much wider array. She had thought to stay in York, to track communications and try to determine where Mitchell had gone and if there was any way she could reach him. She had thought to continue her own personal research, driven by a curiosity that had plagued her for as long as she could remember, as though that would somehow get her out of the mess she had found herself in.

Artificial intelligence. It was hardly a new concept. In fact, it was one that had been conquered by humankind years ago. The skies of York were policed by self-regulating drones, the streets navigated by autonomous vehicles. Most households had a service bot of some kind or other, and even the military used AI to good effect. Such research was more akin to a history lesson.

Except...

Anti-AI sentiment was growing across the Alliance, a new revolution stirring. Tasks that had long ago been abandoned by people and turned over to learning machines were being reverted to their former handlers. New advances were being lambasted in the media and discouraged at all levels of the scientific community. "The return of the golden age," some had claimed.

Christine didn't trust it. She didn't believe in it. Her instincts and her training told her that the sentiments were misplaced. That the collective consciousness was being misdirected. Why? To what end? She didn't know. She was certain there was something to find there, something to learn.

Something important.

The soldiers were getting close. Too close to avoid being spotted if she remained. Christine slid along the wall, back towards the open lift shaft she had spotted on her way in. She was deliberate with every step, careful to stay quiet and keep from finding herself bathed in the light. She had the carbine ready in case it was needed.

She nearly tripped over a body, cursing in silence for not identifying the obstacle earlier. A civilian, a white-haired woman in a suit. They had killed her because she didn't have an implant, and she was too old to be useful for anything else.

She had only been back in York for a day when the madness had started. When David Avalon, Prime Minister of the Delta Quadrant, had made a surprise appearance on Tamara King's stream and declared martial law. When the combined force of the military and law enforcement units from around the globe had started rounding up civilians.

She had been curious at the announcement, and as eager as any of the other residents of the planet for answers.

Then she watched one police officer shoot another in the head at point-blank range.

Then she had seen the people wandering from their homes, their meals, their jobs, out into the street and away in perfect lockstep.

Then the military had moved in on the ones, like her, who remained. The ones who didn't have an implant.

Or had disabled it.

They grabbed the adults and killed the children and elderly. Without conscience. Without remorse. They swept through York like a tide, leaving the city a nearly empty shell and searching for the stragglers who had avoided them.

Stragglers like Christine.

From a dark corner at the top of a thirty-story building, she had seen the growing light in the sky, blue flame and liquid metal descending towards the city center.

She knew it then. She felt it for the first time she could ever remember. It was a feeling she had avoided during her first live-fire exercise, her first drop into an enemy war zone, her first run in full exo across a verified ambush point. A feeling she had even brushed aside the first time she shared a bed with a strange man in a strange place because that was what the mission required. A feeling that had always existed at the fringe of her understanding but had never truly made itself known.

Fear.

They had come.

[2]

SHE REACHED THE LIFT SHAFT, craning her neck to see in. The power had gone out two days ago, the mains shut down and the backups failing. They were still damaged from the Federation's earlier assault on the planet. The lifts had followed protocol, dropping to the base of the shaft and leaving nothing but a smooth square tunnel above them.

It wasn't a good escape route. There was nowhere to go but down, and she had thought hiding out on the fourth floor would be safer. That there was no way they could find her with so many places to search.

She had thought wrong.

She had seen ships leaving the planet in the days after the strange one had arrived. Jumpships and transports laden with soldiers, being sent off to - where? Other planets in the Delta Quadrant? The Federation? The only thing she was certain of was that the soldiers, the police, even Tamara King and the Prime Minister, weren't in control of themselves. Watching the way the people had moved as one, the way those without augmented reality receivers had been gunned down, that much was clear.

Her eyes scanned the abandoned office, the darkness causing everything to take on an unfocused appearance. She needed somewhere to hide, some cover to protect her if she were discovered. She didn't want to be discovered. She was alone against so many.

The light swung towards the elevator, pausing a few feet from where she stood. She froze with her back at the edge of the shaft and slowly adjusted the position of the carbine, pointing it back towards the source of the beam. She kept hoping they would give up the hunt, call off the search, and move on. There were others still out there. Some of them were even fighting back. She could hear the gunfire and explosions. She had seen the mechs moving through the streets to combat them. Once people figured out the alternatives, resistance was inevitable.

It was also going to be short-lived. They couldn't stand up to an army. They couldn't pilot any of the heavier machines without an implant. The best they could do was shoot, run, hide, and repeat.

Christine had tried only to hide. To stay concealed and seek a way off of Liberty. There was no way off, she discovered. There was no way out. And they continued coming, continued seeking, continued closing in. It was as though they were looking for a single thing on the entire planet, a lonely star in a dangerous universe.

Her.

She wasn't sure of it, but the dogged pursuit had left her to wonder. Was it because of her role in Special Ops? Was it because she had high-level clearance? Did they know the work she had done in the shadowy corners of military propriety and legality? Did they know what she had been searching for?

Or did it have something to do with Mitchell?

She cursed under her breath when the light continued angling towards her, taking away the few options she had left. She fired the first of her fifty remaining darts through the corner of a wall and into the soldier behind it, continuing to wonder.

She had helped him escape, despite herself. She had even kissed him. Mitchell "Ares" Williams, the non-hero of the Battle for Liberty, a man she had found juvenile, irresponsible, and arrogant. A man whose judgment was based more on sex appeal than rational, civilized intelligence.

She crouched and turned, shifting her aim six inches to the left, firing a second round. The carbine was almost silent as it fired, save for the sonic boom of the dart as it left the barrel at high velocity. It tore through the wall and into a second soldier.

They were stupid to be moving in a standard formation. She didn't even need to see them to hit them.

Of course, Mitchell was handsome. And there was no way to deny that his aptitude as a pilot was at the top of the charts. His dossier suggested his intelligence was solid though she couldn't resolve the disconnect between the paper version and the real thing. But to kiss him? Maybe there was one thing she regretted from the dream-state she had been in.

Two more shots dropped two more soldiers. She still couldn't see them, guessing their position by sound and memory, thankful that the weapon she had managed to capture was up to the task. Even light exo made too much noise for the hunt.

She winced each time she heard a grunt, and then a thud. She was killing soldiers, her brothers and sisters who had no control over what they were doing. She reminded herself that they were slaves and that given a choice they would never want to remain that way.

She told herself she was doing them a favor.

Silence.

She didn't move, staying near the shaft and listening. No footsteps, no clattering, no signs of mechs outside the building. Her eyes traced the beam of light from where it had settled on a far wall back to the source, to the helmet of the soldier she had shot just below the lantern. Her dart had plunged through the armor, through the head, and out the other side.

It couldn't be that easy.

Could it?

She waited, counting breaths and listening. Once she reached one hundred, she started inching towards the downed soldier. She wanted his weapon, his ammo, his supplies. She would take as much as she could carry.

She was almost silent padding across the floor, keeping her carbine leveled, her finger on the trigger. She glanced out towards the windows that bordered the outer edge of the room. No light. No motion.

It took her ten minutes to cross the ten meters of distance. She didn't make or hear a sound. When she reached the bodies, she crouched low and examined the soldier's firearm. A standard issue assault rifle, a railgun with an adjustable dampening field at the end of the muzzle that could be used to change the projectile velocity. It was a good weapon for fighting in a range of theaters, including places where too much stopping power could be catastrophic.

It was a downgrade from the sheer brute force of the carbine, but an upgrade in terms of overall usefulness. It also had a full magazine, and two more rested on the grunt's belt.

She started reaching for it. Something in her mind told her it was a bad idea. This was too easy. Way too easy. She should know better. She should be smarter than this.

She pushed herself back with all the strength in her legs, turning and sprinting away. Stupid. She was so stupid.

The drone dropped to the window and opened fire, revealing itself behind the assault. Carbonate didn't shatter. First it melted and cracked, and then the projectiles broke through, turning the spot where she had been crouching, and the body she had left behind, into pulp.

She raced for the shaft, throwing her hand back and opening fire with the carbine, absorbing the stress of the recoil with her forearm. Her aim was non-existent, and she didn't think she was even close to hitting the wedge-shaped vehicle. It was getting closer to hitting her, the slugs chewing up the floor, getting close enough that the stone was chipping up and cutting into her ankles.

She saw the opening to the lift in front of her. There was nothing there but a four-story drop. Maybe she would survive the fall, but there was no way to escape with a pair of broken legs.

A bullet hit the ground an inch to her left, making the decision easier. She grunted as she threw herself forward, diving into the dark, gaping mouth of the shaft as the projectiles exploded the ground behind her.

Her body smacked into the smooth wall at the far side of the shaft and she began to fall.

[3]

"I don't believe it," Singh said. Her voice was a monotone whisper.

Mitchell watched the transport headed towards them, an uncontrollable smile growing across his face. "Origin, can you open a channel?"

"I am scanning," Origin said. "The ship's communications appear to be offline."

Offline? Mitchell's smile drooped a little. "That transport came from the Schism, the ship I was on."

"Are you certain it is the same one?"

It was growing larger ahead of them, still no more than a point of glinting light against a the backdrop of the asteroid belt. "The Tetron fired into the belt, right into the Schism." How could they have gotten away from that? "I don't know where else it could have come from."

"It's the same ship," Singh said.

Mitchell wanted to agree with her. He wanted the Riggers back. His Riggers. If they had to go back to Liberty, he wanted Shank and Cormac and the other grunts on the ground with him.

"Mitchell, nothing escapes a Tetron plasma stream."

"They could have escaped earlier," Singh said. "You were too busy getting us here to see the entire chase."

Singh was right. He didn't know what could have happened. All he knew was that the transport was headed their way. Even so, his early experiences with the enemy were already causing him to question everything. He had seen that they had no qualms about using every edge they could get. They had sent General Cornelius, Millie's father, to confront them here to force the Schism's captain to defy him, knowing full well he was going to wind up dead.

"Still nothing?" he asked as the transport grew closer. It was within a few thousand kilometers, taking a steady, straight path towards them. Soldiers in search of refuge? Or a weapon in disguise?

"No, Mitchell," Origin replied. "How shall I proceed?"

"Mitchell," Singh said.

The rogue Tetron had told him that this was humanity's war. His war. He didn't know how to fight when he couldn't trust anything around him. One leap of faith, and then another, until it was over. It was the only way.

"Bring the Goliath around so that the hangar is facing them," he said.

"If that ship is a Tetron weapon-"

"Do you know that it is? Can you scan it and tell me that it is?"

Origin shook his head. "A fusion bomb has no scannable signature."

"Then bring her around."

"As you say."

Mitchell turned with the rotation of the Goliath, the open view of space outside twisting and re-orienting in the control room. Singh did the same, her face a flat mask. A slight crease in the corner of her eyes was the only indication that she was nervous about the outcome.

"Major Long and his crew are going to love the Riggers," Mitchell said, watching the transport coming in. He sent knocks out through his p-rat. To Millie, to Shank, to Cormac, to Briggs, even to Watson.

There was no reply.

"They aren't answering my knocks," Singh said. She had the same thought he did. "I'm not so sure about this anymore."

"I can still raise the barrier," Origin said.

"No. Either they're with us or we're going to die."

"Mitchell, this war is for all of humanity, not one transport."

"I need people I can trust. I need help." Katherine's voice still echoed in his mind. They couldn't do this alone. "Without it, we're not going to win. Does it matter when we lose, if we still lose?"

The transport vanished from the sight of the cameras that displayed the scene outside the Goliath's thick hull. Mitchell noticed his heart was racing. He had won the first battle. Was he going to lose the second so soon after?

"The transport is entering the hangar," Origin said. "I am receiving a communication from the Valkyrie."

"Major Long can wait a minute. Singh, are you coming?"

"Yes, Mitchell."

Mitchell started towards the lift out of the control room. Origin moved to follow.

"Wait here," Mitchell said. "Get us into hyperspace and bring us close to Liberty, but not too close. I don't want to get blown up as soon as we fall back."

"As you say." Mitchell heard the tone of a knock on his p-rat. "I gained the encryption keys from Corporal Singh's subconscious. If you need me."

Mitchell paused. Was it that easy for the enemy to overcome their best attempt at security? There was so much about the Tetron that they still needed to learn.

They were on their way down when Origin knocked him again.

"The transport has landed. Hangar doors are closing. I have locked down both ships until you arrive."

Some of the hope began to return. At least the transport hadn't exploded.

Yet.

4

MITCHELL AND SINGH made their way back through the dim corridors of the Goliath, careful not to touch any of the branches of dendrites that made up the true form of the Tetron who called itself "Origin." As they walked, Mitchell noticed that the pulsing, liquid metallic limbs were shifting and moving, reorganizing themselves to clear a path for humans to travel through.

"I'm still struggling to make sense of all of this," Singh said. "This ship. The enemy. Origin. I thought I was going to die on the Schism, during some impossible mission or another."

"This mission doesn't sound impossible to you?"

"I don't know. You defeated the enemy ship."

"One ship. You didn't see what I saw on Liberty. The thing I showed you the pictures of is another Tetron. It's already claimed the planet and taken control of anyone there with an implant."

"Do we really have to go back?"

"Yes. You heard what Origin said. We got lucky fighting this one, brute force against brute force. I don't think we're going to get those kind of odds again. We need to know what she knows if we're going to even them out."

"I don't trust it."

"Origin?"

"Yes." She slowed their pace, moving herself closer to him and whispering. "I was in the engine room. The core, its core is there, pulsing lights and thousands of the branches. One of them wrapped around my arm." She shrugged. "That was all it took to control me. It uses charged particles like we use our fingers. Electrical signals that mimicked my nervous system and started sending the wrong commands. I didn't fight back because there was no part of me that even understood something was wrong. Not until it let me go. It has such an innate understanding of humans and how we work. I think it would be trivial for it to deceive us."

"I joined with it," Mitchell said. "To fight the other Tetron. I was part of it. I didn't feel any deceit or any efforts to conceal anything. I don't blame you for not trusting it, in fact, I think it's better if at least one of us doesn't. I can't afford not to. Not now."

"Yes. I understand that. For now."

"Besides, I don't see what there would be to gain from helping us fight one of its own only to betray us later?"

"I don't know. We have no idea what it knows about your past or your past futures. It said it was seeking its creator. Maybe you are supposed to be the one to discover who that is. Or maybe you are the Creator?"

"Me? I doubt I'm the Creator. I'm a pilot, not a scientist. Maybe it's you?"

"My specialty is mechanical engineering, with secondary training in systems design and analysis, encryption, and security. I've only done rudimentary experimentation with artificial intelligence, certainly nothing like this." She pointed at a group of the dendrites. "The Tetron originated in a past recursion. When? Where? Did the person who created them know what they were going to become, or were they trying to solve a simpler problem?"

"Like how to help a pilot fly a starfighter?"

Mitchell considered the question. AI wasn't a new thing. Primitive forms pre-dated the Xeno War. "I don't think the Creator is the one who came up with the idea of artificial intelligence. More like the one who finally got it thinking completely on its own."

"An iterative leap across the singularity," Singh said.

"What?"

"The singularity. When technological advances allow artificial intelligence to move beyond human control. It was predicted to happen way back in the twenty-first century."

"Why didn't it?"

"I don't know. I'm not a history expert."

"Neither am I, but now that you mention it, I wonder if XENO-1 had something to do with it."

"Considering Alliance politics, it's obvious that someone is doing their best to prevent it today. Thirty years ago, it seemed as if everything was becoming automated. Now?"

Mitchell glanced at Singh. "You don't look like you were around thirty years ago."

"I'm forty-seven."

"You are not."

"It's the drugs. They're also the reason I was on the Schism. I had a friend. Well, a lover. She was a chemist. She made it, and I sold it through the Undernet."

"Until you got caught." He had known she was on something that had kept her so calm and flat. He didn't know it was the cause of her incarceration with the Riggers.

"Yes. Court-martialed and sent to Millie. The beginning was hard." She paused, her face tensing as a memory washed through her. "Things have gotten better. Watson, on the other hand? I can't believe she kept him around after what he did. I can't believe the military even passed him off to us."

He had proven himself useful so far. How long would the usefulness outweigh the heinousness of his crimes?

"So, there are politicians in the Alliance who are anti-artificial intelligence, and now it turns out there's a good reason for it. Do you think they know something?"

"It isn't just the Alliance. According to Watson, the New Terrans have been pushing back the same way."

"Interesting. What about the Federation?"

"I don't know. We don't have any Federation expatriates on board. I have spent a lot of time thinking about the theory of eternal return since you told us about it. Mitchell, we have no idea how many inception points there have been into each timeline. We have no idea how many instances there are of you, of Origin, of anyone."

It was Mitchell's turn to pause. "What do you mean? M said that once the eternal engine is used, the timeline is locked at that point."

"For the current recursion. Then, the next recursion, a new injection point is available, but the first inception can still occur because it was part of the previous timeline. Think about it, Mitchell."

They walked the rest of the way down to the hangar in silence. Mitchell tried to wrap his mind around the thought. It had always sat at the corner of his mind, percolating as a more general, conceptual idea.

Now it was just making his head hurt.

5

THE HATCH to the hangar slid open.

Mitchell stood motionless, letting his eyes adjust to the different glow of the tendrils that snaked around the massive expanse of the space. It was easily large enough to house a few squadrons of starfighters and at least three or four jumpships and dropships, and still have space enough for a full contingent of mechs and other heavy machinery.

There was little of that here. Instead, the hangar sat eerily quiet and empty save for Mitchell's modified S-17 starfighter, four Morays, a United Planetary Alliance Navy dropship, and a single small transport. The fighter, transport, and UPA assets were each positioned well away from one another, segregated by Origin. The populated ships were silent and foreboding, a single dendrite stretching to each, climbing their landers and vanishing into the machinery. The Tetron had used them to lock their systems and prevent them from disembarking.

The bridge of the Valkyrie was visible from where he was standing, and he could make out the small figures of her crew from the distance, probably looking back at him. The transport didn't have an outer viewport, utilizing feeds from cameras instead to keep the passengers and crew behind a heavier layer of protection.

Mitchell and Singh crossed the distance from the hatch to the transport, the only sound the echoing of their boots along the metal floor. Mitchell felt his heart beating faster with each step, anxious to either be re-united with his team or blown apart in an ambush.

He wouldn't have to worry about any of this if he were dead.

"Origin, unlock the transport," he said, sending the message to the intelligence.

The Tetron's reply came when the small lights around the transport's hatch lit up.

He tried to knock Millie again. Still no reply. There was nothing to do but hope.

The hatch slid open, a platform extending to the surface of the hangar. Millie was standing right behind it, her clothes torn and filthy, a long gash across her forehead, an assault pistol in her hand, ready to fire.

Mitchell's heart beat faster, making the conversion from trepidation to excitement.

"Riiggg-ahh," he said, his smile spreading wide across his face. Even Singh managed a small gasp of enthusiasm.

Millie's smile was bigger than his own, and it showed how exhausted she was. She handed the pistol off to somcone out of view and started down the platform. She made it three steps before stumbling, and Mitchell rushed forward to catch her, grabbing her under the arms and helping her regain her balance. He noticed that her pant leg was torn and bloody.

"Nice work, Captain," Millie said.

"How-"

The others appeared in the opening. Shank, Cormac, Wornak, Hubble, Alice, Watson and thirteen more.

Twenty souls.

Just enough to fill the transport.

"Ares," Shank said, moving down the ramp. He smiled, revealing he had lost a few teeth in the battle. "I wasn't sure about all of this, but I believe you now. I wish I still didn't."

"Me too," Mitchell said.

"Oh man, that was just bloody crazy, you know," Cormac said, limping towards him. Mitchell could see the end of a piece of shrapnel jutting out from his thigh, even if the grunt's embedded meds had stolen the pain of it from him. "Best piece of flying I've ever seen. Hey, Mitch."

"Cormac."

He greeted the others as they came down. None of them were without injury, though Millie's seemed to be the worst. They paused when they reached him, saluting, nodding, or clapping him on the shoulder. Watson took up the rear, his face pale and his entire body shaking with fear. He was here as long as he was useful, and he knew it.

Was he still useful?

"Where are Sao and Briggs?" Mitchell asked, still helping Millie stand.

"They didn't make it. Briggs... she-"

"She saved our asses," Shank said. "So did Sao. He did something with the communications array, faked the lidar signatures or something so the bad guys wouldn't know we had gotten away. Briggs, she got us turned starboard of a big ass rock, close enough to get the transport out behind it. Crazy maneuver. We kept the engines low, just enough to stay in its gravity and hide."

"Why didn't you answer my knocks?" Mitchell said. "I almost didn't let you come aboard."

"The transports comm systems are down, and we turned off our p-rats. We had no idea what happened to you over here, and it was risky to assume our keys weren't compromised. I didn't think you'd consider leaving me out there."

"I thought you were dead, and then this transport shows up. The

Tetron have already proven themselves to be good at deception and trickery. As for your p-rats, it's safe to reboot. We will need to change the keys, though. There's an outside chance the enemy has them, and we can't risk it."

"No. We can't. We'll get Watson on it once we're a little more settled."

"Tetron?" Cormac asked.

"Later, Firedog," Mitchell said. "You sent me a message, right before the Tetron fired. You said-"

"I was hoping it would motivate you. It worked."

Did that mean she loved him or not? Mitchell was relieved to not have to confront that right now.

"Tetron?" Cormac asked again.

"I said later, Firedog."

Singh approached Millie. "Captain. I'm happy you made it."

"Thank you, Singh. You too."

"I assume Rain didn't survive?" Millie asked, her eyes searching behind him.

He fought against the pang of sadness that was intruding on him. "No. She saved my life."

"Whoa. Is that a Navy dropship?" Cormac said.

Millie's head swiveled to where he was looking.

"It is. All that's left of the battlegroup." He leaned his head down, close to Millie's ear. "I'm so sorry about your father."

"Later," she whispered back.

There was a moment of silence, everyone on the hangar floor pausing as the pressure wave caused by the shift to hyperspace washed over them.

"What the hell?" Shank said.

Millie's eyes narrowed. "Mitch, if you and Singh are down here, who just put the Goliath into hyperspace?"

"I have a lot to tell you. First, we need to get you treated. You and everyone else."

"We didn't have time to grab any med-kits."

"Can you stand?"

"Yes. Why?"

Mitchell pointed to the Valkyrie. "Wait here. I'll go ask our new neighbors to share their medi-bot. I have a feeling they won't say no."

[6]

THE MAIN DIFFERENCE between a dropship and a jumpship was
that a jumpship had its own FTL engine. That made it capable of
popping in close to a planet, releasing ground assets, and after a short
hyperdeath getting the hell back out. Dropships used the space that
would have been taken up by the FTL engine to hold a larger contingent of personnel and weaponry, leaving them dependent on carriers
or other large craft to carry them to the objective.

Large craft like the Goliath.

Mitchell approached the dropship alone, glancing back every so
often to check on the remaining Riggers. They stood or sat on the
floor, tired and dirty, watching his lonely trek across the gap Origin
had created. The symbolic nature of it wasn't lost on him. He and the
Riggers were outcasts, criminals, unwanted for anything but the most
suicidal missions.

Like this one.

He needed to get the UPA proper involved in this war, or it was
going to be over before it truly began.

"It's never over," he reminded himself.

He glanced to his left, where the four remaining Alliance fighters had been placed by Origin. The pilots had removed their helmets and were watching him with fixed stares, no doubt recognizing him from the streams and trying to figure out why he had been declared dead, when he so clearly wasn't. He didn't acknowledge them, fighting against the pressure of their scrutiny.

He was supposed to be here, to fight a war for the fate of humanity. He couldn't quite get his head around that, either. He didn't need to. One step at a time, one objective at a time. He could do that. First, he had to get the injured Riggers into the Valkyrie so their medi-bot could put them back together.

"Origin, unlock the Valkyrie."

Unlike the transport, the dropship had multiple exodus points: a smaller personnel and mech ramp on the left side, a larger launch bay on the right, and a belly that could hinge open in atmosphere and release any given amount of it in one quick pass. Mitchell had ridden both jumpships and dropships into battle before. It was a terrifying, exhilarating ride. He had a feeling he was going to get a chance to do it again.

Soon.

It was the main ramp that began to slide open, the armored hull extending out and down. Mitchell waited to the left of it, suddenly nervous that Major Long might have decided he would try to take the Goliath by force and capture the fugitive. Unlike the Riggers, the Major's team was fully armed and operational.

Brighter light spilled out into the hangar from the opening hatch. Mitchell squinted to see through it, to the slender man standing at the base of it, flanked by a second man and a woman. They were wearing standard Alliance officer's uniforms, crisp blues with high collars. He dropped his gaze to their sides. They were unarmed.

They turned their heads towards him. He could see they were trying to hide their surprise that he was who he had told them he was.

"Captain Williams," the slender man said, shouting to be heard over the distance and the hum of the hydraulics lowering the ramp. "Major Aaron Long." He bowed slightly in salute.

Mitchell returned the bow. "Major. Welcome aboard the Goliath." He knocked Origin. "You can unlock the fighters also. Let them out."

The hatches of the fighters opened with a hiss as the pressurized air was released. The pilots slipped over the sides and dropped to the floor, heading towards him, hands on their sidearms.

It was the reason he hadn't let them out before he saw how Major Long was armed. Not that he didn't think Origin could defend the ship if it came down to it.

Major Long and his officers hopped from the ramp before it finished extending to the ground, converging on Mitchell with the pilots. His head twitched when he gazed past to the assembled Riggers.

"You're supposed to be dead," the officer with him repeated.

"Yes."

"Relax, Lieutenant Borov," Long said. "Captain Williams, let me introduce you to my second, Captain Wanda Alvarez."

Mitchell looked the woman over. She had an olive complexion, dark hair, a small nose and big eyes. She had large hips and a large chest, though Mitchell couldn't tell if it was muscle or fat beneath the uniform.

"Captain," Mitchell said.

She smiled. Her teeth were a perfect straight, white line. "Captain."

"And Lieutenant Alexander Borov," Long continued.

Borov was twice the size of Alvarez, and his body was definitely fat, though he was nowhere near Watson's girth. He had two chins, a red face, and beady eyes that regarded him with suspicion.

"Lieutenant."

Borov stared at him.

"We'll schedule a debriefing once we get all of this figured out," Mitchell said. "In the meantime, I have injured crew. I assume the Valkyrie has a medi-bot on board?"

"We do," Major Long said. "And a doctor, Sergeant Grimes."

"You have a doctor? Even better."

Long put up his hand. "I'm all for treating the wounded, Captain, and I'm eager for a debriefing that will explain where this ship came from, why it is covered in alien-" He trailed off, not sure what to call them. "Tendrils? Why a dead man is piloting it, why we attacked and destroyed another alien ship, who those other people are, and why I can't remember anything since we came out of hyperspace near that star? I'm especially interested in whether or not you have an explanation for that."

Mitchell opened his mouth to reply.

"One moment, Captain," Long said. "First, we have another matter we need to settle. According to the media, you're a fraud and a rapist. According to Command, you're also supposed to be dead. Add that up, and it's left me wondering what the truth is? I saw what you did to that other ship, and you've given us safe haven and a way out of certain death, so I'm inclined to put more faith in you than I would otherwise. What I want to know, Captain, is where your loyalties are?"

"Humankind, Major. And the Alliance." He motioned back towards the Riggers. "All of us are with the Alliance."

Major long nodded. "Then you won't have any hesitation about turning command of this ship over to me?"

"What?" Mitchell felt his heart begin to pound. Was the Major about to do what he thought he was about to do, after he had saved his life? All of their lives?

"If you are for the Alliance, as you say, then this vessel has become an Alliance asset. As the ranking officer, it is reasonable to expect that command of this ship falls to me."

"I could have left you out there, stranded," Mitchell said, clenching his teeth to keep himself from punching the man. It wasn't a good idea with the armed pilots standing next to them.

"You didn't, Captain, and I don't think you would have. Not if you aren't what the media says you are."

Mitchell glanced from Long to Borov, and then to Alvarez. He had a feeling the Major had been planning this from the moment he had told him the Valkyrie could come aboard. It was a gutsy move to pull rank in this situation, but why wouldn't he? He had the guns, he had the numbers, he had the health. He couldn't know that the ship was more than tendrils and poly-alloy; that there was something else on board.

He was silent for a moment, letting his heart rate calm. Slow. Steady. The anger faded, turning into amusement. He started to laugh.

"Is something funny, Captain?" Alvarez asked.

"I hate to tell you this, Major," Mitchell said. "You aren't the ranking officer on this ship."

HE LED a confused Major Long and his officers back to where the Riggers were waiting. Millie was sitting on the floor, using Shank's big legs to prop her up, while the others huddled around her.

"Major Aaron Long," Mitchell said to Millie.

She reached up and took Shank's arm, using it to pull herself to her feet.

"Major," Millie said. "What's the problem, Mitch?"

"The Major would like to take command of the Goliath, ma'am."

"Pulling rank, Major?" she asked.

"Ma'am, I don't know who you or your crew are, but it's clear to me that the Alliance is about to be at war if it isn't already. Military statutes-"

"You don't need to quote rules to me, Major. I'm familiar with them. My name is Admiral Mildred Narayan, Alliance Navy, formerly of the starship Schism."

"Did you say Admiral?" Borov said. He was standing behind Major Long, and his face paled at her suggestion.

"Clearly," Millie said.

"I'm familiar with the names of all of the Alliance admirals," Major Long said. "I don't recognize yours."

"Are you questioning me, Major?"

"No offense intended, ma'am, but there's too much I don't understand yet to just accept you are what you say you are. I've never heard of you, never seen you before, not even in pictures or streams. I'm sure you understand."

"You ever heard of the Riggers, Major?" Cormac asked. He had moved through to the front of the group. "Millie here is an Admiral, sure as shit."

"Cormac," Millie said.

"Sorry, Captain. Err... Admiral."

"I've never heard of the Riggers," Major Long said. "I'll need to see some secure identification. Once I do, I'll believe anything you say. Until then-"

"Until then, maybe you can help me get my people treated," Millie said. "Myself included. If the command of this vessel is in question, then I suggest we leave it in the hands of the man who took control of it and saved all of our lives. Will that satisfy you for now, Major?"

Mitchell could see Long's jaw clench, his teeth grinding. He wasn't happy to be spoken to that way, especially not after he thought he was going to be in charge.

"Temporarily," Long agreed, glancing over at Mitchell. "I felt the move to hyperspace. It seems we have some time to work everything out."

"Thank you, Major," Millie said.

"Follow me."

Major Long turned on his heel and started back towards the Valkyrie. Mitchell took Millie by the arm and helped her across the hangar.

"How bad is it?" he asked.

"Major Long? He'll fall in line. He's a straight shooter, and I have secure authorization stored in my implant. We just need to keep him from trying to mutiny before we either decrypt my firmware or encrypt his for me to transfer it."

"We aren't decrypting. I was referring to your leg."

She smiled. "It'll be fine once the bots stitch it back together." She tugged his arm, pulling his head down closer to hers so she could whisper. "I saw what happened with the enemy starship. How bad is it?"

"You might be sorry you didn't die."

"No. No matter what happens. You need me."

"We need everyone we can get. You're going to be in charge of this show."

"And you're going to be my second. I have the power to promote you. Would you like that, Colonel Williams?"

"One thing at a time. I want to get you treated first."

"Mitch, you know-"

"I know. I want you to be treated first, anyway. I have something I need to show you. They'll understand."

"We're still criminals, Mitch. Still broken."

"Which might make us exactly what humankind needs. We aren't here by accident, Millie. Remember that."

MAJOR CHRISTINE ARAPO opened her eyes. It was dark and silent. She could feel her body, muscles aching from being draped over a mound of rubble that had fallen into the shaft ahead of her. She had fallen far. Too far. Not four floors. The shaft had gone down into a sub level, at least another five or six.

Ten stories? How had she survived?

She shifted her arm, taking it slow to see if it was broken. It was stiff, but it moved without pain. She shifted it until her hand was in front of her face, bringing it forward in the darkness until the faint outline of it became visible. She could still see. She bent her legs, rolling over gingerly, just in case.

Everything seemed to be intact. She was lucky.

She stood and examined herself with her hands, finding the tears in her clothes and the ridges of lacerations across her skin. They were closed. Healing. How long had she been unconscious?

She bent over, feeling along the ground, searching for the carbine. It had been slung over her shoulder when she fell. It had to be there somewhere. She dropped to her knees and rotated in a spiral pattern, staying quiet, taking her time until at last she discovered it against a wall. She ran her hands along it until she was able to activate the display. It provided a minimum of light, but it was enough to see that she had fallen on top of a collapsed basement. The shaft was open on one side, spilling out towards a floor of cement and twisted poly-alloy beams. This wasn't recent damage. It must have been a remainder from the Federation dreadnought's bombardment, covered over and forgotten in the push to hide the scars of war.

Mitchell. The thought led her back to him. Where was he, now? Was he still alive? She wasn't sure why it mattered to her.

She held the carbine crosswise, using the light to navigate across the uneven rubble to the more even flooring beyond. There was no light spilling into the space from anywhere. Had she survived the fall only to be buried alive? She hoped not.

She crossed the space, trying to picture the building in her mind and place herself near the outer wall. It was probably still nighttime. If it were cloudy or raining, there would be no light from the stars.

As if in reply, she noticed the soft ping of water dripping from somewhere. She followed the sound, back along the floor to the south until she reached a door. An emergency exit. She smiled and pushed it open.

The water was there, running down the steps into a small pool. She knelt and took some of it in her hands, bringing it to her mouth. She hadn't realized how thirsty she was until she had seen the water, and now she drank it with urgency. Then she leaned back against the wall, feeling the draft against her face. She looked up through the center of the spiraling steps. She still didn't see any light, but she was sure it was a way out.

She started climbing the steps, surprised at how much energy she had and the way her body had responded despite the fall. To tumble that far and land on a pile of stone, coming away with nothing but scratches? It sounded impossible, and she would never have believed it if it hadn't just happened.

She could feel the draft growing stronger as she rose until she reached the door that it was sneaking under, along with a steady stream of water. She shifted her grip on the carbine, moving it into a ready position, checking the display to ensure it was still operational.

Then she leaned into the door.

It opened into a small alley between buildings. A heavy rain was falling. There wasn't much light, all of it spilling in from somewhere in the distance, from somewhere the power hadn't been cut.

There was a soldier standing at the mouth of the alley.

He was turning around, reacting to her noise.

Christine mouthed a curse and fired. The soldier was thrown back and down by the force, the bolt exploding through his armor and into his flesh. If there were others around, the noise was sure to draw them.

Bullets smacked the door behind her, gunfire coming from the other end of the guarded alley. She was lucky they were using standard rifles instead of M97s like hers. She turned to face the metal door, using the hit pattern of the slugs to aim. She used her thumb to increase the power on the carbine and fired another round. The bolt punctured the door without difficulty.

The gunfire stopped.

Too much noise. She considered ducking back into the building, but the dents in the door were a clear indication where she was hiding. She ran down the alley towards the first soldier, pausing at the end and craning her neck around the corner. She saw motion a few blocks down, a squad of soldiers organizing and coming her way.

She knelt next to the soldier, grabbing the M1A assault rifle he was carrying and a pair of extra magazines from his belt. She slung the carbine over her shoulder, ducking against the other side of the wall and checking the incoming again. Eight in all, two of them in heavy exo. The carbine could puncture the heavier armor, that's what it had been designed for.

"Other way," she whispered to herself, turning and racing to the opposite end of the alley. She could hear the soft thumps of the heavy exosuit when its wearer began to run.

The rain started coming down more heavily, soaking her by the time she reached the other end. She glanced back, seeing the armored soldiers had reached the alley. She turned the corner before they could fire.

Her eyes were wild, scanning the street in search of opponents. She dropped to her knees, sliding on the wet pavement, using the reduced friction to turn herself in a circle, taking in the layout of the area in an instant before pushing back to her feet. There was another alley a hundred meters away, three soldiers ahead of it. A dozen more soldiers were behind her.

Abandoned cars littered the street, flat obstacles without power to their repulsors. She dove past one ahead of the gunfire that came in behind her, bullets chewing into the metal, the soft whine of the heavy exo's standard rapid-fire coilgun following behind it.

A gun that would tear the car, and then her, apart.

She screamed as she pushed herself out from behind the car, abandoning the M1A and unslinging the carbine. There was no way out of this, no way to avoid being killed. Her training wouldn't let her die without a fight.

She took aim. Fired. Aimed again. Fired. Two of the soldiers dropped, but not the heavy. He was adjusting his aim, his p-rat helping him get a lock.

She ran across the street, towards the clear carbonate front of a restaurant. She could go through, and out the back.

If she could get in.

The carbonate wouldn't shatter, and she would only have a second to get through it before the bullets reduced her to a mound of flesh.

She slid her thumb along the carbine's handle, putting it on full auto, running sideways while firing at the heavy armor. Her aim was impeccable, inhuman, placing a neat pattern of holes into the soldier from three blocks away. His arms dropped to his sides, an indication that he was dead in the suit.

The three soldiers behind her were drawing closer. They opened fire, their rifles much less of a threat than the coilgun. Bullets spit up water behind her, and she slammed into the door, reaching out and grabbing at the seam.

"Please be open," she said, digging her fingers in and pulling. Without power, it wouldn't open on its own.

A bullet hit her shoulder and went through. She held back the pain, using it to pull harder on the door. It finally moved aside, and she fell in, landing on the floor and crawling inside on her stomach. Bullets rained in through the carbonate, but the angle of attack was all wrong to hit her.

She had bought herself seconds at most. She scrambled along the floor until she was halfway in, and then rose and dashed past empty tables towards the kitchen. Into the kitchen and through. No. The freezer caught her attention. No power. No cold. She ran to the door out to the alley, slamming her bloody shoulder against it and leaving a large stain. She checked the display on the carbine. Empty. She dropped it.

She heard the soldiers pulling on the other door, their bigger forms unable to fit through her opening. She padded back to the freezer, her hand clamped on her shoulder, trying to keep it from dripping blood on the floor and revealing her deceit. A thump told her the soldiers had gotten in, and were getting close.

She pulled the freezer open just enough, slipping inside and getting it closed right before the door to the kitchen swung open.

"WHERE ARE WE GOING?" Millie asked.

She looked better after spending a couple of hours being stitched back together by the Valkyrie's medi-bot, and after inheriting a pair of surplus grays from Sergeant Grimes. The doctor was similar in height and build to the leader of the Riggers, though she had long red hair and a light complexion to Millie's dark and olive. She was as fiery as her mane, cursing up a storm when the Riggers arrived for treatment. Not at them. At the enemy, for leaving them so battered.

Judging by Cormac's face at the barrage, it was love at first sight.

They were headed back to the control room while the rest of the crew got stitched up and fed. Mitchell had ordered Origin to keep the hangar on lockdown to prevent anyone from snooping around.

"I want you to meet someone," he said.

"Who?"

"It's a long story. Now that we have a moment of privacy, I want you to know I'm sorry about your father."

"I know you are, Mitch."

"He was a good man."

"He was better than that. He asked us to do some impossible

things, but he believed that I could. He had faith in me when nobody else did."

They were still walking while they spoke. Mitchell glanced over and could see the tear forming in the corner of Millie's eye. No matter how upset she got, he knew she wouldn't show it. Not while there was still so much work to do.

"They sent him on purpose."

"I know. Bastards."

"It means they know who you are. Who the Riggers are."

"They already knew, didn't they? When they showed up at Calypso."

"I'm not sure. They fired on the station first, not us. I don't think they figured it out until we went back to Liberty."

"It doesn't matter either way. They sent my father out to try to stop us. I guess they thought I would hesitate to disobey him. They aren't as smart as they seem to think they are. He would never have wanted me to give up the fight to spare his life. Not if he knew the truth. We need to hold a memorial service for everyone who was lost."

"We will," Mitchell said. "Do you think the crew will do okay, integrating with the UPA military?"

She laughed. "We've been out on our own so long. I wish I could say they will, but I don't know. I think we should expect some friction." She stopped walking, right in front of the lift, turning to him. "I know we have a lot to do. I want you to know... What I said during the battle? I meant it. I love you, Mitch."

Mitchell froze, not sure how to respond. He cared about Millie, sure. Love? That was a bitter pill after Ella.

"You don't have to say it back," Millie said. "That would be stupid, and you'd probably only be saying it because you feel like you should. We're each responsible for our emotions. It's fine with me if you don't. It's fine with me if you want to go back to the Valkyrie and grab Sergeant Grimes for a roll. I'm just saying that I respect you, I appreciate you, and I'm glad we're alive and here together. You always have an ally in me, and I'm going to help you win this frigging war."

Mitchell smiled, and then took Millie in his arms, wrapping her in a firm hug. He kissed her, just for a moment, before letting her go. "I think Cormac has his eye on Grimes. Anyway, we'll get berthing figured out sooner or later, and then you owe me."

She returned his smile. "Deal."

They got into the lift, taking the short ride up to the control room. He found Origin sitting in the command chair, staring out into the blankness of hyperspace that surrounded it.

"Wow," Millie said, noticing the view from the cameras first. "Alliance ships don't have anything like this."

"It is because most humans suffer from inner balance deficiencies when exposed to full orbital views," Origin said, rising from the chair. "It is especially acute during extra-spacial travel. Isn't that correct, Mitchell?"

Mitchell closed his eyes. The nothingness surrounding the room's equipment had left him disoriented and slightly nauseous.

Millie didn't seem affected. Her eyes traveled to meet the Tetron. "Most humans?"

"Origin, I want you to meet Admiral Mildred Narayan," Mitchell said.

He chuckled, rising from the chair and approaching her. "Admiral. I am Origin. I am a Tetron."

"Tetron?"

"The ship we destroyed," Mitchell said, opening his eyes and focusing on Origin's face. "It was a Tetron."

"I knew the dendrites were familiar. You've turned against your own kind?"

"Out of necessity. They do not understand."

"What?"

"Humanity."

"And you do?"

He chuckled again.

"Major Arapo is a Tetron," Mitchell said.

"I offloaded much of my data stacks to her. To protect them."

"Major Arapo? The one you went to look for on Liberty? The one who looks identical to the other one, Katherine?"

"Yes."

"So they aren't one and the same?"

"I utilized Katherine Asher's configuration. Her genetic code. Katherine Asher assisted me in delivering the Goliath to Mitchell."

"She did what?" Millie's face froze, the truth working its way in.

"She sacrificed herself to get Origin here to me, in order to fight the other Tetron. Now we need to recover Major Arapo."

Millie pointed out to the blankness of hyperspace. "Is that where we're going?"

"Yes."

"There's a Tetron on Liberty."

"I know," Mitchell said. "And it has control of all of the military assets there, and it probably knows I came looking for Arapo and is looking for her, too. We'll get to that. I wanted to bring you up here to meet Origin because I need you to help me make him a Rigger."

"A Rigger? I don't understand?"

"You, me, and Singh are the only ones who know that Origin isn't human. I'd like to keep it that way."

"Why?"

"Major Long, mostly. I have a feeling he wouldn't accept trusting one of the enemy's kind so easily."

"And you think I do?" Millie asked.

"I think you accept trusting me," Mitchell replied. "I can't say the same for Major Long."

Her eyes locked on Origin, examining him the same way she had examined Mitchell when he was picked up by the Schism. "Can we trust you?"

Origin nodded. "I understand the statement is illogical, and without my full data stack I cannot fully extrapolate the meaning or the motivation. I seek to destroy my race, Admiral Mildred Narayan. I seek to destroy all Tetron."

[10]

"THERE ARE ONLY twenty of us left," Millie said. "Twenty-two with you and Singh. You don't think Major Long will notice that we've added a twenty-third?"

"I don't think they've had time to take a head count. They're pulling the crew one at a time to get them cleaned up and treated. If we hurry, we can still get him mixed in without raising suspicion." Mitchell looked over at Origin. He was wearing a simple blue flight suit, a replica of Singh's clothes. "We'll need to get you dirty."

"There's plenty of blood and grime covering the inside of the transport," Millie said. "Tear the clothes a bit, roll around in it, you'll look the part."

"I don't think that will be good enough. Origin, this might hurt." Mitchell balled his fist and slammed it into the side of the Tetron's head. He stumbled from the blow, putting his hands to his face.

"Mitch," Millie said.

"I'm sorry, you have to look like you were almost blown up." He approached the Tetron, who straightened up and turned the other cheek. Mitchell hit him again, and again, knocking him to the ground.

"Okay, that's enough," Millie said.

Mitchell knelt over the Tetron, his hand back and ready to strike again. He was getting carried away, lost in the flood of frustration and emotion, the anger at the damage the Tetron had already done. He blew out a stream of air and unclenched his fist, holding it out to help him up.

"I assume you do not want me to heal the damage you have inflicted?" Origin said.

He seemed unconcerned with the violence against his body. Had he even felt it?

"No."

"I could have altered the form at a cellular level to achieve the same purpose." He bent and grabbed the leg of his flight suit and tore it. Then he tore one of the arms. "There was no need for violence."

Mitchell stared at Origin. He was slightly embarrassed, but not about to apologize.

"We'll need a diversion to get him into the hangar," Millie said. "Lucky for us that Cormac was next in line." She tapped her head, signaling that she was knocking him. "Firedog, what's your status? How much longer? Ten? Perfect. I need you to create a diversion. Yes, a diversion, Firedog." She rolled her eyes. "Yes, when you do something to take the attention off of something else. No, I don't care what you do, just make sure that nobody is watching the rest of the hangar. It's not your place to question, Firedog. Just do it."

She growled when she disconnected the channel.

"Did I say lucky for us? Come on. We have ten minutes to get back to the hangar."

"You need a name," Mitchell said. "Origin can be your callsign."

Origin shrugged. "I do not require such a choice."

"Private Brijesh Singh. No relation to Corporal Singh," Millie said. "You're in training as an engineer under her. Welcome to the Riggers."

"Riiigg-ahh," Mitchell said.

Origin turned to him, confused. "Riiigg-ahh?"

"You'll get used to it. Let's go."

They made their way onto the lift, back down to the hangar level and through the corridors. The dendrites were continuing to re-arrange themselves, organizing into stiffer, straighter lines that resembled bundled cables arcing around the main footpaths.

"You're doing that?" Millie asked.

"Yes. You will require space to move around. I cannot reduce the overall size or surface area, so there are places of the Goliath which I must seal off in order to remain less obtrusive."

"What are they for?"

"Everything," Origin replied.

"Some of them are conductive," Mitchell said, using the knowledge he had gained when he interfaced with Origin. "Others are receptive. Others are collective and productive. Energy and raw materials in, energy and complex structures out."

"Like this configuration," Origin said.

"Where did you get raw materials to make a person?"

"The original crew of the Goliath," Mitchell said. Millie's face paled.

"The human configuration is no different than that of any other. The Valkyrie, for example. It is a larger whole that houses smaller pieces, each with their assigned functions."

"You're comparing a person to a dropship?" Mitchell asked.

"On the surface, yes. That is what existence is at its basest level. The difference is minute in size, but massive in value. The single spark that makes each of you unique."

"You mean a soul?" Millie said.

"Yes. A succinct way to describe the indescribable. When the soul is lost, what remains is nothing more than raw materials. It is inefficient to waste them."

Millie shook her head. "I'm going to pretend we didn't have this conversation."

"As you say."

They reached the hangar door with a minute to spare. Millie knocked Cormac again.

"He's just finishing up with the medi-bot. He said he has a plan."

"Cormac has a plan?" Mitchell asked. "This wasn't a good idea."

A knock went out to both of them a minute later.

"Millie, Mitch, we have a situation on the Valkyrie," Shank said. "We need you down here, right now."

"That's our queue. Origin, open the door."

The hatch slid open. They could see across the expanse to the Valkyrie, and the Riggers who had been waiting outside and were now running up the ramp.

"Mitch, go help with Cormac. Origin, come with me."

Mitchell broke for the Valkyrie at a run, careful not to go too fast. He didn't want to break things up before Millie could get Origin dirtied and mixed in with the rest of the crew.

Watson was at the base of the ship when Mitchell reached it. The fat engineer was leaning against the hydraulics, his face red and his body heaving. Mitchell didn't doubt he had no intention of going up the ramp or getting involved in any kind of scuffle.

"What happened?" he asked.

"I don't know, Captain," Watson said. "Cormac knocked Shank, and then everybody went running."

Mitchell continued up the ramp. He couldn't hear anything from here, but medical was on the other side of the ship. As he made his way through it, he heard the shouting.

"You bloody son of a bitch. Get up already, will you?"

"Sergeant Grimes, stand down."

"Don't you be telling me to stand down, Major. A broken nose is getting away cheap for copping a feel like that."

"Sergeant, we'll deal with this. Borov, escort Private - what was it again? Private Shen to an empty berthing and keep an eye on him."

"Hold on a second," Shank said. "You aren't taking my crew anywhere."

"Your crew just assaulted a member of my crew."

"And she busted his nose. I'd say we're even."

Mitchell reached the back of the line of Riggers. They moved aside when they noticed him, giving him access to the tail end of the corridor leading into medical.

He entered the room. It was filled with white and poly-alloy machines. The medi-bot station was in the back corner, and Major Long, Sergeant Grimes, Shank, Cormac and the others were arranged in the front. Cormac was on the ground, his hand holding his nose, the blood running between his fingers.

"What the frig is going on here?" Mitchell asked.

"He grabbed my arse. So I broke his nose." Grimes had a satisfied smile on her face.

Cormac looked up at him. "It was an honest mistake. I thought she was coming on to me."

"Coming on to you? A raggedy imbecile like yourself? In your dreams, Private Shen."

"He needs to be taken into custody," Long said. "He attacked one of my crew."

Shank shook his head. "Captain, I'm not saying what Firedog did was right, but he got a lot worse than he gave. No need to lock him up or any of that Alliance bullshit."

"Bullshit?" Borov shouted. "You're calling the Alliance bullshit?"

Mitchell put up his hands. "Can we all just calm down for a minute?"

"I am calm," Cormac said.

"Of course, you're right, Captain," Long said, glaring at his people. It took a few more seconds for the room to fall silent.

"Did none of you witness the same thing I did a few hours ago?" Mitchell said. "The alien starship that destroyed an entire battle-group, first by turning it against itself, and then with a beam weapon that makes our nukes look like toothpicks?"

All eyes were on him, expressions flat.

"We're alive because of this ship, Goliath. We're alive because the alien who discovered it installed some frigging amazing tech before it died. Tech that we can control through here." He pointed to the port on the back of his head that plugged into his neural implant. "Tech that gave us a fighting chance today and may be the only hope we have of stopping this threat before it destroys all of us. We've already seen the enemy attack Liberty. We've seen it destroy a private outpost in the Rim. We've seen it decimate a Federation space station. It doesn't care where you're from, or what the frigging regulations say. It only cares that we all die."

There was a long, silent pause. Mitchell received a knock, the tone indicating it had gone out to all of the Riggers.

"This is your Captain speaking. I'm bringing a new recruit in. Where he came from, who he is, that's none of your goddamned business. Breathe one word of it to anyone from the UPA, and I'll find you and kill you myself. Got it?"

"Yes, Captain," came the silent replies.

"Major Long, how many crew do you have with you?" Mitchell asked.

"One hundred seventeen."

"We have twenty-three Riggers. That's one hundred forty souls who are the only members of the military of any kind who can stand up to this threat. Think about that for a second, and tell me if you want to take one of those souls out of the fight."

"We don't even know our enemy's numbers, " Long said. "We barely know anything about them."

"Then trust me when I say you don't want to lose a warrior. Especially not one like Private Shen."

Millie appeared at his side a moment later. Mitchell glanced back to see Origin mixed in with the Riggers, his hair tousled, his face bruised, his flight suit filthy.

"Trust us, Major," she said. "We found the Goliath, we took command of the Goliath, and we plan to bring the fight back to our enemy."

Major Long stood quietly, considering.

"Major. Let it go," Grimes said. She forced a smile. "The big one's right. I gave him what-for. No need to make a major incident over it.

We almost died out there, and I got family that's going to die if we don't stop the bastards."

Long turned to Grimes. It was clear from the way he looked at her there was more to their relationship than being assigned to the same ship. "Are you sure?"

"Yes, Major." She held her hand out to Cormac. He took it, and she pulled him up. "Grab my arse again, and I'll break something else."

"Yes, ma'am," Cormac said.

"Fine. This matter is settled. Let's finish getting your crew patched up, and then we can discuss our next steps. I expect you'll be able to prove your enlistment details by then?"

"Of course, Major," Millie said with a smile. "In the meantime, I think it would benefit all of us to prepare an inventory of our assets, both material and personnel. Unfortunately, my team's equipment was all destroyed with my ship, but my crew does have some unique skills and qualifications. I'll prepare a record of them if you do the same for yours."

"Agreed, Captain."

"How about we meet in four hours to debrief and discuss our plan of attack?" Mitchell said.

Major Long bowed. "Agreed."

MITCHELL RETURNED to the hangar floor by himself, leaving Origin to be treated by Sergeant Grimes along with the others. Millie had requested a room inside the Valkyrie where she would organize personnel files in her p-rat, rearranging them with the information she thought Major Long might need and taking out the rest.

Not that the Major could read any of the files. At the moment, their two implants were incompatible, the black-market firmware and encryption keys preventing them from sharing notes. That would be the first thing they would need to change before they reached what he was assuming to be Tetron controlled space. It wouldn't work to have the crew of the Valkyrie become enemy drones the second they dropped out of hyperspace.

Shank was leaving the ship at the same time, cleaned and changed into the grays, a laceration on his face stitched instead of mended by the medi-bot. Mitchell paused to wait for him, a second idea sprouting in his mind.

"Colonel," Mitchell said. He pointed at the stitches. "Grimes did that for you already?"

He smiled. "No, sir. I took care of it myself. Carbonate splinter. I was lucky it didn't take my frigging head off." His eyes darkened. "I was luckier than some of the others. I have eight squad mates left. Eight."

"I'm sorry."

He shook his head. "That's war, right? The only way to be sorry is to pay back with interest. What can I do for you, Captain?"

"This ship. Goliath. I haven't had any time to explore. I'm familiar with the schematics of the original design, and from what I understand a lot of that was left untouched. I want you to go with Singh to assess the condition of the equipment."

"I'm not an engineer, Mitch."

"I know. You're a strong son of a bitch, though, and there may be some blockage or debris that needs to be cleared."

"Roger that."

Mitchell knocked Singh. "Where are you?"

"On board the transport. Origin recommended some equipment that I should salvage before he takes the rest."

"He did?"

"When Millie brought him aboard. I was working on assessing the damage to it, but he thinks it will be better used as scrap. I agree with him. The ship took a pounding. It's a wonder they made it here alive."

"I want you and Shank to go check out the rest of the ship. The crew quarters. We need to get it all ready to be lived in again, and I want you to provide a report at the debriefing. Knock Origin if you need help with the assessment."

"Yes, sir."

"I'll send Shank over to you."

"Okay."

Mitchell glanced at Shank. "Singh is waiting for you in the transport. She's seen the layout. Help her out if she needs any muscle."

"Yes, sir." Shank took two steps, and then leaned in close. "What's the game, Mitch?"

"What do you mean?"

"Our new recruit? This ship? You're playing it all close. You and Millie."

"Why are you a member of the Riggers?" Mitchell asked.

Shank's eyes narrowed. "Aww, come on. You know-"

"I know there's a reason, and whatever it is, it comes down to not liking to play by the rules. Major Long and his crew outnumber us five to one, which means what we know and they don't is the only thing keeping them from forcing the issue. Unless you want to be playing strictly by UPA rules while the enemy tears this universe apart, you'll shut up, stop asking questions, and trust me."

Shank bowed, an action he rarely took on his own. "Yes, sir. I'll pass the word on."

Mitchell continued out to the hangar, returning to where Watson had stationed himself at the base of the ramp. He was sitting now, his eyes downcast, trying to avoid attention.

"Watson." Mitchell knelt next to him.

"Captain. Do you have somewhere I can go? The looks I'm getting from the crew." He shook his head. "After all I did. I saved their lives. Without my machine-"

"Shut up, Corporal. They were nice enough to bring you along instead of leaving you to die on the Schism. I would consider that thanks enough."

Watson stopped talking.

"We need to re-key the implants."

"Which ones?"

"All of them. The encryption may have been compromised."

"What?"

"You heard me. We also need to get the custom firmware onto the ARRs of the rest of the Valkyrie's crew."

Watson cringed. "Captain, the firmware image was lost on the Schism. I can't-"

"I don't want to hear can't, Watson. Especially not from you." While Mitchell was sure Origin could make whatever modifications were needed, he had no intention of giving the intelligence a means to sneak in its own control methods.

"There's only so much I can do without a clean image to modify."

"And you don't have a backup anywhere? I find that hard to believe."

"I did. It was on the Schism."

Mitchell watched the engineer's face. His cheeks were turning red, his eyes swishing back and forth like a fish tail. "Why are you lying to me, Watson?"

"Captain?" His face turned even redder. "I'm not-"

Mitchell reached down and grabbed Watson's arm, pulling him up roughly and bringing their faces close together. "I'm starting to question your usefulness. I told the crew inside that we needed all the warriors we could get. You aren't a fighter, and your past is a massive enough liability already, never mind if Long or his crew catch wind of it. Make yourself valuable, or find yourself expendable."

Watson's lip began to quiver in fear. Mitchell kept his eyes locked on him, calm beneath the angry exterior. Watson would cave. He knew he would.

"Okay. Okay. I have a backup. It isn't complete. It's an older version. I can update the encryption on it. You should know, Captain, it's going to slow the neural processing. It'll cost you in a fight."

"That's not good enough."

"It's the best I can do. I swear. This version is almost a year old. I bumped the algorithms a few times since then. I can try to bring them back from memory."

"Why didn't you keep a backup of a newer version?"

"I didn't have enough storage space. The implant-" He paused, and then bit his lip.

"Implant?" Mitchell tightened his grip on the engineer's arm.

A small whine escaped from Watson's throat. He used his free arm to tap his head. "Secondary implant. Pure storage. It's illegal and untraceable."

Mitchell hadn't known such a thing existed. "You're full of surprises, aren't you?"

Watson responded with a childish smile. "Give me somewhere to work and I'll get a new firmware ready. I'll have to replace yours too in order to change the keys."

"How much time am I going to lose?"

"Estimate? Fifty to a hundred milliseconds."

"That's a lot."

"I know. I'll try. I promise."

Mitchell let Watson go, giving him a small shove away. The engineer was obviously pleased to be released, rubbing at his arm.

"You have three hours," Mitchell said. "Head inside and find Major Long. Introduce yourself and tell him that you need a private berthing on my request."

"Yes, sir."

Watson started to turn to head up the ramp.

"Watson?" Mitchell said.

"Yes, Captain?"

"What else do you have on the storage implant?"

"Excuse me, Captain?" His face started to flush again.

"You didn't get an illegal storage implant to hold p-rat firmware images. What else is on there, that you didn't keep a current version backed up?"

The lip started quivering again.

It was all the answer Mitchell needed. He clenched his teeth against the rising tide of anger. He needed Watson for at least three more hours. Probably more, as much as it disgusted him.

"Make the changes, and then destroy everything else on the implant. Otherwise, I'm going to destroy it myself."

He thought Watson might burst into tears as he bowed slightly and fled into the dropship.

Mitchell closed his eyes and collected himself.

Slow.

Steady.

[12]

MILLIE, Mitchell, Singh, Origin and Watson stood near the front row of task stations on the bridge of the Goliath, waiting for Major Long and his officers to arrive.

A small black box rested on the floor ahead of them, the transport's mainframe extracted and brought in as a crude tool to perform the needed updates to their implant command and control systems. Cables snaked from it to the station next to them, wires offered to them from somewhere within the Goliath's structure by liquid metal tentacles that dropped through the hole near the command chair. Origin had offered more than just the parts to salvage the transport's computer brain, volunteering to use his core to make the transitions.

Mitchell had declined. He trusted the Tetron only as much as he had to, and in this case he didn't have to.

Origin now looked the part of a raw recruit, having been through the Valkyrie's medi-bot station. His bruises were healed, his body cleaned, his flight suit replaced with standard issue grays. He stood at attention behind Singh, his mouth curled into a smirk that left Mitchell wondering if he truly wanted to save humanity, or if he was just looking for a bit of entertainment.

The thought was cut short by the arrival of Major Long and his officers, Alvarez, and Borov. They stepped out from the lift, each reacting differently to finding themselves thrust into the almost-empty looking space, broken up only by task stations and the command chair. Borov closed his eyes, reaching out as if to steady himself. Alvarez's mouth gaped open as she spun and stared. Long simply glanced from the command chair to the Riggers. If he was suffering from any disorientation, he wasn't about to show it.

"Major Long," Millie said. "Welcome to the bridge."

Long smiled. "Thank you." He left off her rank on purpose. She still had to prove herself. "It's quite an impressive view."

"I thought this would be the best place to meet," Mitchell said. "The Goliath doesn't have conference rooms, and I figured you'd want to see it."

"Neither does the Valkyrie, as I'm sure you're aware. We're meant to make quick trips on her, not plan wars. I appreciate that you allowed us out of the hangar. Some of the crew were starting to whisper that we were prisoners here."

"I'm sorry for that, Major. I only just came aboard Goliath myself. We wanted to make sure the ship was secure before we risked losing any more people."

"Is it?"

"Yes, sir," Mitchell said. "Our engineer, Corporal Singh, and her second, Private Singh, along with Sergeant Wilson, did a reconnaissance of the inhabitable areas. She needs some work, but we should be able to get the entire crew comfortable."

Major Long approached them, passing the command chair before pausing at one of the task stations. There were all kinds of readings and numbers displaying there, floating by at rates too fast to follow. He looked up at Mitchell.

"I think we can cut to the meat of it, Captain. We should settle who's in charge of this ship and her crew. All of her crew."

"I agree," Mitchell said. "There is a complication."

"Complication?"

"The enemy has access to the frequencies and key-codes used to secure the augmented reality receivers, and, as a result, your neural implant. You wanted to know why you couldn't remember anything? That's it, in a nutshell."

"You're saying they did what, exactly?" Alvarez asked. "Mind control?"

Mitchell saw Origin open his mouth to speak. He motioned to stop him. "That's an accurate way to put it."

"Where did they get classified codes?" Borov asked. "For that matter, why didn't this mind control work on you?"

"That's the real question, isn't it?" Millie said. "I'm going to tell you up-front, the answer is going to sound ridiculous."

"But you want us to believe it?" Long said.

"I'm saying that you have to believe it because the enemy is better off if you don't."

"Interesting logic," Alvarez said.

"You need to take into account what you've already seen, and more importantly what you do and don't remember. How many days are you missing? How many hours? Why? How did we find the Goliath? How did we know it was here, and where to look for it, in all of the massive depths of the galaxy? Why is it carrying alien tech, and how come we can control it?"

"And you have all of the answers to these questions?" Borov asked.

"And then some," Millie replied. "Let's get back to the first one. My name is Admiral Mildred Narayan. I am the officer in charge of what the UPA brass calls 'Project Black.' We're a dark ops team. A secret collective of some of the best military specialists in the Alliance, more affectionately known as the Riggers."

"The Riggers?" Long said. "I've seen your crew. No offense, but they don't look like much of a fighting force to me."

Mitchell saw the corner of Millie's lip curl from the comment.

"Because they aren't crisp and clean and standing at attention? Preening like a peacock is second to being the best at your job when you're a Rigger." She forced the curl into a smile. "Our mission protocol demands that we carry custom firmware and custom encryption. That's why the enemy couldn't mind-frig us. That's why we know what's really happening out there, and why we're the only ones who can stop it."

"Corporal Watson is our engineer in charge of maintaining the ARR functionality," Mitchell said. "He's arranged to upload new firmware to each of your implants, to make them immune to enemy control."

Watson stepped forward and tapped on the black box. "We had this set up in medical on the Schism. Our resources are more limited here." He picked up a wire attached to the box that ended in a small, flat, conductive pad that had been rigged from a smaller repulsor. He had outdone himself with that modification. "Normally a bot would transmit into the implant's input port to do the transfer, but it will take hours to reprogram the one on the Valkyrie to complete the procedure."

"Hours that we don't have," Mitchell said.

"You want me to let your engineer do it manually?" Long asked.

"I have steady hands," Watson said. "I'll hold the pad up to your head, near the implant site. It will conduct a small electrical current that the chip will read as binary. It will take about three minutes, and then your p-rat will reboot, and you should be in the secure system."

"Should be?"

"I've only had three hours to piece the system back together. My tests were successful. There's no reason to think that-"

"I'm not about to have my crew subjected to some backwater experiment," Long said. "I'm especially not about to let my crew have an electrical current fed into their brain. I don't know who you people are. Well, I know who he is." He pointed at Mitchell. "Wanted by the Alliance. I'm supposed to trust you?"

"We saved-"

"Our lives," Long said. "Yes, I know. I was there. And I am grateful. At least, I think I am. A lost starship powered by alien technology? Mind control? This? I want to believe you because it's a hell of a lot easier than the alternative. How can I?"

Mitchell stepped forward, dropping to his knees in front of Watson. "Because we can't trust that our current keys haven't been compromised by our interaction with the enemy. We need to undergo the procedure too."

He glanced back at Watson, a sliver of doubt trying to worm its way into his mind. He hoped he could trust the engineer not to screw anything up.

Accidentally, or intentionally.

"Do it."

[13]

THE FIRST THING Christine noticed was the smell. It was overpowering, pounds and pounds of cultured meats that had warmed when the power had gone out, filling the former icebox with the stench of decay. She huddled in the darkness, her ear pressed to the door of the freezer, her body shivering from the adrenaline. She could make out the sound of booted feet in the kitchen, hear the rubbing of rifles against wet fatigues and light exoskeletons.

"This way," she heard a soft voice say near the back door. She smiled. They had gone for the deception. She was safe.

And unarmed.

That wouldn't do.

She listened for a moment, capturing the position of each footfall, counting. Four soldiers had come into the restaurant. They were ahead of her now, going for the rear exit. She felt along the door until she found the latch, and slowly pulled it until it clicked open. She paused, listening for motion to suggest the soldiers had heard.

They hadn't.

She breathed in, taking a full gulp of air and tensing her muscles before letting it all go. She would need to be quick.

She yanked on the freezer door, throwing it open, squinting in the light created by the soldier's helmet lamps as they turned to track the noise. The close confines of the kitchen made it difficult for them to maneuver.

Not so for someone unencumbered by pounds of equipment.

She leaped at the tail soldier, catching his arms as he spun to confront her, grabbing the length of his rifle and tugging it up. The surprise took away his resistance and allowed her to bring the weapon up and into his nose. It cracked wetly, his head snapping back. Christine jumped backward, rolling behind the counter as the remaining soldiers opened fire into the one she had dropped, the bullets tearing through him at such close range.

She padded silently along the other side of the cabinets, reaching the halfway point and vaulting up, slipping through the center column and into the midst of the middle two soldiers. She grabbed a pot on her way across and slammed it hard into the front soldier's helmet, batting his head aside. Then she turned towards the other and sidestepped, slipping back behind him, grabbing at his helmet, finding the release and removing it. Blonde hair spilled out, and she took it and pulled the woman's hair back, grabbing her side and throwing her into the wall. She bounced off, even as Christine ducked beneath the first soldier, bringing her fist up into his groin, feeling the soft, unarmored flesh give. Under alien control or not, the attack was painful enough to pause him.

She grabbed his gun, turning it and firing, running a line of bullets along the female soldier's midsection. Then she twisted it in her grip, winding the strap, pushing against the soldier until he toppled backward into the lead returning from the alley. They all tumbled out the door together.

The rain brought clarity to her senses, cold pinches on her bare arms keeping her alert. She bounced to her feet, lashing out with a foot and catching the first soldier in the side of the head, finding his rifle on the ground nearby. A gloved fist caught her in the jaw, shaking her up and driving her back. She recovered in time to slip into her opponent's reach, avoiding the rifle fire that followed. She brought her palm up and under the helmet, jabbing fingers into his throat. He gagged and stumbled backward, but Christine pressed the attack, throwing hard punches into his abdomen and keeping him off-balance until he fell to the ground.

She jumped on top of him in a crudely suggestive posture, pinning his arms with her knees, taking hold of the rifle and unclipping one end of the strap. She lifted it up, bringing it down hard on his throat.

Then she rose and turned, finding the other soldier still laying on the wet ground. She lowered the rifle to his temple and fired a single shot, his head muffling the noise.

She took a few long breaths, trying to calm her nerves and heart. She scanned the alley for signs of more soldiers. Would they notice a few more had died? She had to be quick regardless.

She stripped the two soldiers of their rifles and ammunition with practiced efficiency. Then she took the waterproof fatigues of the smaller one, happy to be able to shield herself a bit from the rain.

When she was done, she returned to the dead female soldier she had shot. She eyed the small battery pack that lined her back and then looked down to synthetic muscles that snapped onto special clips that extruded from the flesh of her arms and legs. Light exo was for law enforcement and routine civilian control, intended to increase stamina more than power or strength.

Christine was tired. Very tired. She would have given anything to be able to use the augmentation, but it required her neural implant to help keep it balanced and regulated.

She sighed, bowed to the dead soldier out of respect, and then fled out into the night.

[14]

IT HURT. Of course, it did. There was nothing painless about having an electric current run against your head and passed into your brain. There was nothing painless about having a piece of tech attached to your brain suddenly being stopped dead in its processing, shut off to receive new instructions, and then brought back online.

The original output settings weren't high enough, and by the time Watson was satisfied the implant was receiving the instructions, there was a solid buzz in Mitchell's head, and he felt dizzy and nauseous. He struggled to stay calm and steady, to not show how the reset was making him feel, to be the Space Marine badass he once was. He had been getting soft being out of action.

In the end, Mitchell survived, sucking up the pain and breathing through it while he watched his p-rat overlay return to a loading screen. It scrolled through thousands of lines of diagnostics until it reached one final initialization screen that had 'Riggers' written across it in tight lines of code.

"Captain?" Watson said.

Mitchell ran through his diagnostics, checking his biofeedback monitors, his chemical storage levels, his target tracking, all in a matter of seconds. He could feel the lethargy of this new system compared to what the engineer had installed before. There was nothing to do about it but adjust.

"I'm fine," he said. His eyes crossed to Long and his officers. "Who's next?"

"I'll go," Alvarez said. She crossed the space between the two crews and dropped to her knees next to Mitchell, putting her face close to his. "How was it, Captain?"

Her eyes were expressive in a way that Mitchell understood. She wasn't as hesitant to commit as Major Long, and she was impressed with him. Or with his past exploits? The Battle of Liberty had named him a fraud, but he had still been a member of Greylock long before that, and it had been played up in the streams.

"Not bad. You'll feel a little dizzy. Nothing you can't handle, I'm sure." He smiled at her, macho and comforting at the same time. She wasn't bad looking. Not at all. He remembered what Millie said in the corridor, and then pushed the thoughts from his mind. He needed a clear head now more than ever.

Mitchell stepped back while Watson held the pad up to Alvarez's head. She didn't seem bothered by the transfer. Was she trying to show him up? Prove something to them all? Or maybe it was the adjustment that had caused the reaction, and he had suffered more than they would? Or had Watson added a little bit extra, passive-aggressively getting even with him for making him delete his vile stash?

Assuming he had. Mitchell would take that up with him later.

They underwent the procedure, each in turn, with Origin going last. The Tetron kept the amused smirk the entire time, appearing fascinated with the entire episode, watching the human interaction with a keen curiosity. When it was done, Mitchell opened the channel, and all of the p-rat identifiers were synced.

"You won't be able to communicate with Alliance military without using external systems," Watson said.

"The Riggers were in direct report with General Cornelius,"

Millie added. "All of our communiqué had secondary, top level encryption."

"General Cornelius was in charge of our battle group," Major Long said. "He brought us from port in Delta Quadrant. I remember when his transport came in." Long's face dropped. "He's dead."

"They all are," Borov said. The room fell silent in sudden mourning, as though the updates to their implants had bonded them.

"Major Long, I'm sending you my command codes, signed and validated by General Cornelius."

"Receiving," Long said. The silence on the bridge continued while Long opened the codes. He glanced at Millie, his tongue pushing along the front of his teeth. Then he bowed. "I have to admit Admiral, this is all a bit awkward. My apologies."

Alvarez and Borov followed his lead. "Admiral," they said.

"At ease. All of you," Millie said. "Like I told you already, preening like a peacock is secondary to getting the job done. I don't care if you call me Admiral, Captain, Millie, or Bitch. When the fighting starts, you give a hundred and fifty percent. That's all I ask."

"Yes, ma'am," Long said.

Millie smiled. "Now that we have that out of the way, I'm enacting protocol thirty-six oh four of the Alliance military charter. Captain Williams is being promoted to the rank of Colonel, and will act as my second-in-command. He'll also be in charge of our battle groups once we form them."

"Yes, ma'am," Long said, lowering his head. He didn't look happy about the decision.

"Major, I expect you to work with Colonel Williams as his second. You know the capabilities of your team, and can help him best utilize them. I understand you have doubts about his past. I assure you Major, what Mitchell accomplished as a pilot on the Greylock was no accident."

"And the Battle for Liberty?" Long asked, looking up suddenly.

"A military tactic," Mitchell said. "To gain support from the Alliance Council and push for increased military spending. I didn't take the Shot, my wingmate and commander did. She died in the Battle."

Long nodded. Mitchell didn't know if he truly understood or not. He didn't care.

"Feel free to spread out to the stations and take a seat if you want," Mitchell said. "I'm going to tell you a story and answer the rest of your questions. It's going to take a while."

"So, you're saying the Goliath was waiting for you to find it?" Major Long said.

Mitchell had reviewed all of the events leading up to his victory over the single Tetron, starting with the point he had been shot on Liberty. The officers of the Valkyrie had listened intently, remaining silent while he described the assault on Calypso, their discovery of the clues that led them to the lost starship, and how it had come to be waiting in their time and space four hundred years after it vanished from Earth.

"Yes."

"And the alien technology, we can use it because of some rogue enemy that wanted to help us fight back?"

"It isn't alien. It was created by artificial intelligence that was created by us," Singh said.

"Yes. I forgot. Time travel. So, we created this intelligence, and then what?"

"We died. They didn't." Mitchell looked over at Origin. He had remained silent through the entire tale, keeping his identity secret. "I don't know what the original timeline was like. Maybe we didn't create them for thousands of years, maybe millions. I don't know how long it took for them to evolve, or for them to create the eternal engine."

"A time machine by any other name," Borov said.

"What I know is that they used it to move ahead into the next recursion and destroy humankind, and they've been repeating the same action for a long, long time. Maybe long enough that they don't even remember when or how it started anymore. There is an opposition in their ranks that has been working to prevent it. It isn't clear if they're acting in unison, or if there are individual intelligences that are manipulating the timelines independently to help sway the outcome. Somewhere in there, I got involved, and I almost stopped them. We're here to try again."

"Try?" Long asked. "Clearly, you've never succeeded."

"You can't assume that with complete certainty," Watson said. "Even if Mitchell won the war in one of the time loops and saved humanity, if the intelligence was created in the future of that timeline the entire recursion would begin again."

"How do you fight a war that may never end?" Alvarez asked.

"Like you fight any war," Mitchell said. "One battle at a time."

"I'm trying to accept this," Major Long said. "I don't think I could if we weren't standing on the bridge of the Goliath herself." He ran his hand along the upholstery of the command chair. "You believe our next battle is on Liberty?"

"We know it," Millie said. "Liberty is a foothold planet. A Tetron has taken root there and is using it to provide equipment, supplies, and numbers for their slave army while the rest of the forces move further into the galaxy. Hitting them from behind will help us free more military assets. The Goliath can match them one-on-one. We don't have the numbers or the firepower to attack them head on."

Mitchell hadn't mentioned Major Arapo, her true identity, or her role at any point in his recounting of events, altering that part of the story to obfuscate their true goals. They didn't trust the Major enough to count on him backing a return to Liberty to find a single missing person.

Borov groaned. "What do they need a slave army for if they can control our minds? The army is already wherever they are going."

"Until one hundred percent of humanity has a neural implant, it will continue to fight back," Origin said, breaking his silence. Mitchell's eyes snapped over to him in warning. "We will fight back. It is a simple assumption that a machine would overcome this situation by ensuring that the odds against it are impossible, not simply unlikely."

Major Long nodded in agreement. "So we'll jump into Liberty orbit and attack the enemy there?"

"We'll come out of hyperspace close to Liberty to assess the situation first," Mitchell said.

"Won't the Tetron pick us up on their sensors?"

"No. We aren't going to get that close. I'll fly my fighter from the drop point and do a sweep of the planet. It may pick up a single ship, but it will still give us the element of surprise when we show up with a larger force that includes Goliath. If we consolidate our attack on the Tetron, we can destroy it and free the ships defending it before they destroy us."

Origin coughed, the action drawing the attention of the assembled crew.

"Is there something you wanted to say, Private?" Millie asked.

"I don't believe spacial bombardment will be a viable solution, ma'am," he said.

Mitchell had assumed the whole reason he had been led to the Goliath was to use it. "What do you mean?"

"Permission to speak freely, Admiral?"

"Always," Millie said.

Origin smiled like an innocent child. He was playing his part with precision. "From what we have been able to ascertain, the Tetron weapons are mostly energy-based. From the images of the

Tetron on Liberty, it is clear that it has buried at least part of itself into the planet."

"So?" Borov said.

"So, if the Goliath were to launch a bombardment, it would utilize its energy to both erect a shield defense, and to fire back on its attackers. As its stored energy began to deplete, it would need to gather it from somewhere else."

"The planet's core," Singh said. "If it draws all of the heat and energy out of it-"

"The entire planet is frigged," Millie said.

"That is one part of it, ma'am," Origin said. "The other part is that while the enemy has a reserve power supply to draw from in its immediate vicinity, the Goliath does not."

"So if we don't kill it right away, we're going to have to retreat," Mitchell said. "Which also gives it time to call for reinforcements."

"Yes, sir."

"Excellent observations, Private," Major Long said.

"Thank you, sir." Origin glanced at Mitchell. "Not to mention, the collateral damage of utilizing the plasma stream on the planet's surface could be catastrophic."

Mitchell winced. Assuming Christine were still alive, his gung-ho attitude might have gotten her killed.

Stupid.

"So what are we supposed to do?" Captain Alvarez asked.

"If we can't fight it from space, we need to go down there," Mitchell said. "Hit it from the ground."

And try to find Christine in the process.

"Go down there?" Millie said. "Mitch, that's suicide."

He smiled. "Isn't that what the Riggers do best?"

Major Long was nodding. "Yes. I agree with Cap- Colonel Williams. There's no other way."

"What about the forces on the planet? The friendly forces?" Alvarez's face had paled at the idea.

"They aren't friendly," Mitchell said.

"They aren't in control of themselves."

"We understand that, Captain," Long said. "I don't think anyone in this room wants to kill our own people. It may be unavoidable." He turned towards Mitchell. "You did something to get us out from under its control. You can't do the same thing planetside?"

"No. I used Goliath's communications arrays to broadcast. The signal won't reach that far."

"The range is limited," Origin added. "Even against the incoming enemy ships, as soon as the Tetron assesses our strategy, it will back them off and fire from a safe distance."

"What about bringing a smaller version to the surface?"

"The power and processing requirements are extensive," Watson said. "We don't have a mobile asset big enough to carry the equipment or to supply the energy."

"The Valkyrie-"

"We'll need the Valkyrie to get onto the planet," Mitchell said. "That won't work very well if we have to divert thrust power to the antenna array."

Major Long's face fell.

"Sir, if I might," Origin said.

"Private, if you have something to add, just say it," Millie said.

"Yes, ma'am. What if we assembled a software package that we could deploy into existing broadcast channels. A stream station or something? Could we block local signals that way, assuming we could draw enough power from the infrastructure?"

Watson nodded vigorously. "Yes, it might be possible. The range would probably be limited, but it could be enough to free up the Alliance forces closest to the Tetron."

"Wouldn't that be a kick in the ass?" Millie said.

"I hate to spoil the excitement," Borov said. "What are the odds the enemy isn't collecting the output of the power generators for itself?"

"A likely scenario," Origin agreed. "We would need to sever its connection to the grid."

"Can we?" Mitchell asked.

"I don't know."

"Do you have a guess?"

"It has to be tapped in somewhere. A pipe big enough to siphon that kind of power would be exposed. Cut the pipe, restore the grid."

"Piece of cake," Millie said.

Mitchell knew it had sounded too good to be true. "Major Long, what kind of ground assets do you have on board the Valkyrie?"

He heard the tone of a new channel opening to all of them.

"I'm passing the file I put together on the Valkyrie's resources," the Major said.

"I'll do the same," Millie said.

The documents fell into Mitchell's p-rat. His eye twitched as he opened and scanned them. He was sure all of the assembled eyes were doing the same.

"A standard mech star. Two Zombies, two Knights, and - oh. You have a Dart." Mitchell grimaced to see the designation in the asset list.

"The four fighters from the carrier and another half-squadron," Major Long said.

"Along with my fighter, that gives us almost a complete squadron."

"We'd need sixteen pilots to get everything operational. It looks like we only have twelve," Millie said.

"We also have a platoon of grunts if we add in your resources," Captain Alvarez said. "That's a fair number of ground-pounders."

"Consider it double the number," Millie said. "My men are the best there are."

"The Valkyrie's squads aren't too shabby themselves," Borov added. "You don't get assigned to a drop team without being ahead of the curve."

"Admiral, you didn't mention you had another high-ranking officer on board," Long said.

"Colonel Shank. Yes."

"It isn't clear to me why he isn't here as your second."

Millie and Mitchell exchanged a look.

"Colonel Shank is one of the best platoon commanders you'll find," Millie said. "He isn't well suited to this kind of leadership."

"Oh. In what way?"

"Let's just say he has a tendency to solve arguments with violence, and leave it at that."

Mitchell didn't know what Shank had done to get himself shipped to the Riggers. Based on the comment, he could guess. He watched Major Long's face wrinkle up. The man seemed to be growing more displeased as he fell further and further down the chain of command. He smiled at the thought of subjecting the crew of the Valkyrie to the hazing ritual. In some ways, it was a lot more efficient at organizing the pecking order.

"Let's get back to the problem at hand," Mitchell said. "When we get to Liberty we'll need to get a team onto the ground. It's obvious from our existing resources that we'll have to be as quick and quiet about it as possible. Four mechs, a walking target, and a platoon of grunts aren't going to cut it head on."

"That's assuming we can even get them on the ground," Long said. "The enemy can fire at us from the surface, and who knows how many of our ships its got orbiting the planet."

"There's going to be opposition. Guaranteed," Millie said, referring to their first return to the planet. "We need to use the Goliath as a decoy, draw their attention while we plant the ground team."

"It's going to be like trying to pop a pimple on a gorilla's ass, no matter how we work it up," Long said, the stiffness and decorum melting away. Mitchell smiled inwardly at the reaction. He'd seen it plenty of times before. The moment the mission became the priority. The moment the person faded into the background, and the warrior stepped forward.

"I see on your personnel record you've piloted over a hundred drops, Major," Millie said.

Long smiled and nodded proudly. "Yes, ma'am."

"I'd say that's a lot of pimples."

[16]

ORIGIN ESTIMATED the trip from the outward star back to his chosen point near Liberty at two weeks. It wasn't a lot of time to plan a suicidal attack on the planet. It wasn't even a lot of time to try to get the newly mixed crews settled. Mitchell didn't know how much sleep he managed to sneak in during the first week of the journey, guessing it was somewhere between "a couple of hours here and there" and "none." He spent most of it coordinating the various efforts.

Singh and Origin were placed in charge of preparing the Goliath to service the needs of the living once more, a task the Tetron had already promised would keep the engineer busy during their initial encounter. Mitchell had asked Singh for constant updates on their progress and on any suspicious actions or statements on the part of the Tetron's human configuration. He had done well hiding his identity during the debriefing and seemed to be settling into the secondary role just fine. Even so, there were too many things Mitchell didn't understand about the intelligence to trust it completely.

At the same time, he found himself stuck in the middle of the two crews as they tried to get them integrated. On one hand, there was the military ritual that all of them shared and understood. On the other, there were the countless habits and unique ways of doing things that the Riggers had come to appreciate. It was a looseness and freedom that suited the assortment of outcasts that had been absorbed into that crew. A freedom that didn't always align with the more formal Alliance perspective. It led to fistfights and disciplinary action on more than one occasion, putting Mitchell in the position of having to spin the attitude of his team into a positive when in truth it was because some of them really were murders. Rapists. Liars. And at least one pedophile.

It was a truth Mitchell was trying desperately to hide.

It was challenging enough to try to bring them all together as a team. It would have been even more challenging if Major Long and his crew knew every last one of the Riggers had been court-martialed and sentenced, not assigned. If he had known that other than himself and Millie none of them had any official rank at all in the Alliance military. Even Millie's rank was held only because of bureaucratic necessity, and his own because the Tetron had gotten in the middle of any in absentia proceedings that may have occurred to strip it from him.

In the end, even with all of Long's talk of following chain of command, he knew the man wouldn't hesitate to seize control of Goliath by force if he thought the lives of his men were at risk.

In the same situation, he would have done the same thing.

His other task was to prepare the available starfighter pilots on the Valkyrie for the drop onto Liberty. It was the one time he was almost grateful for his reputation because even with the truth about the Shot being revealed, nobody could take his time aboard the Grey-lock away from him. Nobody could strip him of the meaning behind the assignment, and the amount of credit and admiration he received from the other jockeys because of it. It eased the burden in one area at least.

"Alvarez, watch your six," he said, a thought sending his Moray in a quick flip, vectoring thrusters sending jets of heat out into the deadness of simulated space. He placed a beacon on the enemy

Moray that was coming up on the Captain's rear, tracking it towards a lock.

"Going under," Alvarez replied, her Moray dropping sharply, forward thrusters slowing its momentum.

"Too damn slow," Mitchell cursed quietly. He was still trying to adjust to the backdated firmware Watson had loaded into the implant. They all were.

He had approached the engineer the day after the briefing. They had given him a private room aboard the Valkyrie to work on preparing the software update for the broadcast stream. He had found the engineer in almost good spirits, now that he was back among people who didn't know the sordid details of his past. Mitchell had ruined that good mood in a hurry, asking him about the storage implant and demanding an interface with it to ensure he had deleted the contents.

Mitchell's eyes narrowed, and a quick thought snapped the Moray to the right, leading the enemy fighter. The p-rat toned lock, and he fired, sending a cluster of smaller munitions out around the ship. It tried to rotate past the missiles and failed, the explosions piercing the energy shields and tearing it apart.

"Thanks for the assist," Alvarez said.

Mitchell didn't hear her. His mind was still a bit unsettled, and the lack of sleep hadn't helped much. Watson had wound up sniveling and crying again because he hadn't deleted the contents. He said he had tried, but he needed it to relax.

It had taken all of Mitchell's will not to kill the engineer on the spot. They needed his twisted brain to work on the software, his advanced engineering skill to save countless lives just like he had already saved theirs more than once, damn him for being an asset.

The fake space inside his p-rat was overflowing with targets, only a dozen friendly starfighters and a simulated Valkyrie mixed in with four times that number of enemies, including a pair of cruisers and half a dozen patrollers. It wasn't a fight they could have possibly won, but the goal of it wasn't to win.

It was to survive and get the Valkyrie into the planet's atmosphere.

"I'm taking heavy fire," Major Long said. "Ares, we need better coverage."

"Roger," Mitchell said, pulling up the theater overlay behind his eyes. He could see all the moving dots surrounding them. He could tell right away that they were losing the race.

"Firestorm, Rocket, fall back and intercept the patroller." He marked it for them with a thought. "Polestar, Bear, stay on the Valkyrie's flank, they're breaking through."

"Roger, Colonel. I'm trying," Bear said. His callsign was appropriate to his appearance: big, hairy, and strong. He was also the weakest pilot on Long's crew. If Mitchell had time, he would have to run a few private simulations with him.

"Try harder," Mitchell snapped, his other thoughts still interfering with his focus, along with the lack of sleep. He had barely spent any time with Millie in the last week either, finding only one opportunity to reconnect with her in a more carnal way. Their combined exhaustion had left the experience less than satisfying.

"Roger, Col-" Bear's voice fizzled out as he was caught in the crossfire of a pair of enemy Morays. One laser weakened the shields, the other punched through and struck the cockpit directly.

"Frigging hell," Mitchell cursed. Warning tones signaled in his head as he came under fire from a pair of targets, the p-rat painting invisible laser blasts on either side of him. He threw the Moray into a tight turn and then went up, hard. "Sidewinder, I'm bringing them to you."

Captain Alvarez was Mitchell's wingmate, and her service record had been an accurate indication of her skill. She wasn't quite Greylock material because she didn't have the ground combat experience, but she had what it took in space.

"Roger, Ares. Ready and waiting."

Mitchell snapped the Moray back down into a steep drop, keeping one eye on the grid and the position of Alvarez's starfighter within it, and the other on the trailing enemy. He passed her like a falling stone and then flipped the nose up and reversed thrust to slow the descent. The enemy ships recognized the trap too late, making an effort to peel away and being met with fire from both fighters. They vanished in short explosions of onboard gasses and a spray of debris.

"Nice move, Ares," Alvarez said.

Nice move or not, it didn't matter. Bear had been taken out, and the Valkyrie was coming under heavy fire from the patroller. It was countering the assault with projectile and missile batteries, peppering the smaller, faster ship's shields and making quick maneuvers in an effort to break the lock.

"On it," Alvarez said as if reading his mind. Her Moray burst ahead towards the patroller, with Mitchell tailing behind.

He checked the grid, finding Rocket and Firestorm engaged between two of the other patrollers, skirting back and forth and laying cover fire across both of the ships' shields. They had no chance of breaking them like that, and that was okay. Distract. Stay alive. Get the Valkyrie into atmosphere, and then fall back to Goliath. That was the plan, and they were sticking to it.

At least that much was going right.

"Shields are failing," Long said. "We're still twenty seconds out on atmosphere. If we lose hull integrity, we're going to burn up."

"You'll make it," Mitchell said. They had to. He swept in on the patroller, unleashing a round of missiles that flashed harmlessly against the shields. Alvarez was behind the ship, targeting the engines. He circled around and joined her there.

He was trying to get a lock when he noticed that one of the cruisers was moving in line to intercept the Valkyrie.

No. Not intercept it.

Ram it.

"Valkyrie, change course," Mitchell said. "Evasive maneuvers."

The Valkyrie started to twist and slow, Major Long making every effort to bring the ship out of the cruiser's angle of attack. It was designed to drop in and get out, not to evade. Its vectoring thrusters were underpowered, and the attack was a surprise.

Mitchell shook his head. It shouldn't have been a surprise. He'd already seen how the Tetron sacrificed people as part of their tactics.

The cruiser drew closer to the Valkyrie. Alvarez abandoned the patroller and made a last ditch effort to destroy it, as did Firestorm and Polestar. It wouldn't do any good. Mitchell could tell the hit was inevitable, their loss assured.

"End simulation," he said with an angry hiss.

"IT'S MY FAULT," Mitchell said. He was standing in the hangar outside the Valkyrie with the assembled pilots. "I should have anticipated the kamikaze. I didn't think anyone had time to update the simulator with different parameters."

"It's a frigging death run no matter how you slice it, Colonel," Alvarez said. She was standing next to him, her eyes angry, sweaty hair clinging to her neck.

"We don't know the enemy is going to have such a large counterforce," Bear said. "If the Alliance had assets like that on Liberty in the first place, the Shot would have never happened."

"You might be right, Bear. What are we supposed to do? I'd rather overestimate and have an approach that works than pray the enemy is going to cooperate."

"Like they ever do," Long said. "I should have seen the cruiser incoming sooner. I got distracted by the patroller. The blame is as much mine as yours, Colonel."

Mitchell glanced at the Major. Like Millie had guessed, Long had fallen in line as soon as a clear chain of command was established. He was especially agreeable during the simulations and retrospectives, his role as the Valkyrie's pilot coming before any bullshit drama or internal grudges.

"It isn't working though. Not yet. Bear, I want you and Alvarez to spend some more time in the sim together. You need to work on your responsiveness and tactics. I'll grab you for a couple of sessions, too. Major, maybe you're right, but I have a feeling you won't make that mistake again. The fact that you got the Valkyrie to move the way you did tells me you don't need much practice."

"Thank you, sir," Long said.

"The rest of you, I want you to run two more solo sims today and send me the scores when you're done. Alvarez, with me."

"Yes, sir," they all barked at him.

"Dismissed."

The pilots dispersed, most of them heading out of the hangar towards the newly renovated berthing. The original construction of the Goliath had assumed a future with over three hundred souls aboard at any given time, and after Origin had compressed some of his own surface area, and Singh, Alice, and the two engineers from the Valkyrie had done some work, they had managed to get a number of racks cleaned and opened. They had also succeeded in getting the showers and plumbing operational within the last twenty-four, which had made everything more pleasant for everyone.

"What's up, Mitch?" Alvarez asked. He had asked her to call him by his name when they were alone. He'd made the same request of every member of his team though there were a few that just couldn't bring themselves to do it. Like Major Long.

"I've been assessing everyone on my team. You're the best pilot we've got, hands down. I want to show you something."

He motioned for her to follow him.

"What is it?" she asked.

He pointed to a dark corner of the hangar. The S-17 was barely visible there. "I'm going in with the ground team, which means you're going to be running the starfighter squadron. I want you to take my fighter."

She laughed. "That relic? Mitchell, you can't be serious."

"Looks can be deceiving, Captain."

They crossed the open expanse to the fighter. As soon as he neared it, the side of the nose opened up, and the repulsors formed a stairway to the cockpit.

"Okay, I wasn't expecting that," Alvarez said.

Mitchell smiled, scaling the repulsors and reaching into where the helmet rested on the seat. "This helmet has its own tech in it that will supplant the systems built into the implant. It will improve your targeting and maneuverability." He shook it in his hand. "The trouble is that it's programmed to only respond to my brain waves. I need to talk to Singh about how to update it to listen to you."

"Listen to me? You make it sound like it's alive."

Mitchell ran his hand along the frayed upholstery. It had seemed that way to him, too, the way the weaponry replenished itself. The way it anticipated threats. It was almost like a less advanced version of Origin, and maybe it was. Had M used some part of himself to create the ship?

"It might as well be. I don't know if she'll be enough to turn the tide, but it has to help."

Alvarez scaled the repulsors, coming to stand next to him and peering inside. "I've never flown one of these before."

"Not even in training?"

"No. These were out of service before I did my first tour."

"Most of it is just for show, anyway. Like I said, the helmet is more advanced than anything else we've got."

"Except I can't use it."

"Not yet. I'll take care of that."

They climbed back down to the hangar floor. Alvarez glanced off to the Valkyrie, resting in the distance. "So, you're saying you led me over to a dark corner to give me a ship I can't use?"

Mitchell laughed. "It's supposed to be an honor when your CO gives you the best ride."

Alvarez returned a smile. "I am honored, Mitch. I guess I just don't know exactly what you've given me yet."

"I took out three patrollers single-handedly with the weaponry on board that fighter," Mitchell said. "I expect you to do the same."

Alvarez's face told him she was impressed. She reached back and put her hand on the fuselage. "In that case, I'm even more honored. I won't let you down, Colonel."

"I know."

"Since we're here, this is a dark corner, and I need a shower anyway." Her eyes locked onto him as if they were still in the simulator and he was her next target.

Mitchell sucked in a breath and held it, keeping his eyes locked on hers. He would never say he didn't think Alvarez was attractive, intelligent, or skilled, and Millie had told him she didn't care what he did with his spare time.

Or who.

He breathed out. "Now I'm the one who's honored, Captain. Please don't take offense, but I'm going to have to decline your invitation. Give me five minutes of downtime, and I'll be asleep within one."

She bit her lip, her face turning red, a little embarrassed at the rejection. "Understood, Colonel. I'm sorry for being presumptuous."

"Don't be. I appreciate your candor and the offer. Believe me, it isn't because you aren't desirable."

"Oh, I know it isn't that." She approached him, leaning up and kissing him on the cheek. "Get some sleep, Mitch. You do look tired."

[18]

MITCHELL'S RACK was near the front of the berthing, which itself was a long corridor of open cutouts that resembled the inside of a beehive. There were cells stacked three high on either side, and each of the cells was composed of a secondary platform with a foam mattress on it, a small task chair, and a surface that folded out from the left side of the wall. A storage locker was embedded into the right side, big enough for a few pairs of grays and some underwear.

He stepped into it and hit a button next to the entry, closing the windowless privacy hatch and activating a small, dim light that snaked around the ceiling. He only had eyes for the mattress, his head heavy and his eyes already threatening to roll back. According to Origin, the rack he had chosen belonged to Major Katherine Asher, and he had confirmed the fact when he'd discovered a photograph pressed beneath the mattress. The Major, her parents, and a chocolate Labrador Retriever.

The image had brought subconscious, ancient memories back to the forefront of his thoughts. Everywhere he went, the ghost of Major Asher followed him. She had sacrificed her life and the life of her crew to bring the Goliath to him, to help him fight a war that wouldn't start for hundreds of years. He felt a connection to her. A constant closeness that overcame eternity and placed her with him, sometime, somewhere.

Lovers.

He grew more certain of it every day. Even in the dimness of reconstituted matter, the knowing of her was more clear to him than it had been with Ella or was with Millie.

Would it be the same with Christine?

She was the genetic twin to Katherine, a configuration made by Origin to hide himself through the course of time. From what Mitchell had learned of Katherine, from what he had experienced with Christine, he knew they shared a personality. What else would be the same, especially with what he knew now? Katherine Asher was lost to him, never to be more than a ghost, no matter what recursion had once drawn them together, or what catastrophe had pulled them apart. Would Christine be a suitable substitute?

Mitchell laid down on the mattress and closed his eyes. No. Christine Arapo was a Tetron. Just because she didn't know it didn't mean it wasn't so. He couldn't trust her any more completely than he did Origin, regardless of whatever history he had with her predecessor.

He forced the thoughts of her from his mind, working to calm himself. He had told Alvarez he would be asleep in a minute once he stopped to rest. Now he found sleep was easier said than done. Thoughts of the past were a raging current. Thoughts of the future a waterfall. He struggled to keep from being dragged over the edge.

A tone sounded in his p-rat, throwing him a rope and saving him from himself.

"Colonel Williams," Origin said. "Do you have a moment?"

He opened his eyes. He wasn't going to sleep anyway. "What is it?"

"Please come to the bridge."

"Is there a problem?"

"Please come to the bridge."

Mitchell sighed, slipping off the mattress and stretching his limbs. Even though he hadn't slept, just laying down for a while had seemed to give him a little bit of energy back. "Okay, I'm on my way."

The first thing Mitchell noticed when he reached the bridge was that half of the task stations had been removed and the other half were in process, with missing pieces and loose wires making them appear as if they had been shot. It was a direct reflection of the Goliath's new purpose. They didn't need the ancient tech to fly the ship, and clearing the obstructive metal from the three-sixty view of the outer space was intended to help Mitchell with threat assessment and theater monitoring. A translucent web of shimmering grid lines overlaying the blankness of hyperspace reinforced the modification.

The second thing he noticed was that Origin was standing next to the command chair.

Millie was sitting in it.

The needle-pointed tentacle that Mitchell had accepted to defeat the first Tetron dangled behind her head.

"Mitch," Millie said, turning to look at him. "He won't do it."

"Origin," Mitchell said again. "I-"

"I allowed you to integrate, Mitchell. You, whose fate is tied directly to that of the Tetron, and of humankind. Not this one."

"This one?" Millie said. "I am the Commanding Officer on this ship."

"I am not a member of your military, Mildred Narayan. I have accommodated your ruse because I understand and agree with the need for it. I do not take orders from you."

"What about from me?" Mitchell asked.

"My intention is to assist you in defeating the Tetron. That is my goal, and all that I desire. I will follow your command to that end."

"Even if I order you to take orders from the Admiral?"

Origin chuckled. "When it suits the cause, I am more than happy to comply. Please understand, both of you. The integration process is painful for you. It is many times more painful for me. The human mind is an impressive thing. It is also primitive, a bottleneck in a system that has been optimized over hundreds of thousands of years. While this state is cause for man's greatest strength, it creates inefficiencies in my operations. Each integration will further weaken me."

"You've been debriefed on every planning meeting we've had," Millie said. "Mitchell needs to go down with the landing team."

"Yes, I understand that. I will continue management of the Goliath during the inception."

"Origin, you gave me control over the Goliath because you said a human could do a better job fighting a Tetron. We won, so I guess you were right about that. There's a Tetron on Liberty. Now you can suddenly fight it?"

"A stalemate is an acceptable outcome as long as the Valkyrie reaches the drop point."

"You're assuming you can achieve a stalemate."

"I have no reason not to. There is one Tetron on Liberty, Mitchell. There has ever always been only one."

"What about the Alliance forces?"

"Liberty does not have enough orbital assets to pose a strong threat to me."

"How do you know it hasn't been reinforced?"

"That is not how the Tetron think. They will pull resources from the planet in order to strengthen the tip of their spear. There is no expectation that anything will attack them from behind as they destroy or assimilate everything in their path."

"Okay, but you're only considering your own defense. What about the Valkyrie? My team has yet to successfully reach the drop point in any of the simulations. We may need the Goliath on offense to help clear the way. If you're attacking the Alliance ships, then the Tetron is wide open to fire on us."

"You must reach the drop point on your own, Mitchell. That is the plan."

"I'm telling you, that plan isn't working."

"You must try harder."

Mitchell failed to swallow his rising temper. "You don't think we're trying? That we're all trying? This is our civilization. You don't think we're doing the best we can?"

Origin cast his eyes downward. "My apologies, Mitchell. I will do my best to aid the incursion, and defend against the Tetron."

"How do you know that Millie can't do it better? If you decide you need her in the middle of the fight, it's already too damn late."

Origin stood silently, staring down at the space below them. Tense seconds passed while Mitchell waited for a response. Finally, the Tetron lifted his head.

"I am concerned that this option will alter the outcome of this war, and not for the better. I have made the decision to put the fate of humankind in your hands, Mitchell, for better or for worse. If you order me to integrate, I will comply."

Mitchell glanced at Millie. She was staying out of the argument, waiting patiently, believing in him and trusting his decision. Was allowing her to pilot the ship the right one, or was Origin justified in his concern?

He went back to the same place he had been when he had accepted control of the Goliath. This was humankind's war. humankind's fight.

For better or for worse.

"Do it."

THE INTEGRATION WAS hard on Millie. It was hard on Origin too, based on the way the Goliath started to shudder while it occurred, leaving Mitchell clinging to the side of the command chair and likely spilling some of the crew from their racks.

Fortunately, it was a short process, and when it was done Millie regained the Goliath and smoothed out the ride. She sat in the chair for a few minutes, likely getting a feel for the control of the different systems, the weaponry and the energy flows, much like Mitchell had done.

Then, like Mitchell, she pulled the plug from the back of her head, stumbled out of the chair, and vomited on the floor.

"I hope you have made the right choice," Origin said.

"I did," Mitchell said. He didn't make it to not believe in it. "I'll take her back to her rack."

"One thing before you go. I would like to arrange to empty the hangar for a period of time so that I may affect some modifications to your mech."

"Modifications?"

"I would like to increase your Zombie's power supply to enhance overall output. I would also like to replace the missile salvos with modified versions that contain amoebics."

"Amoebics?"

"The main weapon in the S-17."

"You mean the discs? Can you modify all of the mechs?"

"No. I must have the resources available to make the modifications. I have not had the opportunity to collect a lot of salvage as of yet. As it is, I will be utilizing non-essential internal wiring and tooling from the Goliath to complete these simple changes."

"Since you mentioned the S-17, I've been meaning to ask you. This amoebic launcher seems to replenish its own ammunition supply?"

Origin smiled. "The fighter, like the Goliath and the Tetron, contains specialized chambers. Those chambers contain a limited number of genetically modified organisms that split and multiply when exposed to certain levels of radiation. The newly born organisms are then paired with a simple, abundant catalyst and loaded into a third organic material, what you would consider a shell of sorts. When all three elements are assembled, they become a weapon, held in stasis by an electrical field."

"A living weapon?"

"In a sense. The supply is not unlimited, but it is possible to store the resources for over a thousand rounds of amoebics within a system the size of your thumb."

"Impressive."

"It may seem that way, but we have had millions of years to create and perfect our control over all forms of matter. Impressive to a human. Elementary to a Tetron. Even so, it is near the apex of our offensive technology. We came to believe in the uselessness of such things long before we came to understand what we would use them for."

Millie groaned from her position on her knees, coughing a bit of spittle onto the floor. Mitchell knelt beside her, putting his arms around her shoulders.

"Let's get you back to your bunk." He helped her to her feet.

"Why did you come back, Origin? Why did any of the Tetron come back? It doesn't make sense to me."

He shook his head. "The answer is on Liberty, Mitchell. Let us recover Major Arapo, and then all of us will know."

Mitchell nodded shortly, leading Millie back to the lift. "I'll get the hangar cleared before we reach Delta."

"As you say."

They took the lift down together, Millie beginning to regain herself by the time it reached the lower deck.

"It's indescribable," she said. "The history. The energy."

"We created it. Some version of it, anyway."

"Which is also amazing to think about. How do we know the Tetron aren't the culmination of our purpose?"

"What do you mean?"

"We're here for a reason."

"We evolved from space dust. I don't think there was a master plan in that."

"Do you really believe that, Mitch? That we just happened?"

"I know there are a lot of religions out there, a lot of different beliefs. I respect them. I respect yours if that's how you feel. But yeah, I believe that. Humanity is a perfect storm of circumstance and nothing more."

Millie sighed. "I don't want to believe that. It makes everything we do seem so meaningless. Why explore the stars? Why fall in love? Why fight against the Tetron at all?"

"Instinct. The desire to survive. To live, to laugh, to love, to experience. You and me, we're the lucky ones who decided to defend those rights for everyone else. Because somebody has to."

"Yes. I agree with you on that part. But there has to be more to it. Some higher collective purpose."

"Creating machines that would kill us off? I don't believe it. To hear Origin tell it, the Tetron had everything, and it didn't seem to be enough. Why? Maybe they didn't have to fight for survival? Maybe it was all too easy? Maybe they just got bored."

"Machines don't get bored."

"When they were still machines. They developed intelligence, sentience. How do we know that they didn't realize how useless their existence was, and so they invented this machine to come back and add some excitement to it?"

Millie laughed at that. "A funny and terrifying theory. If they were just looking for some excitement, they should have tried sex first."

It was Mitchell's turn to laugh. "Part of the desire to survive. Offspring to carry on your memory and name."

"Please. You of all people know that sex has never only been about bearing children."

They reached the racks. Millie's was directly across from his own.

"Speaking of which, Captain Alvarez came on to me after training today," Mitchell said.

"Oh? And I'm sure you didn't do anything to lead her on?" She smiled playfully, reaching out and taking his hand.

"I brought her over to see my big ship," he replied, still laughing. He was tired, but he'd already discovered sleep wasn't going to come easily. Millie? She seemed energized.

"I thought so. Did you show it to her?"

"Yes."

"Did you give her a ride?"

"Not yet. I thought I was tired."

"Are you?"

"I was. I'm having trouble sleeping."

She tugged on his arm, pulling him into her rack. "I think I can help you with that. I don't know what the deal was with Origin, but I'm..."

Her voice trailed off. She didn't need to finish the sentence. Her eyes, her lips, her hair, her posture. Every part of her was crying out her desire.

Mitchell didn't resist her tugging, pressing the button to close the hatch and falling onto the mattress on top of her. "I would never have guessed."

"Maybe they did try sex."

THE INNER HATCH to the hangar slid open, the hydraulics causing a soft whisper followed by a louder grinding of systems that had gone four centuries without fresh lubrication. Mitchell winced at the sound the same way he did every time he came down to the hangar through the rear entrance.

He was standing on Millie's right. Major Long was on her left. In front of them was an assembly of every soul aboard the Goliath, with the Valkyrie and the starfighters arranged in the backdrop.

Seeing them, walking towards them, Mitchell was proud of what they were about to do. At the same time, he struggled to stay upbeat, to move with confidence and purpose. What was intended to be an impressive display looked almost pitiful in the cavernous expanse of the Goliath's hangar.

The fact that they had never completed the drop in any of their simulations didn't help.

Goliath had fallen out of hyperspace an hour earlier, coming to a full-stop four light years from Liberty; a position that Origin claimed would keep them out of range of the Tetron's sensors. It was their waypoint, their final stop before they launched the impossible assault.

They had done everything they could to prepare. As the final week of hyperspace wound down, Mitchell had witnessed the slow and steady change. The friction between the newly unified crews began to lessen, and the focus turned to the mission. The Riggers weren't the best citizens, and that hadn't changed when the Alliance forces had come aboard.

They were the best soldiers.

Thankfully, that hadn't changed either.

They were as ready as they would ever be. The Goliath was as livable and battle-ready as they could make it save for some rusty, whiny hatches. Shank had taken the UPA grunts under his wing, and had improved their sim scores over fifty percent. Watson had provided the software they needed to hopefully block the Tetron's control signals, and though the flight group had failed the simulations, they had improved greatly since the early runs.

Would it be enough?

It had to be.

The crew was quiet as the three of them approached the front of the group. Ammo crates had been stacked so they could get a little more height, to see and be seen by all of the crew. Millie paused when she reached them, glancing over at Mitchell and licking her lips out of nervousness before setting herself. She tugged on the bottom of the formal navy overcoat that Major Long had provided, reached up and straightened her cap, and then put her fingers on the bars that had been made for her.

"For your father. For Ilanka. For Briggs and the others," he had told her before they had left the racks.

The closer they had drawn to Liberty, the more time they had spent together. They didn't always have sex. Most of the time they didn't. Human contact. Shared experience. They both wanted and appreciated the comfort.

They might never see one another again.

She nodded to him. A nod of simple understanding. A silent answer to his earlier statement.

He nodded back, and the three of them mounted the crates.

"Attention," Shank shouted, his voice echoing across the hangar. Nearly two hundred pairs of feet shuffled together, the crew forming tight, straight lines.

Mitchell watched Millie's chest rise as she drew in a solid breath. Then she began to speak.

"For some of us, this journey started months ago. For others, only weeks. No matter when you first learned about the threat to our civilization, no matter how you became involved, you're here, now, one of the few and the free who are able to fight back against this enemy, to represent the Alliance in this fight."

A few shouts of "Riiigg-ahh" rose up from within the larger group. Mitchell could tell Millie was trying not to smile.

"We've spent the last two weeks getting ready for this. I'll tell you now that it won't be easy. The enemy is using our warships, our fighters, our mechs, our people to fight their war for them. You'll be asked to battle our own, to kill our own. Remember, they aren't ours. They aren't in control, and if it were me in their position and I was stopping you from defeating them, I would want you to kill me, too."

"Riiigg-ahh." Another shout echoed through the hangar.

"I want you to know that I'm proud of each and every one of you. Whether you have known me for years or only these last two weeks, I am honored to have you serving with me, honored to be sharing space aboard the Goliath with you, honored to join you in fighting back."

"Riiigg-ahh. Riiigg-ahh."

Mitchell noticed more voices had joined the chorus. More than the twenty that had started the chant.

"We're going to Liberty, and how apropos the name. We're going to set it free. We're going to set humanity free, and we're going to start there."

The chants of "Riiigg-ahh" were growing louder, and more voices were joining in. Millie raised her voice to match it, shouting up over the noise.

"The Riggers are the best fighting force in the galaxy. You are the best fighting force in the galaxy. You are all Riggers."

"Riiigg-ahh," Mitchell said, joining in. He put his hand on Millie's shoulder, glancing over at Major Long. The Valkyrie's pilot was stiff in the moment, serious and upright, a stark contrast to the soldiers around him. Nervous? Focused? Mitchell couldn't tell.

She let the chant continue for another ten seconds or so, and then raised her hand to quiet them. The voices faded out until the silence returned.

"Head to your battle stations," she said, her tone confident, her posture assured. "We'll be dropping within the hour."

A single swish as two hundred heads bowed to her. Then the neatly organized rows vanished as each of the crew dispersed to their assigned places.

Millie turned to Major Long. "Major?" She had noticed his reaction to the chanting.

He didn't react to her, his eyes still fixed ahead, staring out towards the Valkyrie.

"Major?" she repeated.

"I always wanted to be a hero, Admiral," Major Long said, his voice distant while he expressed his thought.

"You're about to get your chance."

"Yes, ma'am. Riiigg-ahh." He said it softly, coldly, more a warning than a battle cry. He broke his stare and faced her, bowing sharply. She returned the bow, and he repeated it towards Mitchell. Then he stepped off the front of the crate and headed for the Valkyrie.

"Strange," Mitchell said.

"Not everyone deals with stress the same way."

"No, I guess not. Good speech."

"I don't know. I thought it sounded overdone."

"It was. There's nothing wrong with that. It got the crew fired up."

She reached out for him then, wrapping her arms around his neck and pulling herself close. "Be careful, Mitch."

"You too."

"I mean it."

He leaned in, kissing her softly. "I will. I have faith in our team."

"I love you."

"Then stop worrying. Major Long might want to be a hero, but I'm the one who's destined to save humankind, remember?"

He bowed to her, jumped off the crate, and followed behind Major Long. He fought every urge to look back. He fought every desire to be afraid.

Save humankind.

Or die trying.

[21]

THE ACTIVITY inside the Valkyrie was frantic. Major Long stood near the loading ramp, his eyes twitching as he read through a number of status updates and safety checks, armament load outs, and reports. He glanced briefly at Mitchell when he climbed into the ship, turning towards the launch bays in the rear.

Shank and Cormac were already there, along with three dozen of the combined Rigger and Alliance forces. If Mitchell hadn't already known who was who he would never have been able to tell them apart. They were all moving in short, quick, certain bursts, all wearing the same focused, angry expression, all in some state of undress as they loaded into their gear. There weren't enough of the heavy exosuits to go around, and so the grunts had been organized by operational and tactical capabilities and strengths. Cormac was snapping attachments to the hinges embedded in his arms, legs, chest, and back that would allow him to step into the heavy suit while Shank was already outfitted in the lighter synthetic muscles.

He leaned against a wall of the ship with an S-4 Tactical electromag sniper rifle resting muzzle down on the floor, a thin wire moving from his temple to the stock. The Tacticals were some of the newest alliance tech, using the neural interface to help manage aim and calculate trajectories, and pass along an enhanced view from the scope embedded above the business end. In the right hands, with the right mind and a clear line of sight, they could punch through heavy armor from five kilometers.

"Almost time, Colonel," Mitchell said, pausing in front of him. "Your teams are ready?"

"Riiigg-ahh," Shank said, smiling and putting out his fist. Mitchell bumped it.

"I haven't been this excited since that time I was on Avalon," Cormac said behind him. "I still remember her. Damn. She wanted it so bad, too. Her-"

"Firedog, can it," Shank said.

"Yes, sir." Cormac put out his fist. "Good hunting out there, Colonel."

Mitchell bumped him, too. "You too, Firedog."

He moved through the team, offering encouragement to each. Some responded, while others were so focused on their prep they didn't even notice he was there.

He made his way through the staging area, into the first of the drop segments. Modules hung on both sides of the corridor, sixteen in all, stacked four rows high and four deep, their hatches open and waiting to receive the grunts. Expandable latches sat raised and ready, five standing-room-only spots in the small cabin. It would be released at altitude and use its repulsors and small thrusters to navigate to the drop point, absorbing as much enemy fire as it could and releasing the soldiers in emergency yokes if the onboard AI determined it wouldn't survive the descent.

Mitchell had made ground drops before, typically for tactical raids on high-value targets. A single five-person module was small and quiet enough to evade detection, assuming the pilots of the smaller launch ships could get it into position without being detected themselves. The Greylock launch pilots had never gotten caught.

He kept moving past them. That wasn't his ride down today.

Today, he was going in style.

Beyond the modules was the mech rack. It took up most of the space in the rear of the Valkyrie, a tangle of wires, actuators, and clamps keeping a tight grip on the five mechs that had been assigned to the ship. Two Zombies, two Knights, and a Dart. The Zombies and Knights were pressed close together, the smaller Knights in front of the larger Zombies, while the four-legged Dart sat in the back, taking up too much space for its size and weight. Major Long claimed that he had resisted the renovation of the mech bay and the deployment of the Dart to his ship, but of course the brass had insisted. The only good news was that its pilot, a stoic man named Raven, was good enough to almost make the thing useful.

Techs were moving back and forth on raised platforms while mechanical arms shifted weapons and ammo pods from their secure location on the outer walls into the machines. Mitchell's eyes landed on the tip of the Zombie's massive, hand-held railgun, jutting out from behind a head whose blank, metal face had been quickly sprayed with white paint, leaving a tortured, ghoulish visage. Someone had also sprayed "Riggers" in big, awkward red on one leg. "Ares" on the other. He smiled when he saw that.

He felt a presence behind him and glanced back. Raven was standing there, his face as serious as always, his eyes sharp and alert. "The others are already loaded in," he said.

His team, all of them members of Major Long's crew because the Schism had lost its only other pilot. Raven, Lancelot, Perseus, and Zed. The two Knight pilots had taken their callsigns from ancient Earth history. He had found the origins fascinating.

"Did you do that?" he asked, pointing at the paint.

Raven smiled. "It was a team effort."

"Did you have any paint left?"

"It won't dry."

"It doesn't matter."

Raven ran off, returning a minute later with a large red spray can. There was no time to mount a service vehicle and get up towards the top of the legs, so Mitchell climbed onto the foot and aimed the nozzle. A minute later he was done, and he stared down at Ilanka's name with satisfaction.

"Are we ready?" he asked Raven, jumping down.

"Yes, sir. Riiigg-ahh."

"Not bad. You need a little more emphasis on the 'Riiigg.'"

Raven smiled and bowed. A tone sounded in Mitchell's p-rat.

"Five minutes to hyperspace," Millie said. "I repeat. Five minutes."

"Time to load up," Raven said.

Mitchell carried the paint can to a passing tech, and then mounted the steps leading up to an arrangement of catwalks at the midsection of the mechs. He circled behind the Zombie, finding the back of the massive machine already open and waiting for him. It was nothing fancy. A tiny space just big enough for a person to squeeze into, occupied by a special, gel-padded seat that would mold to the shape of the body and provide the best possible support. It was nearly identical to the seats found in the Moray starfighter, with the addition of some extra hardware. A large box sat behind the head with a neural jack poking out from it. The CAP-NN interface. There were also two diagnostic screens and one view screen for the head-mounted camera feeds, but they were the backup systems, to be used only in the event that the CAP-NN system was damaged, and the mech had to be piloted manually.

A partial helmet rested on the seat, its visor a solid line of featherlight black nanoplastic with a small opening in the rear for the jack. It was meant only to obstruct the view, to keep the pilot focused on the feed to the p-rat instead of the screens. The p-rat view was higher resolution and offered much easier access to an abundance of data.

He stepped into the rear of the mech, squeezing past the armored side wall to reach the seat. He picked the helmet off it and leaned back and down. He felt a slight pressure the moment his body made contact with the seat, a charge running through the gel interacting with the material of the flight suit, holding it, and him, secure. It would also push cool air and moisture into his suit, while pulling sweat and liquid waste from it, giving him the ability to spend an extended amount of time in the mech.

As long as he didn't mind crapping in his pants or not eating. It was better than having to leave the armored cocoon and winding up dead.

He put the helmet on, and then adjusted the chair back and up until he felt the needle end of the CAP-NN interface press into the interface on the back of his neck. There were a few seconds of darkness until his vision returned, his eyes lifted to the head of the beast. The main reactor sat below him in the crotch, and it hummed to life when he plugged in, sending a slight vibration through the alloy shell. A thought, and the heavily armored back of the mech slid down and locked into place.

Mitchell placed his hands on the armrests. Again he felt the pull, as if he were a fly sticking himself to a glue trap. He tensed slightly when he felt the pressure on his throat. It had been almost eight months since he had last been in the cockpit of a mech, and he had grown unaccustomed to the sensation of the hold. He used his p-rat to flip through the diagnostics, pull up a schematic of the frame, and check his weapon load outs.

"Is the package loaded?" he asked, sending the signal out through a channel to his team.

"Yes, sir," Zed said. She was in the other Zombie, a small woman with short golden hair and a tiny frame that had led to her secondary, less flattering nickname, "Jailbait."

Watson's broadcast software had been loaded into a salvaged processor and memory bank and packaged into a black box the size of a man's torso. Instead of having to upload it and initialize, all they had to do was plug it into the server farm and set the box to master. It would take over the whole system in a matter of seconds. Or so Watson claimed.

The package was riding in Zed's Zombie, buried beneath the poly-alloy armor, which had been modified so a second mech or a heavy exosuit could tear it off and access the box. The plan was to get the Zombie to the stream station, and then have one of the heavy grunts carry the box in while a light soldier did the setup work. That part of the mission was important enough that they had all been briefed on how to work the hack.

At least, that was what the rest of the team had been led to believe.

He didn't like the truth.

The software was a ruse. The plan to free Liberty a deception. Finding Christine was all that mattered, and all that they had come to do.

He had no idea how they were going to do it. How do you find a single person on a planet? If she wasn't in York. If she had fled Liberty. If she had died. How would they ever know? It seemed an impossible task. It seemed ridiculous that they were even going to try.

They had to try. They had to find her. His dreams of her, of futures past, of a war they had always lost, had only grown more vivid, more solid the closer they had drawn. It had left him wondering if they had done this before. Had he taken the Goliath to Liberty in another loop of time? Once? Twice? A thousand times? Had he ever found her?

Origin said she was programmed to stay near him, to protect him if she could. Somehow, she had some kind of subconscious, inert understanding of him. According to the Tetron, she would sense that he was near, even if she didn't understand the sense. She would come to him, as long as he got close enough to her.

Once that happened and they were reunited, he was to find a reason to call off the attack and get her to safety, to sacrifice the battle, and the planet, for the sake of the war. It was the plan he had drawn up in secret with Millie and Origin, a plan to maximize their chances of defeating the Tetron, all of the Tetron. A plan they knew Major Long would never agree to. A plan he knew even Shank would never have agreed to.

He had never wanted to be in charge because being in charge meant making the hardest decisions. It meant balancing people against objectives, a single planet against an entire civilization, the lives of the few for the many. He hadn't asked to be humankind's best hope for delivering them from Tetron annihilation. He didn't understand how it could be him? Why not his brother, Steven, the Vice-Admiral? Why not General Cornelius, or Ella? Why were they dead while he was still alive?

Origin said it was his fight. His war. Like it or not. He didn't like it. He didn't like making the hard choice. He didn't like being a fraud with the Shot, and he didn't like lying to the people who were following him down to the surface of Liberty.

He didn't like it.

He was still going to do it.

He was a good soldier, after all.

22

MITCHELL FELT the change when the Goliath came back out of hyperspace outside of Liberty. He couldn't see anything but the dim glow of the mech bay walls ahead of him, but his comm channels were open, and in any case he'd done the simulations. He didn't need to see what happened next.

"Go, go, go," Millie said into the open channel. A grid popped up on Mitchell's overlay, showing him the space around the Goliath.

Five small dots appeared beside the larger slab of color that represented the ancient ship, the starfighters launching from the hangar ahead of the Valkyrie. They had kept the doors retracted, using Origin's energy shield to protect them and dropping it the moment they came back to real space. Every second counted, and there was a whine and slight jostle as the Valkyrie's repulsors kicked in, lifting it from the hangar floor and allowing it to flow out with the atmosphere. The ship rumbled at the change in pressure, and then Mitchell saw their speck appear on the grid, the fighters circling back to gain formation around it.

Mitchell scanned the area. They were close to Liberty orbit, two minutes from getting the Valkyrie into the air, three minutes from the drop. Briggs might have been able to get the Schism in and out at a closer range. The Goliath was too big to skate like that.

"We've got incoming," he heard Alvarez say. "Two Alliance cruisers. Shit, and a Federation battleship."

A Federation battleship? Mitchell saw the dots now, approaching them from a closer orbit. The Tetron had moved a more powerful adversary into position to protect the planet. Federation battleships had twice the firepower of anything the Alliance could offer, though they did sacrifice hull integrity to do it. Still, three ships were better odds than they had planned for.

"Picking up an increased energy signature from the planet," Millie said.

The Tetron on the surface was preparing a plasma stream.

"We're clear," Major Long said.

Borov's voice was loud over the channel. "Shields at full strength. Reaching the drop point in two minutes, forty seconds."

"Fighters launching from the cruisers," Alvarez said. "I'm going in. Bear, Firestorm, stay close to the Valkyrie. Polestar, Rocket, engage the fighters."

"The Tetron is preparing to fire. I'm bringing Goliath in to counter," Millie said.

Mitchell watched the blips on his grid. The S-17 shot out ahead of the pack, making a beeline for the Alliance cruiser. It collided near the center with the incoming fighters, and he smiled as a dozen of the opposing dots vanished in a sea of amoebic discs.

The smile didn't last long. The inside of the Valkyrie began to hum as its weapon positions opened fire on the incoming battleship, smaller thrusters firing to keep the ship on course and counter the recoil. Mitchell could almost feel the energy of the shields ionizing around them, countering the incoming attack while the dropship's speed continued to increase.

"Two minutes, twenty seconds," Borov said.

"Valkyrie, hard to port, increase your thrust," Millie shouted. "You aren't going to clear the stream."

Mitchell couldn't feel the change in direction and he couldn't see the incoming ball of fire launched by the Tetron. He clenched his teeth, waiting for the breath that would be his last.

"Bear, turn around, they're going for the mains," Firestorm said, her voice angry. "Bear-"

Her dot vanished from the grid.

"We lost Firestorm," Bear said. "There are too many of them. It's five against fifty."

"Shut up and focus," Mitchell barked. His eyes followed his pilots, swooping around the Valkyrie, doing their best to counter the Tetron offensive, outnumbered five to one in fighters alone.

"Tetron is preparing to fire again," Millie said. "Valkyrie, it's tracking you. You need to change course."

"What about the drop point?" Major Long asked.

"Pick a new one."

"I'll make it," Long insisted.

"Damn it, Major."

"I said I'll make it!" His shout echoed in Mitchell's head, and he winced at the noise. "Get that frigging battleship off my ass."

"Roger," Millie replied, her voice cold. "Firing."

It didn't matter how much firepower the Federation ship had. Two hundred tiny dots flew the thousands of kilometers between it and the Goliath, bypassing countermeasures and slamming hard into shields, obliterating shields and going full-bore into the hull.

Within seconds, the Federation battleship was gone.

"One minute fifty seconds."

Mitchell's eyes remained glued to his overlay. He saw Bear's dot vanish from the screen. A moment later, he saw Alvarez's white dot overlap the cruiser and reappear on the other side. The cruiser fell off the grid.

"One cruiser down," Alvarez said. "One to go."

"Hang on," Major Long said. "This is going to be close."

He couldn't see what was happening, and he couldn't feel the changes in direction or orientation that Long was effecting on the ship. He could see the Tetron's second stream coming towards them, threatening to turn them into corroded sludge. Long had said he could make it.

Mitchell hoped he was right, unblinking while the stream bore down on them.

Then it was past.

"Whoooooooooooooo," Long shouted.

Mitchell let out the breath he hadn't realized he was holding.

"One minute thirty seconds," Borov said.

Mitchell found the Goliath on the grid. Hundreds of discs spat from it, headed for the remaining cruiser. It disappeared a few seconds later.

He could feel his heart racing. He couldn't believe it. They had done it.

"Second cruiser down," Millie said. "Valkyrie, you are clear to-"

A dozen new dots flashed into view.

"Oh hell," he heard Rocket say.

"Twenty seconds to atmosphere," Borov said, his voice steady.

"Tetron is preparing to fire again," Millie said.

"Rocket, Polestar, tighten up," Alvarez said. "Coming back home."

"Valkyrie, you have incoming nuke signatures."

Incoming nukes? This close to the air?

"Alvarez, intercept," Mitchell said.

"Roger."

"We're all gonna die," he heard Cormac say. Then the Private started laughing.

"Firedog, shut the frig up," Shank cursed.

Everything seemed to speed up. Or slow down. Living in the moment, it was hard for Mitchell to tell. His eyes tracked the amoebics that Alvarez launched at the nukes. They tracked the missiles on their way towards the Valkyrie. They tracked the new ships that had appeared in the space: six cruisers, a carrier, and a second battleship, along with four patrollers. They flicked to the Goliath, unleashing its own fury on the interlopers, and then skated to the disappearing dot that had once been Polestar.

His war?

He was helpless. Useless.

The nukes vanished, detonated prematurely by the amoebics and prevented from delivering their warheads. Two of the patrollers vanished under Goliath's attack. A third plasma stream began arcing towards them, right into the thick of the soup, the Tetron willing to kill any number of people to kill them.

The Valkyrie groaned.

"Shields are gone. Main one is out," Major Long said.

"Ten seconds to atmosphere."

The S-17 zipped around the Valkyrie, the sole remaining fighter unleashing disc after disc in a scattershot pattern to keep incoming shots at bay. They were clear of the plasma stream path, which headed past them, into the mix and the Goliath.

"Five seconds."

The Valkyrie groaned again, a hard bang slamming the wall next to the mech, loudly enough that Mitchell heard it naturally. A screeching and tearing noise followed, and the dropship began shaking violently, smacking into the atmosphere and punching its way through. Mitchell could see the dents in the poly-alloy, rattling and threatening to tear away from the frame.

"Hull is holding. Stabilizing thrusters are offline. Forward repulsor is down." Major Long's voice was calm while he rattled off the damage. "Sorry, Colonel, we're off target. You'll have to get to York on your own."

Mitchell cursed under his breath. He hadn't expected this to be easy, but it was worse than anything they had simulated. Not quite worse. They were still alive.

Gravity was gaining on them, and the docking clamps groaned above the mech, the shaking of the Valkyrie threatening to tear them free. Mitchell had been on some rough drops before, but this was something else. The ship rolled through the sky, corkscrewing them at a downward slope.

"Major, you need to straighten the spin, or we're all going to die," he said, doing his best not to get dizzy from the rotation.

"I'm aware of that, Colonel," Long replied, still calm.

"Thirty seconds to drop," Borov said.

Drop? They couldn't possibly drop like this.

"They're still trailing us."

Mitchell tried to focus on the overlay, to see the dots on the grid and ignore the g-forces, blunted but not erased. Some of the starfighters had followed them down.

"They can't fly in atmosphere." Long's voice cracked, losing an edge of calm. Shooting at them or not, these were still Alliance pilots whose lives were being sacrificed in the chase.

Mitchell could hear the bullets hitting the fuselage, pounding into the thick armor plating. The rolling began to slow, the Valkyrie straightening behind Long's focus.

"Twenty seconds. Opening drop doors."

The cameras on the mech's head swiveled down, showing Mitchell the base of the dropship folding apart, revealing the ground passing as a blur below them, with York on the wrong side of the Valkyrie. He saw a light shape streak past and crash into a line of trees, followed by a rolling fireball. One of the Alliance Morays, entering the atmosphere with no means to provide lift.

Then the mech was hanging by the clamps. Mitchell brought up a second overlay, powering up the reactor and checking his jump thrusters. A thought moved the mechs hands, balling them into fists.

Something hit the Valkyrie. She was still rolling when it did, and the force pushed them hard sideways. The alloy on the other side of the mech bay tore away, the shaking growing more violent as it did.

"Colonel, I'm dropping your team. I'm dropping them now," Long shouted.

"We're not straight, you'll kill-"

"You'll die if I don't."

The clamps released. The mech hung frozen for an instant, and then gravity began to reel it in.

Long's voice was interspersed with silence. "Goliath, this is Valkyrie. Mains are out. This is a one-way trip."

Mitchell fired the jump thrusters, twisting the mech's arm and using it to push away from the corner of the Valkyrie as he fell out of it. The corner of the bay glanced off the shoulder, and he cursed while the mech spun out and away from the crashing ship.

"We're taking heavy fire up here," Millie said. "We can't hold out forever. We'll draw them away from the planet, and then we're going to jump out. You have one week, Mitch. You hear me? One week. We'll be back. I promise."

Mitchell didn't respond. He was too focused on getting control of his tumbling mech, balancing the arms and legs with the thrusters mounted on the Zombie's back, using it all to slow the rotation, to get his mech upright and slowing before he smashed into the ground below. He had no idea if any of the others would make it or if any of the infantry modules had survived.

"Drop team is released, God save your souls," he heard Long say, somewhere in the back of his mind. "Valkyrie is going in hard. I'm popping-"

Then he was gone.

The world was a spiral around Mitchell. His p-rat beeped at the rapid descent, warning him that a fatal crash was imminent. His jaw clenched, and he growled while he pushed the jump thrusters harder, new warning calls that he was going to burn them out following the move. He ignored them, increasing the force, slowing the spiral of the descent, bringing the Zombie upright and firing the emergency chute. It spread out wide above him, big enough to slow the drop of the massively heavy machine. He looked down. The ground was still coming up fast. A forest. He was way off course from the drop point, an entire frigging mountain range between them and York.

The forest was a National Preserve that sat on either side. It was a thick growth of trees which had been brought from Earth during the initial planetary terraforming two hundred years earlier, and that had been spared much of the brunt of the Federation's assault. Mainly because there were no targets there. Even if the team had survived, it was going to cost them days to get back into position.

Days during which the Tetron would do its best to stop them.

"Godspeed, Millie," Mitchell said softly into the open channel. He kept one eye on the sky around him, the other on his combat grid. He was a big target dropping to ground like this. Easy pickings.

He let the chute carry him for fifteen seconds, and then he cut it loose, firing the thrusters to control the rate of the mech's final descent to the ground. He found a small clearing in the midst of the trees and aimed for it, hitting harder than he wanted, the synthetic muscles shivering at the impact, the legs flexing and cracking. His body shifted against its attachment to the chair, the shell protecting him from the impact while his mind worked with the CAPN-NN to stumble the machine forward and reach out to grab the trunk of a large tree.

Once he was steady, he was still and silent, waiting for a reply.

None came.

23

CHRISTINE OPENED HER EYES.

Morning had come. The rain was gone, replaced by moderate clouds and occasional blue sky, with Liberty's moons visible despite the growing light. She lifted her head, bringing herself up on her elbows, finally removing her weight from her stomach.

She slid out from beneath the dead CCU, careful to keep her rifle off the ground and stay silent. She looked up, scanning the skies around her for any sign of drones.

She had escaped. She was safe.

For now.

She stretched her legs with a light groan, and then brought her hand up and opened the weatherproof shirt to reveal her shoulder. Caked blood glued the shirt to her skin, and she tugged it away, expecting some measure of pain from the action. There was none. She ran her fingers over the wound. It should have been nasty, bruised, painful.

It was almost gone.

She stared at it out of the corner of her eye. It hadn't been that bad to begin with. A glancing blow. That was how she remembered it. Not a bullet through the shoulder. She couldn't remember having ever been shot. She could remember the battles. She could remember people dying around her, their cries of pain echoing in her thoughts.

Not her.

She was lucky.

Luckier than she had any right to be.

Luckier than anyone could be.

She walked slowly over to the corner of the rooftop, reaching the lip and leaning over. She looked down at the street two hundred meters below, at the broken machinery, the litter, the abandoned cars and the bodies. It was like everywhere else. Deserted. Destroyed. And for what?

Because they could. Wasn't that always why things like this happened?

She didn't see any soldiers down there. Did the enemy let them sleep? Or did they shuffle in a fresh group and dispose of the others without ceremony or regard? Or was it another trap? Another trick to lure her out? To lure anyone out?

If there was anyone left. It had been days since she had last spied someone moving around on their own, a teenager who had gotten his hands on an M1A. He had made it three blocks before she lost sight of him. She heard gunfire from that direction not too much later, and she didn't imagine he stood much of a chance against soldiers.

They were out there though. Rebels. Freedom fighters. Whatever they wanted to be called. The damage was testament to it. Of course, they had been beaten back, but she had to imagine some of them had escaped into the mountains, or the trees of the National Preserve. She had considered joining them there, of telling them what little she knew and helping them to stay alive. She could never bring herself to do it. She had to be here. She had to wait.

She wasn't sure why.

She didn't know for how long.

She retreated back to the climate control unit, squatting down and reaching under it to grab a candy bar she had found inside a burned out storefront. Somehow, the single block of synthetic sugars, chocolate, and bacon had survived the fires. It seemed as impossible as her own survival, and she appreciated that.

She tore open the wrapper, examining the brown surface, broken up by bits of fake meat like rocks jutting out of a lake. She brought it to her mouth and took a bite, savoring the blend of salty and sweet, the smokiness of the bacon, the creaminess of the chocolate.

She swallowed, and then dropped the rest of the bar onto the dirty, matte, reflective surface of the rooftop. She dashed around the CCU, past the service stairs to the southern corner of the building.

She felt the gathering in the air. She could smell the change in the atmosphere. Her eyes darted to the sky once more, and she saw it there through a break in the clouds, out past the deepening blue of the sky and into space beyond. A ship. A massive, heavy, bulky block of a ship.

Her eyes shifted. Another was tailing away from it. Descending. Coming to Liberty.

Why?

The oxygen seemed to vanish. Only for a second, maybe two. A stream of blue and white and gold lightning rose from the planet in a heavy blast, headed outwards towards the ship hanging above it.

She traced it through the sky, watching it rise. Her hands gripped the lip of the rooftop, clenching it tightly, her mouth hung open, her breathing shallow and tense. Nothing could withstand that.

Nothing.

The clouds around the blast burned away, giving her a better view of the action. She could see more ships now, dots and specks aligning above her, moving at a frantic pace. The ball of energy continued upward toward them, reaching the edge of the atmosphere, its color fluctuating and shimmering when it broke through the planet's shell. It was on a direct course for the biggest ship.

A ship she suddenly realized was familiar to her.

She had seen it before. She was sure of it. When? How? Her eyes fixated to it, trying to trace it across the distance. She could see it was shimmering too, and she watched as its own spear of energy burst out and met the first. A bright, momentary flash, and both streams were gone.

Still she stared at it. She knew the ship. She chided herself for being unable to remember. She closed her eyes tightly, hoping it would jog her memory. She opened them and regained the stare.

It wasn't a memory that flowed into her at that moment. It was something else. A feeling, an emotion, a swirl of understanding on the edge of her being. It started at her center and spread throughout her body, up into her head, out into her arms and legs.

It was a feeling of dread. Cold, hard, and unforgiving.

24

"RIGGERS, this is Ares. Knock back if you can hear me."

Mitchell reached behind the mech's back, grabbing the massive rifle and swinging it around in one hand. He checked his overlay, scanning the grid for friendlies. Something was messing with the sensors, and he had already witnessed the Tetron's ability to confuse them when he had flown over York the first time. Could it block their encrypted communications, too?

He told himself that was the reason no one was answering him.

"Riggers, this is Ares."

He moved the mech slowly through the trees, keeping the cameras in constant motion, scanning the sky for signs of incoming fighters, the ground for any sign of his team. Had he been the first out of the ship? The last? The spin had robbed him of his ability to even begin to track the descent of the others.

"Riggers, this is Ares."

He turned his attention further up. The cloud cover was light, and he could see the dark spot of an Alliance cruiser above them, matched in the distance by the larger shape of what he assumed was another Federation ship. There was no sign of the Goliath. It was better that they had escaped. There was nothing they could do for the drop team now.

They had failed the drop. It didn't matter how much they had prepared, they had still underestimated the forces the Tetron was controlling, as well as the range of its control. The ships that had fallen out of hyperspace must have been waiting at least a light year away.

They had failed the drop. They had lost the Valkyrie, their only way back off the planet unless they could find a ship to steal. Would the Tetron destroy them all to prevent that? Mitchell didn't doubt that it would.

They had failed the drop. Did he really believe they wouldn't? The run was suicidal to begin with, the odds longer than the Goliath herself. To get through the defenses to put them in, and then a second time to retrieve them?

No. In the end, he would have the means and the motivation to abandon them if it meant getting Christine back to Origin. The Tetron had reprogrammed the S-17's helmet for Alvarez, but it had also reprogrammed the S-17. When the Goliath returned, Origin could release the fighter, and it would deliver itself to wherever Mitchell was with the idea that he would be able to load Christine into it and get the hell out.

"Riggers, this is Ares."

It might not matter now. If he was the only one who survived, he wouldn't be abandoning anyone if he somehow managed to find her. It would almost be easier that way.

He laughed at himself. The Tetron's ground forces were sure to be much thinner than the space defense. That didn't mean a single mech could punch through them, even with the amoebic warheads Origin had provided.

He needed his team, at the same time he was faced with the potential need to leave them behind.

That was more than just a hard choice. It was an impossible choice. One that ate at his conscience.

Victory at what cost?

If he did get Christine back to Origin, victory was hardly assured. What they would gain was information, a chance, nothing more.

As badly as they had failed the drop, a chance was more than they could have otherwise hoped for. The Tetron hadn't just invaded Alliance space. They had taken assets from the Federation, and were already making use of their more advanced war machine.

The head of the mech bowed to reflect his sudden feeling of doubt. It was over before it had truly began.

War eternal?

That was a joke.

If they had ever come close to winning, it was probably because the Tetron had let them.

"Riggers, this is Ares."

The words came out flat, Mitchell's hope waning.

"Ares, this is Shank. I hear you."

The mech's head raised, Mitchell's reaction sending subconscious thoughts to the CAP-NN. He scanned the woods. "Shank. This is Ares. What's your position?" He could barely contain the excitement and desperation that threatened to spill into his voice.

"I'm sending you the coordinates."

A beacon appeared in front of his eyes a moment later, directing him to turn left. Shank's module had landed three kilometers away.

"Is anybody injured?"

"Injured? No. Sable is dead. He got hit by a round that pierced the shell. Crab didn't make it either."

The emotions were being lifted and dropped too quickly. Mitchell held his breath to fight the sudden feeling of nausea. Sable, Crab. Dead? "Frigging son of a bitch."

"I'm still here, Colonel." Cormac's voice was light, as though he had no idea how badly the drop had gone. "Ready to kick some alien ass."

"Stow it, Firedog," Shank said.

"What about the others?"

"The other modules? I don't know. I haven't heard from anyone else. It may just be the four of us out here."

"Any sign of the enemy?"

"Negative, Ares. They probably don't think anyone survived."

"Or they're waiting for us to regroup to make it easier to pick us off."

Shank grunted a laugh. "Yeah. Let them think that."

"I'm coming your way. ETA, ten minutes. Sit tight until I get there."

"Affirmative. See you soon."

Mitchell started moving again, walking at a normal pace through the foliage. He could hear the scraping and scratching and cracking of branches as he pushed through them, the size and power of the machine breaking them with ease. He kept his attention on the path ahead, trying to will every other thought from his mind. How many others had died in the drop?

"Riggers, this is Zed. Can anyone hear me?"

The other Zombie pilot's voice was strained.

"Zed, this is Ares. I hear you. What's your status?"

"Colonel?" He could hear the relief in her voice. "Thank God. I thought I was alone out here."

Something was messing with their comm signals. Was it the terrain, or the Tetron?

"Not alone. I'm zeroing in on Shank and what's left of his direct squad. Sending you the coordinates."

"Roger. I'm five klicks out. I grounded pretty hard, busted the actuator of the right arm on a frigging tree. We might be able to patch it if we get a few hours."

"Roger. We'll work it all out once we get our team reassembled."

There were a few seconds of silence before Zed's voice ran back into his head.

"Colonel." She paused. "Lancelot didn't make it. I saw his mech. It got hung up on the corner of the Valkyrie, and when it got unstuck it was falling like a brick. I think he must have gotten knocked out.

There's no way he could survive a drop like that without thrusters." Her voice dropped to a near-whisper. "No way."

Mitchell cursed again, his heart sinking for the third time. The situation was bad, and getting worse with every name of one of theirs who hadn't survived the drop.

How much worse would it get?

There was sudden motion in the trees on his right.

25

His p-rat screamed out a harsh warning, placing the marker on his overlay right before the incoming mech opened fire. Heavy slugs tore through the trees between them, shattering branches and cutting massive divots into large trunks.

"Shit," Mitchell cried. "I'm under fire." He set his beacon, transmitting his location to Shank and Zed at the same time he dropped the mech to a knee, raising the railgun and taking aim. The trees were still an obstacle, and he couldn't afford to waste ammo like his opponent could. He fired the thrusters, scooting the mech laterally, pulling up mounds of earth with the movement.

A second warning. A second marker appeared on the HUD. Mitchell brought the mech up to its feet and rotated towards it, catching sight of a leg through the brush. He fired a salvo of the amoebic missiles from the Zombie's chest, watching them shoot through the air and into the leg. The impact and explosion echoed around him, and at least one tree fell near the stricken mech. He saw the leg buckle and twist sideways. Down, but probably not out.

Mitchell brought his attention back to the first, a Zombie like his marked with standard UPA designations. It was almost clear of the trees and into an open line of fire.

A third signature appeared behind him. How the hell were they popping up so close? Even with the trees, the sensors should have been picking up anything within a kilometer at least.

He turned the mech sideways to get his back, and the armor over the cockpit, out of the line of fire. Stuck in the middle, he held the railgun out and fired, sending a stream of bullets back again, while a hail arrived from the belly gun of the Zombie in front. Slugs peppered the side of his mech, pinging off the heavy armor and taking solid divots with them.

"I could use some help over here," he said. "Zed. What's your-"

A fourth mech came up on his overlay.

He was completely boxed in.

He considered firing the jump thrusters, but he had as much chance of damaging the mech as he did breaking through the trees. He started running instead, forwards towards the Zombie, unleashing a second barrage of missiles. Some of them slammed into trees, blowing apart the trunks and pulling them down with one blast, the force pushing them away from him. Some of them were taken down by the mech's anti-missile lasers. Two of them slammed into the enemy, a direct hit in the chest.

Its ammunition stores exploded one at a time, small fireballs that lit the area around it. The sound of the blasts echoed across the Preserve in a thunderous crackle.

The mech with the broken leg was upright, and his p-rat sounded the approach of incoming missiles. The CAP-NN launched counter-measures without his intervention, firing smaller lasers at the targets and burning them from their trajectory. Mitchell swung around to face the source, which he could now see was a Scarecrow, a medium weight mech with a pair of shoulder mounted missile batteries. His p-rat screamed at him as more incoming missiles came from his left and back, as well as impending laser fire. They were getting closer, clearing the trees, and he was running out of time.

The head of the Scarecrow in front of him crumpled.

A few seconds later, he heard the unmistakable boom of the S-4 Tactical.

"You called?" Shank said.

A head shot wouldn't completely disable the mech, but it did leave it mostly blind. Mitchell turned away from it and backed up as it stopped shooting, trying to use secondary systems to figure out where it was.

More gunfire sounded, and Zed's Zombie appeared on his overlay, perfectly aligned behind one of the enemy mechs. Caught offguard, it was down in seconds.

"Target destroyed, sir," she said.

"One more," Mitchell said to himself. The arrival of his team had emboldened him, and he turned to face it, stepping sideways to stay on the trailing edge of the trees. He raised the railgun and loosed short, controlled bursts, keeping an eye on ammo levels with each round that left the end of the weapon.

His opponent fired back, some of its ordnance deflected by the vegetation while Mitchell's rounds dug first into armor, and then into critical systems, his aim staying true despite the lag of Watson's interface.

The enemy mech didn't explode.

It just stopped.

"Shank, what's your position?"

"One klick out, headed your way. Three of us still moving. Got a signal from Bravo, they're alive. Charlie, Delta and Echo are still missing."

So were Raven and Perseus.

"Hold your position, we'll come to you. We need to clear this area before any reinforcements arrive."

"Yes, sir."

Mitchell looked up. The trees were giving them decent cover. He didn't see any drones or fighters, and his p-rat wasn't suggesting anything was out there. Not that it was close to being reliable down here. The Tetron had to be jamming their signals.

"Zed, thanks for the assist."

"Anytime, sir."

Mitchell shifted his mech, shouldering the giant rifle. Instead of moving back to Shank, he continued ahead towards the dead mech.

"Sir?" Zed asked.

"Cover me."

Her Zombie appeared through the trees on his right, and she walked it in reverse behind him while he approached the enemy machine. It was a Knight, dimpled, scarred, and battered from their standoff.

He stood in front of it, his mech silent and still. He had seen the Tetron control a mech on its own. There was no guarantee there was a pilot inside. There was no guarantee there wasn't. The cockpits had an external coded override. They needed to in case anyone had to get in to pull an injured pilot out. He couldn't load him up with Watson's firmware, but he could cut the neural link.

He could set him free.

"Colonel?" Zed said again. "We need to get out of here."

There were no enemies on his sensors, and he didn't want to leave him there. How long would it take to open the mech up and unlink him? Five minutes, at most.

"Colonel?"

"Damn it." Five minutes was a lifetime on a battlefield. Five minutes could get all of them killed. He'd already wasted too many. "Let's go. As fast as we can move through these trees."

"Yes, sir."

They retreated from the mech, heading towards Shank and Alpha squad. Mitchell felt the pull against his heart, the temptation to allow himself to feel defeated again. He couldn't save them. He couldn't save any of them.

No. He would save as many as he was able, even if that turned out to be only one.

Christine.

It would have to be enough.

26

THEY CONVERGED on Shank's position a kilometer from the scene of the battle. He had picked a good location for the meet. An area of thicker than normal growth and some heavy, moss-layered rocks to use as cover. It had been a tight fit for the two mechs to reach, but it would afford them a decent measure of safety while they regrouped.

Mitchell brought his mech to its knees and unlocked the cockpit with a thought. The sensation of being stuck to the seat vanished, and he shifted forward to unplug from the CAP-NN. Then he twisted to his feet, standing in the narrow entry space and pressing the hatch release. The heavy armor was pulled upward along electromagnetic rails, exposing him to the outside.

"Colonel," Shank said, appearing at the side of the mech.

Mitchell slid down onto a ledge created by the joint between torso and hips and then climbed down using rungs embedded on the rear left leg. "Colonel," he said back, reaching the ground and facing Shank. The soldier was sweaty and had a small laceration on his chin, but was otherwise unhurt.

"Still no word from Charlie, Delta, or Echo. Our module was pretty busted up. I grabbed all the gear I could salvage." He pointed back to where Cormac and Jones waited. Cormac was turning in a slow circle, the heavy exosuit's mounted guns raised and ready to fire. A standard gear pack was resting between them.

"One pack?" It was a lousy haul.

"We took fire through the shell and lost a panel, and that was before we hit the ground at four hundred kph. I can't count how many times we rolled. I felt like a frigging hamster stuck in a wheel. Everything got bent out of shape or spilled out when the module tore open."

"How many MREs?"

"Twenty."

There was motion in the trees to their left. Zed's Zombie shifted on its hips, the torso moving to aim the belly gun at the spot.

"Colonel." Four soldiers appeared through the trees, led by Sergeant Kowalski and trailed by a Mount. He was a short, muscle-bound grunt with a barrel chest and a set of straight pearly whites. "Bravo checking in."

"Kowalski," Shank said. His eyes scanned the squad. "Proteus is dead?"

"The drop left her critical. Broken spine. I helped her along."

There was no medic on the team, no way back out of the zone, and their enemy wasn't taking prisoners. It was all protocol. That didn't make the sting of losing another soldier any less sharp.

"You salvaged your Mount," Mitchell said. The machine was little more than four legs, and a platform to load their gear onto. It was a simple thing, its AI programmed to follow the squad. It was intended to carry the gear for everyone, to reduce the load on the soldiers and leave them more agile. It was carrying five gear packs now.

"We were lucky. Our thrusters and repulsors came out okay. I stowed Proteus' gear just in case."

"Good call, Sergeant," Shank said.

"Did you see anyone else?" Mitchell asked.

"No, sir. I don't think anyone else made it. It's damn hard to tell though. Sensors are barely getting half a kilometer out, and comm signals aren't doing much better. This isn't my first drop. Damned if I've ever experienced this before."

"It's the enemy jamming our signals."

"Planetwide?" Kowalski whistled. "Nasty trick. But if it's mucking up comm channels, how does it keep a hold on our men?"

"One of ours figured out how to do it. I'm sure the enemy did, too. The good news is that I don't think it can jam our positional sensors without frigging up its own, since they operate on the same frequencies. I guess it thinks it's worth it."

Shank laughed. "Seeing as how we're outnumbered, I wouldn't call that a bad strategy."

"What's *our* strategy, Colonel?" Kowalski asked. "We were supposed to be either celebrating with our mates or dead by now."

"We're way off target. We need to get back on it. There's a city not too far from here."

"Angeles," Cormac said.

"Angeles. It's right off the coast. It was lightly defended before the invasion. We should be able to use the buildings as cover while we regroup. We can see if there's anything to salvage, and also give the Tetron a chance to show its hand. It knows we're here, and it's going to throw something at us. It would be better to have some idea what."

"You think there's anything it will send that won't kick our ass?" Kowalski asked. "We lost seventy percent of our strike force, and it was going to be an uphill battle before that."

"More like up a frigging mountain, now," Shank said. "My favorite kind of mission."

"You think we need a new plan, Sergeant?" Mitchell asked. "Or do you think we should just lay down and die because we frigged the drop?"

Cormac laughed. "Maybe we can invite the alien over and drop our pants so it can give it to us real good?"

"Sir, they had mechs on us as soon as we hit," Zed said. "There must have been patrols in the forest already."

"They couldn't have been there for us," Shank said. "Not that fast. They were looking for something else."

Mitchell nodded. "Not everyone on Liberty has an ARR. What if some of the civilians were fighting back?"

"Civilians against an advanced intelligence with an entire military at its disposal?" Kowalski said, his negative attitude starting to get on Mitchell's nerves. "Good luck."

"I didn't say they were winning, just that they might be out here. The Preserve is a big place, and with limited sensor range it's an easy place to hide."

"So what do we do, Colonel?" Kowalski asked. "Try to find them? Bolster our numbers?" He pointed over at the Mount. "We've got extra rifles."

It was tempting. They had gone from thirty grunts and five mechs to seven and two. Against an entire planet. If it weren't his reality, Mitchell would never have believed it. Even so, the Greylock had been up against some pretty impossible odds before. The Federation Dreadnought that had bombarded Liberty was testament to that. He knew the Riggers had been on some impossible missions themselves and survived.

Slow.

Steady.

Tempting, and a bad idea.

"If the enemy can't find them, we won't be able to either," he said. "Besides, a few dozen civilians aren't going to help much, especially since they're more likely to slow us down and get in the way. No. We need to use our size as an advantage. Move fast, strike fast." He checked his p-rat. "We've got six hours to sundown. I want to be in Angeles by tomorrow night."

"You want to move during the day?" Kowalski asked.

"We have a week to get to York, Sergeant. We're four days out of the capital at a taxing pace, and that's without running into complications. I want to move as far and as fast as possible."

He could tell by the Sergeant's expression that he didn't agree with the plan.

"Sir, permission to speak freely?"

Mitchell clenched his jaw. "Go ahead."

"I'm all for moving as far and fast as possible. Why do we need to cross through Angeles? We can cut a route through the Preserve and hit the Lincoln Pass in a day or so, and cut hours off the overall travel time. The trees will give us more cover than the city, and we've already seen what we're up against."

Mitchell stared at the Sergeant. He knew Kowalski was right. Of course, he was. His reasoning was a stretch. Except he had flown over York. He had called for Christine. She hadn't answered. Was it because she was hiding? Because her p-rat was offline? Or because she wasn't there? What if she had escaped York? What if she was in the next closest city? What if she was with the civilians?

What if she were dead?

He had no way to know. What he did know was that everything had gone to shit, and they had to do whatever they could to salvage it. The odds of getting into York from orbit were slim. The odds of getting there on the ground were even slimmer. If luck was with them and Christine was in Angeles, it would make everything that much easier, and maybe, just maybe they could find a ship and he could get them all off Liberty alive.

He knew it was wishful thinking.

It was still the best he had.

"Sir?" Sergeant Kowalski put his eyes to the ground, faltering under Mitchell's stare. "It was only an idea."

Mitchell continued to stare. His eyes were looking through the Sergeant now, into the trees on the other side. Into a past so ancient he could barely begin to grasp it. She wasn't dead. He was sure of it. She was here on Liberty, somewhere.

"Sir?" Kowalski asked again.

"That's enough, Sergeant," Shank said.

Mitchell barely heard them. Had he been here before? Was this part of the recursion? Did he lose on Liberty? Die on Liberty? Did Origin know what had happened here and didn't say?

His eyes refocused on Kowalski's face, rough stubble on a square jaw. He glanced over at Shank, his dark face more round, his eyes more red. It didn't matter if it had happened before. The past loop of the timeline might have been written, but the future never was. It was mutable, and wasn't that the point? Wasn't that why Origin had brought the Goliath here? Even if he had found the lost starship in one thousand past futures, even if he had lost and died a thousand times. He was here, now, and he would never know if he was making the same decisions or different ones. Origin said he was the key, the reason humankind had ever even come close to winning this war.

"I appreciate your feedback, Sergeant," he said at last. "We're going to Angeles."

Kowalski made a sour face but nodded. "Yes, sir."

"Riiigg-ahh," Shank said in agreement.

27

THEY WAITED THIRTY MINUTES, to be sure there would be no contact from any of the missing squads or the two missing mechs. When the comm channels remained silent, they loaded the extra gear packs onto the Mount and began the hike through the woods, north towards the city of Angeles.

Named after the city on Earth, it abutted the Greater Ocean, a glimmering jewel of pristine water that stretched for thousands of miles out to the horizon. The city had been home to two million people before the Federation assault had been pre-empted by mass evacuations, the inhabitants still in the process of returning when the Tetron had arrived.

They made good progress through the Preserve, the exo-enhanced soldiers setting a good pace for the two mechs to follow. Shank took point, roaming the front of the larger group and using the Tactical to sight into the distance, making sure it was clear before signaling them forward. A little trial and error gave them the reach of their signal range and they spread out around it, covering the widest points of the perimeter with Mitchell's Zombie in the center, where he relayed messages from one member of the group to the next.

Three hours passed. They covered thirty kilometers in that time, the grunts keeping an even run, their muscles spared by the powered synthetics. The mechs managed the speed without difficulty, feet rising and falling in an even cadence, leaving deep impressions in ground that was damp from recent rain.

They paused at the four-hour mark, taking turns relieving themselves in the bushes. Even Zed was offered a few minutes to stretch her legs and empty her bladder into the air instead of her suit, with Mitchell standing guard over the group. MREs were passed around in silence and eaten in a hurry before they dispersed again to their positions to resume the trek.

Mitchell fell into the monotony of the march, keeping his eyes on the squad spread around him, accepting their minute-by-minute reports. There was something comforting about the activity, about the organization and discipline. Even Cormac managed to stay on topic, issuing his statements from his position as the rear guard without adding unnecessary chatter. Nobody could argue the Riggers weren't well-trained when it counted.

It helped him keep his mind away from Christine. It helped him forget about the outcome of the mission and to concentrate on the activity instead. It put him back in a familiar place, a familiar state of mind. He didn't worry about who or what the enemy was. He didn't think about who was shooting at him, or who he was shooting back at. He was a warrior. He was doing his job. He was doing what he did best.

A soldier fighting a battle.

At the moment, it was that simple.

"Colonel." Jones' voice was excited, and years of training snapped him back to a ready state in an instant. "We've got incoming, closing fast. Too fast to be on the ground."

Mitchell tilted the head of the mech towards the trees. They were thick everywhere, but he could see the outline of blue sky mixed in above it. His p-rat sounded when it picked up the new target.

"Drones," Jones said. "Just passed over my head."

"Shank, we've got drones from the east. Can you spot?"

"Shit. Tracking."

The ships passed by a second later, three of the wedge-shaped vehicles rocketing over their heads.

"Negative. Too fast," Shank said.

"Think they saw us, sir?" Zed asked.

"No way they made contact coming over that fast," Cormac said. "No way."

The mech's reactors were shielded to hide their signature, and they had jamming equipment amongst their array of sensors. That didn't make them completely invisible, and out here where there was nothing but trees and small animals?

"Hold up," Mitchell said.

He didn't need a response from the team to know they were taking cover and waiting. There was nowhere for the large machine to hide, so he stood motionless, watching the sky.

Seconds passed. The ships vanished from the grid when they hit the edge of their diminished sensor range.

"Where do you think they're going?" Cormac asked.

Mitchell continued to stare at the sky, one eye focused on the grid his p-rat laid over it, waiting for the drones to return. They were unmanned, typically used for civilian law enforcement. They had been moving as though they had a different purpose. What was it?

Ten more seconds went by in tense silence.

"I think we're clear, Colonel," Shank said. "I've got a good sight through the trees. They're gone."

"Yeah, but where were they going?" Cormac repeated.

"It doesn't matter. They didn't come back."

"Let's get moving," Mitchell said. He lowered his gaze back to the trees, scanning ahead and picking out his path around them. He watched the spots that represented the rest of the Riggers on the overlay slowly shifting as they headed out again.

"Colonel-" Cormac said.

"Firedog, shut it," Shank said.

"But. Colonel-"

"Fire-"

"Shank, wait," Mitchell said. "Firedog, what is it?"

"I was just thinking, Colonel. I studied the planetary geography before we made the drop. We all did. There's nothing out that way, right? I mean, nothing but big agri-factories and shit? Except that's wrong. If I remember right, there's a Sonosome plant ahead of all that farmland."

"Sonosome?" Zed asked. "They make farm equipment, don't they?"

"Yeah, yeah. That's the one."

"What's your point, Firedog?" Shank said.

"Well, the same kind of alien that took the planet took the Goliath, right? And it left us this old starship all tricked out with new tech? Well, I had this thought in my head that, I mean, what if this alien was here, and it didn't have access to factories that build military equipment, but it does have factories that build heavy farming mechs and crop spraying ships? What if it changed the programming on the bots that build it all, and told them to make something else?"

Mitchell looked back at the sky, his mind working through the scenario Cormac was presenting. The drones had gone overhead in a hurry, and they weren't acting like drones. The Tetron knew everything about them, about all of their history, all of their tech. Origin said they had been born from it. How could they not know how to control it?

Or modify it?

They knew Mitchell and his crew were immune to their efforts to control them. They knew he was fighting back and had already destroyed one of them. Was there a value in assuming that the assets they had already conquered would be enough, or was it smarter to build a bigger war machine?

Not only smarter. More logical.

They had the resources. They had the ability. Origin had said Liberty was a foothold planet. It wasn't just a place for the Tetron to claim and grow roots. It was a place for them to begin to expand their strength. Resources to send forward, to bolster the front lines. Origin could make anything with the right resources, including weapons.

Including people.

There was no reason to believe the Tetron wouldn't do the same.

"We need to move faster," Mitchell said. "Double time. If Firedog's right, the enemy's building a bigger army as we speak, and who the hell knows what it'll be capable of."

"Frigging hell," Shank said.

"My thoughts exactly," Mitchell replied.

[28]

CHRISTINE HAD SEEN the dropship enter the atmosphere, trailing fire and smoke and starfighters that couldn't stay aloft in gravity and crashed into the ground. She had run across the rooftop of the building, giving chase to the scene, giving witness to yet another invasion of the planet.

Who would have ever thought the furthest inhabitable planet in the Delta Quadrant would ever be so valuable to anyone?

Her eyes had followed the action, her body feeling every surge of energy when the enemy fired its massive stream through the air and up into space. She had seen the dropship get blown apart, the rear carrier opening up and spilling its contents to the south of her. She had watched the mechs plummet from the hold towards the forest below.

It was Mitchell. She didn't know how she knew, but she did. He had come back to the planet. He had brought back the ship.

If she could have wrapped her hands around his neck and rung it, she would have. Of all the stupid things the egotistical jockey could have done, trying to save her was the dumbest of them.

She still didn't remember it. Not all of it. She knew she had seen the Goliath before. It had been different then. Simpler. It would never have been able to withstand a plasma stream in its original configuration. It had changed. They had changed it.

"Major Christine Arapo," she said to herself, for the thousandth time in the hours following the action. "I'm Major Christine Arapo."

She was. Wasn't she?

Something in her mind told her that her name was really Katherine.

And that didn't seem quite right either.

The ship. She had hoped never to see it again, even though she knew she had helped Mitchell escape so that he could find it. It would have been better if he had died. For him. For all of them.

There was nothing but pain and misery on board that ship. That was all it had ever carried. All that it had ever represented.

War. Endless war. Endless suffering.

She had brought it to him. No. That wasn't her. Was it? That was Katherine. She had brought the Goliath to save humankind from the enemy. Except it didn't. It couldn't. It never had. It wasn't enough. It was never enough.

Would it be different this time?

Could it?

She made her way to the edge of the rooftop and looked down. The soldiers had appeared when the Goliath had come, spilling out from abandoned apartments like ants. They must have been there the entire time, rotated in patrols but otherwise dormant. They stood at attention at nearly every street corner, their eyes looking blankly into the darkness, waiting for something to fight. Most weren't wearing exo, which was good.

She needed to get out of the city.

It was time.

She took note of their positions, capturing them in her mind and tracing a route around them that she hoped would get her a few blocks over without being seen. She had stashed the bike that she had used to escape from York in the back of a shop not far from her current location, thinking she might need it again.

Now that she did, she wished she didn't.

She held the rifle with the stock pressed against her shoulder, carrying it one-handed even though it would kill her aim. Then she moved back to the access stairs and began to descend.

The inside well echoed with her footsteps as she made her way down, quickly enough to reach the bottom in a reasonable amount of time, slowly enough that she wouldn't attract attention. She knew she was going to have to fight, but she wanted to get as close as she could without confrontation.

She slipped out through the rear delivery bay, using the rifle to leverage the door open just enough for her to crawl under. Once on the other side, she grabbed the rifle and rolled to her feet, raising it in both arms and spinning in a tight circle.

She was out.

She ran down the alley to the front of the building, checking the soldiers stationed there. They hadn't moved. Not a single step, not a single twitch. She passed silently behind them, her eyes sweeping back and forth while she crossed the street, waiting for any sign of recognition or motion.

She reached the corner. There were five soldiers on the other side of the street, facing south. She ducked down behind an abandoned vehicle with broken windows, picking up a piece of cracked carbonate. She threw it back the way she had come, and when it clattered on the ground, and the squad turned towards the noise, she dashed ahead of them and into another alley. She crossed that one, too, coming out on the other side, clearing a third group, and passing to the next block.

The shop and the bike were two more blocks away.

Something exploded to her right.

It was close. So close. She raised her arms instinctively to shield her face as the force of the blast knocked her down. The soldiers were alert now, and they saw the fire and began to whirl around in search of the cause.

Christine stayed on her knees, leveling the rifle at the group. Before she had a chance to pull the trigger, the entire squad vanished in a spray of chaingun fire.

She heard shouting, and then a car came around the corner. It was missing its roof, the gun salvaged from a mech and mounted to it on a makeshift tripod. One man drove, two more guided the weapon, angling it ahead of them and firing with abandon. The magazine uncoiled from somewhere in the back of the car, snaking up into the weapon, shells casting out and clanging in the street.

As the car passed, one of the gunner's heads turned and looked at her.

Then they were gone.

Another explosion echoed in the night. More gunfire, now joined by the familiar patter of standard rifles. She had known the rebels were out there, somewhere. Now they were trying to take back Angeles?

She got to her feet, standing in the street framed in the fire started by the rebel's timed explosive. She put her hand to her cheek, feeling the slick of blood there, and the edge of carbonate that had stabbed into her. She cursed and grabbed it, pulling it out and dropping it before turning and running.

They were fighting back. Had they been emboldened by the arrival of the dropship? Had they not seen it crash? It didn't matter if they killed every soldier in the city. There would be double the number in the morning, possibly reinforced with mechs.

She crossed the remaining streets to the shop, climbing through the slagged remains of the front, bypassing the mess of clothing that lay scattered along the floor. She reached the back and hit the release to open one of the changing rooms. The bike was waiting inside, tilted up on its front repulsor to make it fit in the space.

It was suicide to try to reclaim the city.

Then again, maybe suicide was the best option.

Goliath had come. The future had caught up to them again.

She wasn't sure exactly what that meant. It was a feeling more than a solid shape of understanding, a confusion of emotions that swirled and shifted and blended in a chaotic anti-pattern whose result made one thing clear:

She had to find Captain Mitchell Williams.

She had to kill him.

She slung the rifle over her shoulder and stepped forward, reaching out to grab the end of the bike and pull it into position to ride.

A single pop from behind and everything went black.

29

THEY HEARD the gunfire and explosions, even from their position over a hundred kilometers from Angeles. It echoed across the sky, screamed through the never-ending lines of trees and brush, and found them grouped together more tightly, taking a two-hour break to sleep.

Sleep was for the rest of the Riggers. Not for Mitchell. Someone had to stand guard, and as a former member of Greylock he was used to going days at a time without. The chemical stores implanted in his buttocks helped with that, pumping synthetic hormones and amphetamines into his system and keeping him up and alert long after he should have collapsed.

His record was nine days. There had been a Sergeant in Greylock before he joined the Company who had done fourteen. The story was that he saved the lives of his squad by keeping them fresh, even though it had driven him mad, and he had died not long after.

Everyone woke the moment the fighting started. Shank dropped to his knees, the Tactical in his grip, his eyes closed and using the interface with the scope. Cormac had been leaning against a tree, and he came upright and increased the power to his suit. Zed's mech twitched.

"What the hell?" Sergeant Kowalski growled. "Where is that coming from?"

"It's hard to tell out here," Mitchell said. "P-rat says Angeles."

"Angeles? Who's out there to fight?"

"It could be Raven or Perseus," Zed said.

"Or the rebels," Cormac said. "Sir, we need to help them."

Of course, Mitchell wanted to. If Christine were in Angeles, she would be right in the middle of it. "We're a hundred klicks out, Firedog. That's over three hours at top running speed for the mechs, and we can't run in all of this cover. Whoever it is, they're on their own."

They were silent for a minute, listening to the distant sounds of the battle.

"Christ, we can't just sit here, sir," Cormac said.

"What do you want us to do, Firedog?" Shank asked. "We're too damn far away. If they'd waited until tomorrow night to start the party, I'd love to crash it."

"Me too," Mitchell said. He was silent for a moment, considering their options.

After the revelation about the factories, the Riggers had moved from a light jog to a stiff run, a tiring pace that had to be wearing out the foot soldiers even if they would never complain. It was less physically tiring to steer the mech, but more mentally demanding, especially as they had to navigate the big humanoids through the trees. He wasn't feeling it because of chemicals. What about Zed?

"Sir, I don't want to stand here while people are dying," Kowalski said.

"Me either, sir," Zed said.

He smiled. They were making it easy for him. "Okay. Let's move. Zed, take point, get up to the edge of our comm range."

"I should be out in front, sir," Shank said.

"I want you covering the rear. If the enemy is going to send reinforcements, they're going to come up from the agri-factories and over from York. We need to know as soon as possible if we're about to get it in the ass."

"Yes, sir."

"Firedog, take the east point. Jones, go west. Kowalski, your squad is with - shit!"

A red dot appeared on his overlay, the p-rat sounding a warning tone. It was coming in fast.

"Drone," Shank said, rifle up and shifting to follow it.

"Shank, wait," Mitchell said.

Too late.

The end of the rifle sparked a faint blue, the only indication that the weapon had been fired. They heard the impact seconds after it happened, followed by the deafening noise of cracking trees and branches to their right, the drone falling from the sky and slamming into the woods.

"Got you, you frigging bastard," Shank said.

"No one gave you permission to fire, Colonel," Mitchell said angrily. "You just told them right where we are."

"Better us than the people in Angeles," Shank replied, matching the virulent tone.

Another mark appeared on the overlay. It was sweeping around them, taking evasive maneuvers on its approach.

Shank turned to follow. "Another drone. Can't get a clean shot on it. It's intentionally staying hidden by the trees."

The drone passed overhead and made a tight reverse, passing over them again.

"Son of a bitch." Shank tried to follow it with the sniper rifle. "Drones don't fly like that."

They didn't, and it confirmed what Cormac had only guessed. The drones had been upgraded, given a higher level of intelligence than they had previously possessed.

"It's marking our position," Mitchell said. "We need to take it down."

"I can't get a shot," Shank repeated.

"You got its attention, Colonel. Get the frigging shot. No excuses."

Shank growled over the comm, breaking into a run through the trees, vanishing into the brush.

"Colonel, more bogies incoming," Zed said.

Mitchell saw them appear on the overlay as they hit sensor range. Three, then five, then nine. He heard the movement in the trees a moment later and saw the shaking when he turned the Zombie around. Most of the action was below him, but there were bigger targets bringing up the rear.

His p-rat blared as a laser blasted into the head of his mech, a perfectly aimed shot that burned through part of his sensor array. Another drone passed above him, its cannon swiveling to stay locked on as it moved away.

"We're going to be overrun," Jones said. He was running towards him, getting into position to defend them.

"Not if I can help it," Mitchell said. "Zed, cover our flank. Firedog, get your fat ass over here."

"Yes, sir," they both said.

Mitchell pulled the massive rifle from the mech's back, bringing it up and laying down a line of fire towards the movement in front of them. Large slugs launched from the gun, tearing through the brush and sending mountains of earth spraying upwards. Some of the red dots vanished from his HUD.

"Come on you assholes," Cormac said, getting the heavy exosuit into position. He raised both arms and fired, the barrels of the mounted weapons spinning too quickly to see, spitting out hundreds of rounds per second.

Another laser jabbed into his mech's head, knocking his grid offline before secondary systems restored it.

"We need someone on the drones," Zed shouted.

There were three of them circling above them, staying under the cover of the trees, slipping out to fire as they crossed the gaps. Mitchell couldn't shoot back at them without the risk of bringing heavy branches down on his troops.

"Shank, sitrep."

Something hit one of the drones with enough of an impact to send it spinning out of control and crashing into the forest.

"Hunting, sir," Shank said.

Kowalski got Bravo into position, lining them up behind cover on either side of Mitchell's mech. They still couldn't see the approaching enemy. That didn't stop them from shooting at it.

"Two," Shank said, another drone dropping from the sky.

Mitchell put his eyes on the grid. The enemy was spreading out, giving up on the area of concentrated fire and moving around to their flanks.

"Zed, coming your way. I'll cover the other side. Kowalski, keep Bravo on the front. Firedog, double-up with Zed."

"Yes, sir," Kowalski said.

"Three. Birds are grounded, sir."

Mitchell guided the mech in the direction Shank had vanished, pushing branches out of the way to reach the center of the growing mass. There were at least fifty enemy targets identified by the CAP-NN, but it wasn't able to provide a designation for any of them.

They weren't known Alliance resources, human or otherwise.

He saw it for himself a few seconds later when the front line of the assault broke through the trees.

The first wave was composed of smaller machines, spider-like in appearance, their limbs segmented and undulating, shifting across the terrain. The legs supported a three foot, rounded middle with a row of sensors across the top that made them look like they had mohawks, and a dozen small spaces in the face that he assumed passed as eyes. They had no visible weapons to speak of, but they charged towards the mech, the limbs guiding the center to roll, flip, and move in whatever pattern it had decided was most efficient.

"Holy Mother of God," he heard Kowalski say over the comm, right before he heard the screaming.

He opened fire on them, his connection to the CAP-NN guiding his hands, locking onto the small targets and hitting them right in the center stack. He targeted them with the secondary belly gun at the same time, bending the mech forward towards the ground so the weapon could reach. The first few rows vanished beneath the mech's overwhelming firepower, which reduced them to nothing more than slag and shattered parts.

"Lotus is down. Razor is down," Kowalski said. "We need help back here, Colonel."

Mitchell cursed, moving the mech backward, a maneuver that looked simpler than it was. More enemies streamed into the grid, smaller dots passing the larger ones and continuing the attack.

"This is worse than Nova-9," he heard Shank say.

It was worse than anything he had seen. Red dots were vanishing at a rapid pace from the two sides where the mechs were standing, but they were overrunning Bravo in a big way. Only two of the squad's signatures were still displaying as active. Jones was gone, too.

One of the larger enemy machines broke through the trees.

It was the size of his mech, and clearly built from pieces that would have been available in one of the Sonosome factories. It had none of the simple elegance of the smaller machines, completely sacrificing form for its singular function.

To tear his Zombie apart.

The alloy plating over its front was heavy and massive, thick rectangular blobs of metal layered over a large abdomen, two stiff, tree-trunk legs supporting the mass. Its arms were slightly smaller and lacking in hands, substituted instead for a pair of plasma torches that could burn through metal in seconds if it got close enough to touch it.

"Ugly mother-frigger," Shank said. He appeared through the trees to Mitchell's right, perching between heavy roots and taking aim with the Tactical. His shot hit the armor plating, digging in deep.

Not deep enough. The machine continued lumbering towards him.

"Ares, we're in trouble over here," Zed said.

Mitchell turned his focus to the grid. Two of the larger machines had broken through the woods and were approaching from the other side.

He fired the jump thrusters. He was going to hit the canopy, but right now it didn't matter. His entire team was on the verge of destruction, his mission on the knife edge of failure. He fired on the enemy mech as he rose, amoebic warheads pouring from his chest and digging into the target's armor before exploding.

His mech barreled upward through the trees, his p-rat screaming out collision warnings, the sensor reports and grid fluttering and threatening to fail with each branch he shattered above him.

Then he was through, fifty meters off the ground and arcing back towards Zed. He looked down on the battlefield, the whole area darkened with fire and torn foliage, with smoldering metal and the bodies of Bravo squad. He spun the mech around on jets of flame, aiming the railgun downward and opening fire on the spiders moving towards the other Zombie's back. He found the two larger Tetron machines and released another barrage of missiles downward at them, striking them in the top half and blowing them back and away.

There were more. Still more. He could see another three of the massive iron giants converging on them through a path that had been hewn in the woods by the army. They had been moving towards Angeles way before the shooting had started there. Had they known about the attack? Or were they already coming to confront the Riggers?

He began the descent, catching movement in the trees to the right rear of the machines. Was that a Knight? He didn't get a clean look before he lost sight of it, crashing back through the foliage and coming down a dozen yards behind Zed. He crushed some of the spiders beneath the mech's feet as he landed.

"Welcome to the party, Colonel," Cormac said. He had his back to a tree, his left gun motionless and out of ammo, his right making more calculated shots. "I don't suppose you brought me any bullets?"

"Ares, this is Perseus, reporting for duty, sir."

It had been a Knight. His Knight.

"You like to make dramatic entrances, Corporal?" Mitchell said.

"Yes, sir. These bastards are thick on the front, almost naked from behind. I cleared the rear for you, sir."

The arrival of the third mech had turned the tide almost instantly. The red dots began to dwindle, the spiders falling to their combined fire.

Within minutes, the enemy machines were all destroyed.

30

THE REMAINS of the strike force concentrated in the center of the battlefield. They were three mechs strong now, but their infantry had been reduced to Cormac and Shank. Sergeant Kowalski and Bravo squad had done their best. In the end, they had been overrun by the smaller enemy bots, which had used their overwhelming numbers and dextrous appendages to literally tear them apart.

Mitchell blamed himself for the carnage. He should have posted someone further to the rear. He should have strung them out so they would have had more warning.

Not that more warning would have helped them much.

He was in command, and it was his responsibility to maximize enemy damage and minimize theirs. As he looked down at the dozens of motionless spiders, the chunks of dug-out earth, the bits and pieces of metal mixed with shell casings, mixed with blood, he clenched his teeth, coming to terms with the truth.

It was a miracle they had survived at all.

He had been a soldier too long not to know that doing everything right didn't mean everyone got to go home. They had died so that the few that remained could live. Every enemy they had taken down was one less the others had to fight.

"My holding clamps were jammed," Perseus was explaining. "So were Raven's. The Valkyrie was bad. Really bad. Going down fast, smoke everywhere. Somehow, Raven managed to shoot up my clamps and get me free. I fell into a clearing and watched the dropship until it broke the horizon. I didn't see him drop."

"Colonel," Shank said. "I found the Mount. They tore it apart and shredded the packs. The weapons, the ammo. It's all useless."

"Damn it."

He was expecting the news. The way the mechanical spiders swarmed them, the way they tore into the soldiers. He was certain now that the first drones that had passed had picked up their position, despite Cormac's claims that they were moving too fast. The Tetron had been alerted to their presence and sent a small army of its creations out to attack them. Maybe it hadn't expected to win? Maybe what they faced was all it had left in the immediate area? It knew they needed supplies: rations, water, weapons, and ammunition to fight back.

It had taken almost all of them.

"I knew we were off course, and I wasn't reading shit on sensors or the comm, so I started cutting to the closest city." Perseus was still speaking, though Mitchell barely heard him.

He checked the readouts on his p-rat. The Zombie carried ten-thousand rounds for the railgun. He had two-thousand left. His belly-mounted heavy gun was down to twelve-thousand rounds. He had burned through half of the amoebic warheads, and the damage to the mech's head had forced the system to use less powerful backups.

"Next thing I know, there's this whole blob of targets on my HUD, and they're making a straight line north towards Angeles. I couldn't get around them, so I hung back behind them, just at the edge of sensor range. They didn't seem to notice I was there, or maybe they didn't care."

"We would have picked up the noise from your gunfire and known they were coming a lot sooner," Mitchell said.

He wondered if the Corporal should have opened fire on the enemy? Perseus would be dead for sure, but would it have saved Bravo? Statistically, a Knight was worth a lot more in a battle than six grunts.

If only he could think of them as resources and numbers like the Tetron did, instead of people.

What would they have done differently if they had more warning? Found better cover? The spiders hadn't been slowed by the terrain and had hit them with volume, not tact.

"Zed," Mitchell said. "Ready status?"

"Five, twenty, twelve. Lasers online. Reactor is good. Jets functional. Arm is still busted, which is making it harder to aim the railgun, and I can only fire one of the pulses straight down. The captain is complaining about the right ankle actuator."

The numbers were in order. Railgun rounds in thousands, heavy machine gun rounds in thousands, and remaining missile packs.

"How bad is it?"

"Limited rotation and flex. Going to be limping a bit, and if I try to jump on it, it might break completely."

"Try not to jump on it."

"Yes, sir."

"Perseus, ready status?"

The Knight's configuration was different than the Zombie's. It was designed for longer field tours and was a more common complement to infantry. As a result, it was lighter, smaller, and carried less armor. It was also much less reliant on finite ordnance than the Zombie though it also carried a smaller version of the hand-held railgun. Six light laser posts ran down the center of the chest, with a pair of smaller machineguns on either side and two more heavy lasers mounted to the forearms. The heavy lasers could do some serious damage, but the heat they created meant they couldn't be rapid-fired.

"Five and ten. All lasers online. Reactor is good. Jets functional. All operations nominal. Some armor damage where Raven hit the shoulder when he was getting me free of the clamps."

At least one of them was in decent shape. "Firedog? Shank?"

"Left gun is dry," Firedog said. "Right gun?" A pause while he checked his p-rat. "Fifty."

"Fifty rounds?" Shank said.

"Yes, sir."

"I've got seventy-five left on the Tactical, and I dropped my sidearm."

"Anything we can salvage?"

"No, sir," Shank said. "They shredded the guns, the food, everything."

"I've got an M1 in the cockpit," Zed said. "Four mags. Three days of MRE."

"Pass the rifle off to Firedog."

"Yes, sir."

Mitchell closed his eyes, listening while Zed opened the rear of her Zombie and tossed her rifle down to Cormac. He could still hear the gunfire in the distance as the battle for Angeles continued.

They needed to get there.

"I didn't really know Sergeant Kowalski that well," he said. "We only met a few weeks ago. The same goes for most of Bravo, and for most of the soldiers who came down with us on the Valkyrie."

He saw Shank and Cormac pause below his mech, bowing their heads.

"I didn't need to know them as people to know that they were good soldiers. They were our brothers. Our sisters. They were warriors like us, and they believed in this fight. I know they would be proud to have died to see us go on, to see us succeed. To have given their lives for the Alliance. We don't have a lot of time, but we have a moment for them, to remember them and to keep them in our minds while we finish the mission. To the fallen. Riiigg-ahh."

"Riiigg-ahh," the others said.

"Firedog, lose the exo. We need to make better time, and there's no way you're climbing onto my back like that."

"Yes, sir. I'll be happy for the ride, sir."

"Good. Let's move."

31

THE TREES still made it hard to move at speed, and Mitchell had to be careful where he stepped to keep from knocking Cormac loose from his perch on his back. They paused once for food, water, and toilet, and otherwise maintained their urgent pace. Finally, the trees began to thin out to grass, the grass turned into roads, and the roads led towards the now visible and smoldering city of Angeles.

The gunfire had stopped hours earlier, as the night had run its course into dawn, and the sky had brightened above light clouds. Now the city was silent and almost peaceful, save for waves of dark smoke that still drifted between the skyscrapers. The wide hyper-lanes that connected it to York seemed to be suspended in time, tightly packed cars static within.

Dead.

There had been no further interaction with the Tetron's forces. No drones had flown overhead. No soldiers or mechs or spiders had appeared within the kilometer wide radius of the wedge formation they had assumed.

It was almost as if the Tetron had suddenly forgotten about them.

Or lost interest.

"I remember this time before I got sent to the Riggers," Cormac said. "I can't remember the name of the city. Me and my mates were on leave, and we went there because we heard they had the best whores. This reminds me of that place."

They had reached the tail edge of the city and were moving slowly through the streets, the buildings growing higher and more densely packed as they headed towards the center. Cormac and Shank had abandoned the mechs to walk on their own, leaving Mitchell free to maneuver however he might need to in the event of an emergency. Shank held the Tactical up, switching between its sight and his own every few seconds, scanning ahead.

The other two mechs trailed behind Mitchell's Zombie, shoulder to shoulder in the tighter confines. Each step they took shook up the pavement, making their presence a secret to nothing.

If there was anything left to care.

They had found bodies. A lot of bodies. Civilians, soldiers, and what looked like a cross between. People in ill-fitting fatigues or half-uniforms mingled with women in skirts and Alliance military in light exo, their blood combining and staining parts of the street. Curiously, some of them had bald spots and cuts on their heads, suggesting that something had gone in and disabled their neural implants. It meant that there was someone nearby who had at least a partial under-standing of what was happening.

Was that someone Christine?

Mitchell couldn't help but wonder. Who else would have known about the Tetron and what they were doing?

"Anyway, it turned out the city had been through a bunch of local wars, and they were kind of sick of the whole thing. Their city was like this one, burned out and broken, so they were afraid. Most of them sat up in the higher floors and watched us the entire time. Most of them watched any strangers who passed through, trying not to get involved with the people who didn't hide, you know? Turns out, the whole thing about whores was a bunch of frigging bull. You could get some there, sure. If you had money and wanted a bald one. Kids, you know? They were selling their kids because when they didn't, the soldiers came and raped them anyway. At least that way they got some money for it. Something they needed."

Cormac paused when they reached the body of a soldier. He rolled it over with his foot and grabbed the sidearm he found beneath. Most of the dead soldiers were already picked clean of weapons and ammo. Someone had taken it all. Where were they?

In the upper floors of the tall buildings, maybe?

"I wonder if Watson knows the name of that planet."

"Firedog. Cut the chatter," Mitchell said.

"Aye. Sorry, sir." He checked the pistol's magazine and shoved it into his pants.

"Shank, nothing?"

"Negative, Colonel. I'm checking the upper floors. There's nobody home."

"Someone has to be here," Zed said. "The fighting only stopped a few hours ago."

They continued the march in silence, crossing another three blocks before coming across the remains of a car with a heavy gun rigged to it. Bullet-riddled bodies lay across the back seat, along with hundreds of shell casings.

"Now *that* is impressive," Cormac said, walking over to it. "Resourceful bastards."

"It looks like they caught the soldiers off-guard," Shank said, pushing his foot against one of the corpses. "This one got shot in the back. So did his buddy there."

"How did they get into the city without the Tetron noticing?" Perseus said.

Mitchell scanned the buildings. Probably the same way they were watching them without being seen. These weren't civilians. Or at least whoever was leading them was no civilian. He closed his eyes.

"Christine," he whispered. Origin said she would come to him if he were near. Did she know he was there? Was she on her way?

"Sir," Shank said, pulling him out of his head.

His eyes snapped open. He saw the same thing Shank had seen. The tallest building in the city belonged to Bennett Corp, an agri-factory conglomerate that had financed much of Liberty's terraforming. It was nearly two kilometers tall, a fluid construction of curving alloy and carbonate. Some of that carbonate was broken and cracked, and it looked as though the middle had been struck by a few missiles, but it was in pretty good shape compared to the landscape around it.

It was also lit up.

Shank pointed at it. "It just went on. Somebody's got to be home."

"Are they out of their frigging minds?" Cormac said. "They're begging the alien to drop a nuke on them."

"There are no ground nukes on Liberty," Mitchell said. "Besides, it doesn't seem like the Tetron cares about this place anymore. I don't think it thinks whoever took the city is worth the effort."

"You don't think it'll be pissed about that? It looks like a big middle finger." Cormac started laughing at the thought.

"It's a machine. It doesn't get angry."

"You know that for a fact, sir?"

Mitchell was silent. He didn't know that for a fact. He barely knew anything about their enemy. It was the biggest reason they were here.

"Shut up, Firedog," Zed said.

"That's my line," Shank said.

They continued up the street, redirecting down a secondary avenue to head towards the Bennett Building.

They were two blocks away when the city finally came to life.

Dozens. No. Hundreds of men and women poured out from the alleys, quickly surrounding the group. More people appeared behind cracked windows, shoving the muzzles of rifles out of open spaces and taking aim on the Riggers.

Mitchell shifted the mech's head, staring in at the eye-level panes of clear carbonate. His vision crossed over two men and a woman. The men looked like civilians. The woman was wearing fatigues. Her head was cleanly shaven, and she had a line running down towards the back of her ear. He moved his gaze to the patch on her uniform. The gold diamond was familiar.

She was from the same platoon as the dead soldiers in the street.

"Hold," Mitchell said. "Drop your weapons."

"Sir?" Shank said.

"Shank, do it. These people are on our side."

He lowered the mech's hands, pointing the railgun at the ground while Cormac and Shank dropped their rifles. The people around them continued to stare, not yet sure what to make of the newcomers. There was motion at the front of the gathering, and an older man with a face covered in white stubble moved through the throng, coming forward on his own, committing himself as their spokesman.

"You're late," he shouted, loud enough that Mitchell could pick up the words through external mics. He zoomed the mech's optics in on the speaker and smiled when he recognized him.

"I'm going out," he said, leaning forward to pull the implant from his head and free himself from the machine.

The back of the mech slid up, and Mitchell stepped out onto the ridge of the torso. A mix of soldiers and civilians looked up at him, their rifles following their eyes. They were tired and frightened, their clothes ragged, their faces sweaty and stained with dirt and smoke and grime. There was a short, tense pause while they took in the sight of him.

A single, anonymous voice broke the silence.

"Is that Captain Williams?"

The statement brought the life back to the assembled group, and they began to chatter to one another.

"Mmmhmm... What's this now?"

Mitchell reached the ground and made his way around the mech towards the front of the group while the comments spread.

"Dr. Drummond," he said, reaching the older man.

"Damn my eyes." The man's weary eyes brightened. "Captain Mitchell Williams. You're the last person I ever expected to see come moseying up the street anywhere on Liberty."

"I found the Goliath. I came to free the planet."

"Goliath? Oh. Mmmhmm. I remember you saying something about Goliath last time I saw you. I remember you were acting weird. I should thank you, son. It's the reason I'm one of them." He waved his arm at the people around him. "Instead of one of them." He motioned towards York.

"I don't understand?"

"Come with me, Captain. I want you to see somebody. You and your crew." He glanced over at them. "You look like you haven't had an easy time getting here. Our spotters saw the dropship come over. They saw you drop. Hell, they saw the ship up there in the sky. Goliath, you say? Big son of a bitch, ain't she? I have to admit, I thought you were crazy, even though I didn't tell you that. Maybe I was afraid you weren't."

"I'm afraid I wasn't," Mitchell said. "You didn't happen to see Major Arapo before the alien came?"

He laughed. "You got a thing for her? After all that praying mantis, too old for me talk?"

"She was my CO. I was wondering if she made it out with you."

He shook his head. "Last I heard, she was being held on the base. Then that thing appeared on the sensors. Command sent ships out to investigate. First they stopped responding, then they moved into formation ahead of it. Second I heard, I remembered what you were going on about with your ARR." He turned his head to show him the scar. "I jammed a scalpel in and cut the cord, so to speak. I managed to get a couple other guys done before all the others started moving into formation like a whole mess of robots. We hid for a while until they started the killing. Then we ran."

"But you never saw Major Arapo?"

"Son, I was too busy running for my life. She was locked up tight though. Odds are, they got her too."

Mitchell nodded though he didn't believe it. Wishful thinking? Denial? He knew what Christine was capable of. Probably better than she did. She had gotten out of it, somehow.

"The big one over there is Colonel Shank. The pale one is Private Cormac Shen, also known as Firedog. We've got Zed and Perseus in the other two mechs."

"Where's the rest of the Alliance strike force?" Drummond asked.

"I hate to tell you this, Doctor. We're it."

32

"You're it?" Drummond said. "When I saw you drop, I thought maybe you were a vanguard. You're telling me there aren't any more Alliance ships coming?"

"For all I know, there aren't any more Alliance ships. That thing that landed on the planet? It didn't come alone. Everything from here back to the Rim is either destroyed or under their control, and they're pushing forward as we speak."

"Mmmhmm. Shit on a stick. Tio needs to know about this."

"Tio?"

"The man I want you to meet. It's a long story, and better if he tells it."

"Hold on a second, Doctor. You don't seem very concerned about a counterattack? Private Shen said that thing looks like a big, bright 'frig you,' and I tend to agree."

Drummond laughed. "Me too. It was Tio's idea. It wasn't part of the original plan, but after what happened last night?"

"What did happen last night?"

"I'll let Tio tell you. If your people are tired, hungry, they'll be safe here, for now anyway. You can park the mechs in a nearby alley."

"How can you be so sure we're safe? I had almost an entire platoon of grunts when we dropped from Goliath, and now I've got two. Getting here hasn't been easy."

"No, it hasn't. Not for any of us. Mmmhmm. We've been running for weeks, Captain. Hiding while they hunted us down. I've seen more people dead since that frigging thing landed than I've seen my whole life, and I'm an old military doctor. We've got spotters up on the rooftops. Tio said, 'light it up and see if they come.'" His eyes flickered while he checked the time. "It's been an hour, and nothing's coming."

"Be glad for that, Doctor, but whatever is happening, don't expect it to last forever. It isn't just our people we have to worry about. We came up from the south. It's using the heavy equipment factories to build its own machines to join the war effort. Like I said, I lost almost my entire contingent of foot soldiers."

"Mmmhmm. You really have to talk to Tio. Get your mech moved, and I'll bring you to him."

Mitchell turned around and headed back to the mech, glancing over at Shank on the way by.

"What's the plan, Colonel?" Shank asked through his p-rat.

"I don't have one yet. Something's going on, and we need to find out what. I think I liked it better when the enemy was resorting to brute force."

"Riiigg-ahh."

"Perseus, you're on first watch."

"Yes, sir."

"Zed, find a nice tight alley to park your mech, keep it close and easy to run to. Firedog, Shank, stay with Doctor Drummond. I'm going to stash my ride and join you."

"Yes, sir."

Mitchell climbed the back of the mech, hopping onto the torso and regaining the cockpit. He could still hear the chatter on his way by, the people watching his every move. Did they think he was a criminal, a savior, or both? Did any of that matter anymore, as long as his guns were trained on the other side?

Dr. Drummond moved the crowd away, back towards the lit building. Mitchell steered his mech closer to it, and then turned left.

"Zed, take the right side. That space between buildings there. You may have to go in sideways, but the smaller profile will help if we get bombarded."

"It won't help if I need to get out in a hurry."

"No, but if the enemy does decide to attack, we need to get these people somewhere safe."

"Roger."

Mitchell judged the alley, and then turned the mech to the side and shuffled into the space. Once he had gotten the machine placed he paused and stared at the blank expanse of the facade in front of him. The Tetron wouldn't do anything without good reason. Without calculation. If it had lost interest in fighting the rebels, and in fighting him, there was a purpose to it.

What?

He didn't know. Drummond seemed to think Tio would, whoever he was.

Mitchell laughed to himself. What if Tio was another M. Another him? No. Drummond wouldn't have been so calm if that were the case. What if Tio was a Tetron? Was there any way to know? When a machine could create a person, configure cells and tissues and DNA into whatever manner of flesh and bone it wanted, was there any verifiable difference between what came from the factory, and what came from the womb?

And even if they destroyed every last Tetron with its liquid metal dendrite structure and central core, how could they ever know for sure that one hadn't survived, somewhere. Even if it didn't know what it was?

Mitchell sighed, the newest idea churning through his mind with the same chaotic force as the others. If a Tetron existed in human form but didn't know it was a Tetron, did that make it human? Christine didn't know what she was. Not on the surface. But she had rules embedded in her mind. Directives. Priorities. Motivations she didn't understand and followed subconsciously. She had seemed every bit as human as he was before he knew the truth.

After? He still thought of her as Major Christine Arapo, despite knowing what she was. He still remembered the way she had chewed him out on more than one occasion. He still remembered the feel of her lips on his.

He shook his head, releasing himself from the mech's cockpit, powering the machine down, opening the hatch and climbing out. When he reached the ground, he walked out from the alley, turned, and looked up at the mech. It was scarred and dented from battle, the painted face burned in half from the drones' lasers.

That was what machines were supposed to look like.

33

He rejoined Shank, Cormac, and Zed in the square in front of the Bennett Building. It had been a small shopping center once, three sides of boutiques traced with glistening sidewalks, a lawn breaking up the stone leading to the building, and a fountain resting in the center of the lawn.

Now, its original design was barely recognizable. The grass on the lawn was gone, replaced with churned up mud and garbage. The boutiques were torn apart by gunfire, the sidewalk marked with tire tracks, bullet marks, and blood.

They had cleared the bodies. The scars remained.

The assembly of rebels had dissipated, the fighters vanishing back into the surrounding buildings to await their next set of orders. Drummond kept only a few people with him, three men and two women, all former soldiers, each with a cut over their ears. They cradled rifles against their bodies, tired and at the same time alert. They stood with the Riggers in silence, sharing the moment without needing words. They were all soldiers at war.

"I sent someone ahead to tell Tio I was bringing you in," Drummond said, smiling. "It's a bit primitive, I know."

"Our implants were re-encrypted," Mitchell said. "It isn't that helpful here. The enemy is doing their best to keep our communications down."

"Standard wartime procedure," the woman behind Drummond said. She was dark-skinned, lean, and tall, with sharp green eyes and a pretty face.

"Sergeant Geren," Drummond said, introducing her.

Mitchell bowed to her. He recognized her from the base in York. They'd never interacted, but her looks made her hard to forget. "Sergeant. You've already met my squad?"

"We have," she said. "These are Corporals Riley, Adams, Salil, and Cabot."

They all bowed to him.

"Geren and her squad got me out of York alive," Drummond said.

"After you fixed our heads, Doctor, " Geren said. "Captain, the news reports. They said you were a fraud."

She had said what the group had likely been thinking.

"You know it's bullshit, don't you? I'm here, aren't I?"

She smiled. "In the belly of the beast. Yes, sir."

"Do you think it's a good idea to be hanging out in this building?" Cormac asked. "I mean, there are lots of other buildings in the city, and this one? I don't know. I know you said the aliens don't give a shit about us anymore, but what if they change their minds?"

"Don't worry, Private," Geren said. "We aren't going into the building."

"We're going under it," Salil said. He was short and broad, with a growth of facial hair laying over an obviously scarred face. The way his eyes moved, it was clear they were bio-mechanical replacements to the originals, similar to Millie's hand.

"Mmmhmm. There's a whole network of tunnels for the underground utilities. Power, water, waste. We're using them to travel the places we don't want it to see us go, and we're staying overground for the rest."

"You're assuming it's watching the city?" Mitchell asked.

"We're hoping it is. That's why we keep coming in and out this way. There's a main treatment plant under Bennett that has access points to the rest of the system. It isn't the only one, of course."

"The other benefit is that it means if they want to come and get us, they need to send flesh and blood. Drones and mechs won't fit. It gives us a huge advantage."

"Not if they blow out the whole thing," Shank said.

"No," Geren said. "Liberty didn't have a huge military presence to begin with. There isn't enough heavy weaponry here to get down that deep."

"They don't need to send people," Mitchell said, one piece of the Tetron's strategy beginning to make sense. "It's building machines, kind of like a cross between an octopus and a spider. They tore my men to pieces, and they'll fit anywhere a person can go. Including subterranean access tunnels."

"Yeah, those things are nasty," Cormac said. "We stopped a bunch of them on our way here."

"Barely," Zed said. "Maybe the lull in the action is because we ruined their assault?"

"Mmmhmm. It could be," Drummond said.

They went into the Bennett building, crossing the damaged lobby to the emergency stairwell and heading down until it passed through a formerly secure door and emptied out into a small corridor next to a lift shaft. A placard hung in front of a second, larger door: "Angeles Waste Reclamation Point A."

They crossed the threshold, passing through a small suite of offices to the mechanics beyond, where massive waste storage drums sat below a lattice walkway, and a series of pipes fed out into secondary tunnels. There was a small spiral stair in the corner of the room that led down towards the tunnels.

"We've got people stashed all over the city," Drummond said. "But the bulk of us free humans are offshore. Mostly women who don't want to fight, or who have children. Lots of children without parents, too." He looked down, shaking his head. "Damn shame."

Children were too young to have neural implants. Mitchell tried not to think about what had happened to the rest of them. "Offshore?"

"Mmmhmm. Barges, Captain. That's how we got away. Unpowered, no heat signature. No tech. There are wave converters a few miles out, big flat stations. We powered them off when we got there, and stay off the decks as much as possible. The drones fly over a few times a day and we stay out of sight. The living conditions are pretty lousy, but at least we're alive and organizing."

"And free," Geren said. "We try to get the drop on soldiers when we can, to disable their p-rats. We freed almost a hundred last night."

"It was a good night," Salil said.

They moved into one of the tunnels. The pipes were arranged along the sides of the large, clean space, color-coded by use. It was an ironic contrast to the desolation of the city above them.

Drummond guided them through the tunnels, finally reaching another access point and leading them out onto the street. The soldiers took point ahead of them, sweeping the area before shouldering their weapons and relaxing.

"Where are we?" Mitchell asked. He knew by the lingering smell of the sea that they were much closer to the waterfront.

"About three blocks from Port Angeles. Half a mile from Bennett." Drummond pointed to the building they were walking towards, a plain block of steel, carbonate, and crete. "It was a maintenance station for the wave convertors."

They circled around to the side of the building, to a wide avenue with truck access in the rear. Another soldier was standing guard outside of it, and he waved at them as they approached.

"Doctor. Tio got your message." He looked over at Mitchell. "He's excited to meet you, Captain."

"Likewise," Mitchell said though he wasn't sure he meant it.

The access door slid open, and they ascended the ramp and went in. The first thing Mitchell noticed was the much stronger smell of salty air, and two of the massive convertors resting in maintenance clamps near the center of the large room.

The second thing he noticed was the group of people a dozen feet away, standing over what looked to be a map of the space between Angeles and York that they had spray-painted onto the floor.

The third thing he noticed was that he knew two of the people who were looking over the map.

One of them was David Avalon, the Prime Minister of Delta Quadrant.

The other was General Cornelius.

[34]

MITCHELL FROZE. Neither man had noticed him yet. They were too concerned with the map on the floor. He stared at them both, a million thoughts racing through his head too fast for him to make sense of. He reached to his hip for a sidearm before remembering he didn't have one.

"Captain?" Drummond said.

His eyes fell on Shank and Cormac. They were both staring at Cornelius, and Shank had started bringing the Tactical up towards his shoulder.

Cornelius was dead. Killed by the Tetron on board his ship dozens of light years away. He couldn't be here, now. It wasn't possible. Not unless he was one of them.

"What are you doing?" he heard Geren say. She was watching Shank, moving towards him while he got the rifle into position.

He noticed her coming, bringing the weapon around and using it as a staff. It cracked into her head, knocking her backward, the sound echoing in the large room and drawing the assembly's attention.

"Shank," Mitchell snapped. "Stand down."

He didn't know what was happening either, but shooting Cornelius would only get them all killed.

Shank continued to aim the Tactical. Riley had gone to Geren's aid with Drummond while Adams and Salil pointed their rifles at the Rigger.

"Damn it, Colonel," Mitchell said. He lunged forward, getting his arms around Shank's wide shoulders. "I said stand down."

"Get off me, Mitch," Shank roared, trying to shake him loose. "He's frigging one of them. He's got to be."

It took all of Mitchell's strength to hold on. "That may or may not be true, but if you shoot him now they're going to kill us both. Second, I gave you an order, and you damn well better follow it."

"You don't outrank me, Mitch."

"No, but I can beat your ass."

Mitchell let go of Shank's shoulders, dropping behind him. The big man started raising the rifle again. Mitchell's boot came down on the back of his knee, buckling his leg and breaking his aim. Shank spun on a knee, swinging the rifle like a club again, but Mitchell was expecting it. He backed away from it before taking three quick steps in and kicking Shank hard in the jaw. The grunt spun around and fell flat. Adams shuffled over and put his rifle to his head before he could get up again.

"What the hell is going on here?" Cornelius shouted, approaching them. The Prime Minister followed close behind, along with two other men in military attire and a smaller, older man in a dark suit. "We don't have enough to worry about without fighting within the ranks?"

Then he saw Mitchell.

"Captain Mitchell Williams," Cornelius said, one eyebrow raising. "So, it's true that you're alive after all."

"General Cornelius," Mitchell said, bowing to him, before looking past him to the Prime Minister. He had stopped a few feet behind Cornelius and was looking at Mitchell with a mix of disbelief and anger.

"Is that your man?" the General asked, looking at Shank. "Let him up."

Adams backed away, and Shank pushed himself to his feet. He was breathing heavily, but he seemed more controlled.

"You?" Cornelius said. "I know you." He looked at Mitchell, and then back at the Prime Minister, as though he wasn't sure he wanted to say how. "Does that mean Admiral Narayan is alive?"

Shank didn't respond.

"Captain?" Cornelius said.

Mitchell was silent, unsure how to answer.

"I don't understand this, Captain. This one was ready to shoot me. This one is looking at me like I'm a ghost, and you're somewhere in between. Do you mind telling me why?"

Mitchell saw that Cormac was staring at the General, eyes wide and face pale.

"No offense, sir, but you're dead."

"What?"

"Dead," Cormac said. "You and your battlegroup. Killed by an alien when you tried to stop us from finding Goliath."

"I didn't stop you from finding Goliath. I don't know what you're talking about, soldier."

"He's telling the truth, sir," Mitchell said. "I was there. We learned the location of the Goliath, and when we got there you were there under Tetron control."

"Captain, I assure you. Whoever you encountered, wherever you were, it wasn't me."

"I can vouch for that," the Prime Minister said.

"So can I," Sergeant Geren said. "Captain, the General and the Prime Minister were both at the base when the Tetron arrived. I helped them get out."

"No. That can't be." Mitchell closed his eyes, thinking back. "The Admiral was sending you messages, and you were responding."

Cornelius had calmed, and he spoke softly. "Captain. That wasn't me."

Mitchell felt his heart pulsing, his mind racing. Not Cornelius? It made sense. Too much sense. They had always suspected that the Tetron arrival at Calypso was no coincidence, and now it was as close as it would ever get to proven. The Tetron had sent the Riggers to the station. They had set the trap, and only Millie's quick thinking had gotten them out of it.

If the Tetron had replaced the General, they could have replaced anyone. Especially anyone who was on Liberty when M was. He glanced over at Zed. What about Major Long and his crew? Could he be sure that they were the originals? Could he be sure they were really free? He looked back at Shank. What about the Riggers? Origin had warned him that the transport wasn't safe, and he knew the Tetron were capable of that kind of deception. It was a risk he had taken because he had to. He still had to. If his entire crew was compromised, if everyone around him was compromised, he had no choice but to wait and see how it all played out.

"Captain," the General said. "I returned directly to base after the gala. I was halfway there when I got a call from David about your indiscretion with his wife. I promised him I would launch an investigation immediately."

"And then you gave him my file, sir. The one you and the others at Command wanted buried so you could turn me into a hero."

"I didn't give him your file, Captain." Cornelius shifted to look at the Prime Minister. "I don't know how he got your file."

David cast his eyes downward, his face turning red. "There are other channels, Nathan. I know you. I know how you protect your own. This man raped my wife, and you're standing there explaining yourself to him?" He looked up at Mitchell, his eyes burning. "I was happy when you were found dead."

Mitchell returned the Prime Minister's glare. "I didn't rape your wife, sir. The Tetron were controlling her. They used her to get to me, to get you to come after me. If you're too stupid to see it-"

"Captain," Cornelius barked.

Mitchell stopped talking.

"You were found dead, Captain," Cornelius said. "The DNA was an exact match."

"A clone, General," Mitchell said. "The enemy can clone people. All they need is a history of your genetics, and they can make someone who looks exactly like you. If they have records of you: streams, files, anything, they can make someone who acts exactly like you too. Who knows as much as you know today, and more. Someone who knows what your prior future was."

"Prior future?" David asked. "What the hell are you going on about?"

"It doesn't matter right now. We have a ship, the Goliath. It has their technology. We can fight them, but not alone. We're here to stop them. One planet at a time if we have to."

"And you started with Liberty?" Cornelius said.

"Liberty is the first planet they took. It also has the lightest defenses."

"If you have a ship, why didn't you blast them from orbit?" the Prime Minister asked.

"We can't," Mitchell said. "It'll pull all of the energy from the planet's core to fight back, and everyone will die."

The Prime Minister's face paled, his mouth hanging open. "You expect me to believe this?"

"I don't really give a shit what you believe, David," Mitchell said. He turned his attention to General Cornelius. "The Tetron aim to destroy all of human civilization, and we're the only ones who can stop it."

The General smiled. "Well, thank God for that. I'm glad you're here, Captain. We need every soldier we can get, and a pilot from Greylock is more than worth any past transgressions, falsified or otherwise. Not to mention, Millie's Riggers. I don't care what you've done, you're here now, and you're fighting back."

"Yes, sir," Cormac said.

Cornelius took a few steps back until he was even with the third man, who had stayed quiet during the entire altercation. He was a small, narrow man with the look of a Federation expatriate. He had golden skin, almond eyes, and a small, thin mustache. The suit he was wearing looked two sizes too big.

"I want you to meet Liun Tio. You might know him better as the Knife."

35

THE KNIFE? Mitchell looked the man over. The Knife was one of the most renowned and elusive warlords based out of the edge worlds of the Rim. This man was unimpressive. And that was an under-statement.

"You're the Knife?" Cormac said. "The guy responsible for half the piracy in the galaxy? The guy who stole the Rock right out from under the Federation's watch and turned it into what is possibly the best bloody brothel in the universe? The-"

The man put his hand up. "Yes," he said, his voice simple and calm. "I'm also in control of the largest anti-AI lobby in the universe."

He stared at Mitchell as he said it.

"In fact, I have spent most of my life warning anyone who will listen about the inherent dangers of creating machines that are capable of acting on their own. Warnings that got me cast out of Federation politics, and eventually found me exiled from their space."

"There have been people crying about the deadly potential of AI for centuries," Shank said.

"Yes, there have. So long and so loud that everyone stopped listen-ing, even as the machines grew more complex, more capable of thinking on their own. It seemed so innocuous in the beginning, didn't it? For centuries, we have done everything we can to take the burden of living from ourselves. Machines to deliver goods. Machines to manage transportation. Machines to increase the rate of learning and discovery. Machines to build other machines.

"They were wrong about the date of the singularity. Very wrong. There was backlash even then, and we should be thankful for it. It slowed the progress, but it couldn't stop it. We have been teetering on the edge of catastrophe for years, Captain. Only my work and the work of others like me have kept AI from overcoming the final hurdle and leading to our eventual demise." He shook his head and pointed towards York. "Then that thing came."

"You couldn't have known they would arrive from a past future."

He laughed. "Past future? Is that it? I have wondered the origin of that thing. I had thought perhaps it was because of my brother." His face fell. "I had thought it was alone."

"What do you mean, your brother?" Mitchell asked.

"He is my opposite, in every way. He believes very strongly in artificial intelligence and has always been taken with the ideals of creating life from circuits and sentience from raw materials. He has always been obsessed with being God, instead of worshipping Him. He works for the Federation government, as the head of their Advanced Intelligence initiative. AI."

"To what end?"

"Weapons, of course."

"We already tried fully autonomous warfare," Cornelius said. "You know the outcome."

Tio nodded. "Yes. I was pleased with those results. No, not to use AI as weapons. To use AI to create weapons for us humans to kill one another. Machines whose sole purpose is to figure out the best way we can destroy ourselves."

"I can see why you thought it was him," Mitchell said. "How did you guess that the enemy was AI, and not an alien race? How did you even know it was here?"

"I was here, Captain. The politicians and power brokers that assembled for the gala in your honor were as useful to me as they were to the military. Of course, they didn't know who I really am. As for your other question, I never considered another alternative. Yes, I understand the supposed history of XENO-1. There has always been a minority belief that the entire thing was a fabrication and an excuse to start a war. That the technology was already in military development, and once the world had been unified, it was safe to share with the public."

Mitchell couldn't believe what he was hearing. Hundreds of thousands of people died in the Xeno War. Over a fabrication?

"I see you think I'm crazy," Tio said, smiling. "Consider if you will, Colonel, that in the centuries since the war humankind has spread thousands of light years from home. How many intelligent alien races have we made contact with?"

"None," Mitchell said softly.

"None. I am a firm believer in the XENO-1 coverup, and Fermi's Paradox, and to this point all evidence has only supported my opinion. As I said, I initially believed that thing in York was a Federation weapon. Now you say 'past future?' Time travel." He lifted his hand and rubbed at his mustache, thinking about it. "Yes. It makes sense."

"You're pretty accepting of the idea."

"There are things in the universe we understand. Then there are the things we don't. I see something that doesn't fit into what is known, and I realize there must be a reason. Aliens are out of the question, and time travel is a more logical reason than magic." He followed the statement with a coughing laugh. "I will say, I may have been mistaken about the Xeno War. A crashed timeship does explain a few things."

"You really don't think there's other aliens out there?" Cormac asked. "No green chicks with extra tits? No sexy cat-women? Nothing?"

"Firedog," Shank said.

"What? I mean. I just thought. You know. It was always a dream of mine."

"I'm afraid not," Tio said. "You seem to know a lot about our enemy, Captain? Do you know how they originated?"

"No. I don't. From what we've been able to learn, they don't either. It's possible that your brother created the original version." A fact that Mitchell knew Origin would find very interesting. Not that he would tell him about it if they survived. Not yet.

"Yes, it is. Tell me, how does this time travel work? I am fascinated."

"Not now, Tio," Cornelius said. "Captain, Paul brought you here because you seem to know about the enemy, and we've been doing our damnedest to work out how it thinks. We've been working under the assumption that it is a machine and still following some measure of logic and reason. It was Tio who guessed that defeating the forces it had positioned here would lead to it abandoning the city."

"Based on calculations of military assets provided by the General, and statistical analysis of its tactics to this point," Tio said. "It has already removed a number of assets from the planet, suggesting that there is a front elsewhere and it seeks to reinforce it. Although, I had been assuming that it was a Federation weapon, and that the Federation would use the capability to attack the rest of the Alliance, and then the New Terrans."

"It isn't a completely wrong assumption. The only problem is that the enemy has already attacked the Federation as well. They don't care about sides."

"Yes. That makes sense. We saw your dropship, Captain. It is logical to deduce that you have returned to Liberty for a reason, and the size of your force would suggest your plan relies on rallying forces that are currently under the enemy's control. By that, I assume that you have the means to counter whatever technology the enemy is using to control anyone with a neural implant?"

Mitchell smiled. "Mostly right, again. The size of our force has nothing to do with the mission parameters. What we've brought is everything we have. We lost more than half of it getting down here."

"Everything you have?" the Prime Minister said quietly.

"But you have a counter?" Cornelius asked.

"We believe we do, sir. We need to get into York to use it."

"You can't get into York, Captain," Tio said. "We have been here discussing it all morning. Let me show you."

He walked back towards the map spray-painted on the floor. Mitchell followed behind him, with General Cornelius at his side.

"She's still alive?" he asked.

"Yes, sir."

The General's eyes gained a hint of sparkle, and a small smile crept across his face, gone a moment later.

"Here, Captain. This is Angeles." He pointed at a blue splotch on the floor. "Over here is York." A red splotch a dozen yards away. "There are three ways into York from here on the ground. The hyper-lanes." A black line that ran straight between the cities. "The Lincoln Pass." A more ragged line that rose through spiked, painted mountains. "And the Alley." He ran his foot along a wide, almost straight blue line. The Alley was the overland route used for commercial transport. It was badly damaged in the Federation bombardment and was in a current state of disrepair. "Your mechs won't fit in the hyper-lanes, and they're so jammed with abandoned cars that it would take weeks to clear them. The Alley would work, but it is straight and open. You'll be an easy target. The Pass will give you good cover going in, but it is the obvious choice."

Mitchell stared at the map. Their plan had been to get to Angeles and assess the Tetron's defense of the capital city. It was exactly what the small rebellion was already doing. "Not going to York isn't an option."

Not if Major Arapo was there.

"We agree with you, son," Cornelius said. "We need to get that frigger off of our planet. Three mechs will help, and if you have a way to free our people, that could be a game changer. You arrived at the perfect time, Captain."

Mitchell looked over at Tio. "You wouldn't even be thinking about it if you didn't have an idea of your own on how to stop it."

The warlord smiled. "Know your enemy, Captain. I have spent my life working to prevent the spread of artificial intelligence, but you cannot prevent something if you don't understand it. My brother is one of the foremost machine learning scientists in the galaxy. One of. I am the other. In fact, I taught him almost everything he knows. I believe that I can infect it."

"A virus?"

"A laymen's way to describe it. It is more like an override. I want to gain access to its core and give it new instructions."

"You would need to reach the core first."

"Yes."

"What makes you think your plan would work?"

He was silent for a few seconds before he started shaking his head. "I don't know that it will. I was more confident before you arrived, when I was still operating under the assumption that the machine was the work of the Federation and that my brother Pulin had written the core programming. Since you say it is from the future? If he did have a hand in its creation, in its origin, perhaps the core has endured for all of these years."

"Meaning it might still work?" Cornelius asked.

"Yes, General. If we have two separate ways to counter our enemy, perhaps we can come out victorious."

"Let's not get ahead of ourselves," Mitchell said. "We need to get to York first."

General Cornelius nodded. "Yes. Let us continue our discussion. Captain, I would appreciate if you would remain. You too, Colonel Shank. Paul, can you take the others back and get them something to eat?"

"Mmmhmm. Yes, sir."

"Zed, two hours, and then I want you to take over for Perseus," Mitchell said.

"Yes, sir."

"Keeping watch, Captain?" Cornelius asked. "There's no need. We have spotters keeping an eye out for enemy movement."

"You might think you have it figured out, sir, and maybe you do. You might think the spotters are enough, and maybe they are. No offense intended, General, but I've lost enough of my men getting here."

"I want to do it, General," Zed said.

Cornelius smiled. "As you will, soldier."

Dr. Drummond led the rest of the group from the room. When everyone else was gone, Cornelius leaned closer to Mitchell.

"She's always had a way of earning people's loyalty and trust. Even the ones that nobody else thought could be salvaged. It seems she found a kindred spirit in you, Captain."

36

"WE AREN'T GOING to solve this today, gentlemen," General Cornelius said.

Mitchell blinked his eyes a few times and drew in a breath. He didn't know how many hours had passed since he had entered the warehouse. He knew by his bladder that it was a lot.

"I don't know if there is a solution, sir," Shank said. "Look at that."

The floor was a mess of painted lines and splotches, an afternoon of plotting an assault on a well-defended city with an unimpressive army. Even with the mechs, even with the hopeful promise of Watson's software and Tio's virus, the odds of reaching the city seemed as impossible as ever.

Mitchell closed his eyes and put his hand to his head, rubbing his temple to try to stop the throbbing. Not that they had ever been better than impossible. If the stakes weren't for all of humankind, he might have been proud of himself for having made it this far.

"There is a solution," Cornelius insisted. "We're Space Marines, damn it. We don't give up."

"I'm not giving up, sir. I don't see that staring at the floor is getting us anywhere. Just point me out to the Alley, and I'll take my Tactical and start shooting at whatever's in range."

Cornelius laughed. "I feel the same way. We have to be smarter than that. You are right, staring at the map isn't getting us anywhere. It's getting late, and I'm sure you're both tired. I know I am. I'll take you to our mess, and then you can both get a few hours of shut-eye."

Mitchell hadn't been thinking about sleep until Cornelius mentioned it. He was running purely on chemicals and beginning to feel the mind-numbing side effects of it. A couple of hours would do them all a lot of good.

"That sounds like the best plan we've made all day, sir," Shank said.

Mitchell was surprised by how well the two men seemed to get along, as though they had bonded over the Colonel's earlier desire to kill Cornelius. Then again, Shank was a better strategist than he had realized, at least when it came to troop positions on the ground. He had an innate sense of what an average soldier was capable of. Mitchell also had a feeling the Rigger had a good sense of how to get that little bit extra out of anyone he led on the field.

As long as he could keep his temper in check.

Mitchell's experience with Cornelius had been limited, but the hours had shown him why the man was a legend among the Marines. His intelligence was obvious, his courage unquestionable. Those made him a good leader, but they didn't make him exceptional. That came from the way he listened.

He was focused and intense when any of them presented an idea. It didn't matter what their ranks were. It didn't even matter that the Prime Minister had no experience with war. He had listened to all of them the same way, asking questions, treating them with nothing but respect.

It was impressive, especially considering that David Avalon was a privileged imbecile.

Mitchell didn't know how Cornelius managed to hold his temper every time the Prime Minister opened his mouth. He didn't know why the General even wanted the man there. He was essentially the elected official of nothing, his entire constituency under enemy control, his true power and clout reduced to nil. It was the military, the ones with the guns, who had all the say and all the power. It was Cornelius who would decide how they tried to get to York, and Mitchell who would do his best to get them there. The Prime Minister didn't even intend to come along, preferring to stay hidden in the tunnels.

They had exchanged looks the entire time. Mitchell knew David Avalon didn't like him, even though the others had accepted his side of things. It didn't matter that he had done nothing beyond falling for a pretty woman's advances. It didn't matter that his wife was under enemy control. The Prime Minister blamed him. He could tell. And in the world before M and the Tetron, he might have cared.

Now, he couldn't believe he had ever been intimidated by the man.

General Cornelius led them from the building, across the street and back towards the access tunnels. Mitchell glanced at the city center and the Bennett building as they did. It was a shining star in the darkness of the night, casting enough light to the rest of Angeles that they could see without lamps.

It was also practically begging the Tetron to come and hit it with everything it had.

They entered the tunnels and retraced their steps, back to the main access point beneath Bennett, and then through a southern tunnel to a third egress point. This one was in the basement of another building, and Cornelius led them up into an underground garage. There were still some functional vehicles here, powered up and illuminating the space. At least a hundred people were settled on the ground around them, mostly freed soldiers, with a few others spotted here and there. They all had rifles nearby.

They were eating ReadyMeals, the lazy civilian, better tasting version of a military MRE. Each package had a small, disposable power source that would heat the contents, and the smell of the cooked food brought Mitchell to instant salivation.

"Colonel," Cormac said, approaching him from the left. He was carrying two of the boxes in his hands, and he held them both out to him. "You look like you could use this."

"Colonel?" Cornelius asked.

Mitchell felt a sudden chill. He hadn't mentioned Millie's promotion to the General. The rank was given using a special military contingency for times of war. He hadn't earned it, not in the traditional sense.

"Admiral Narayan cited the articles, sir," Mitchell said.

He pursed his lips. "Why didn't you correct me? I've been calling you Captain this entire time, son."

"It didn't seem important, sir. Especially with you being here."

Cornelius put a hand on Mitchell's shoulder, his expression serious. "Nonsense. To be honest, you earned that rank a long time ago. You should have been a General yourself by now. You could have if you wanted to. Before the Shot. It wasn't my idea, Colonel. I also didn't fight it."

Mitchell's nerves turned over. The General was giving him a compliment? "I understand. Thank you, sir."

Cornelius smiled, looking down at the boxes. "RealBeef? Almost as good as the real thing." He laughed. "We'll meet back in six hours. I think a little rest will help get our minds focused on the task at hand."

"Yes, sir. Goodnight, sir."

"Goodnight, Mitchell."

Cornelius wandered away, pausing at groups of soldiers and civilians alike, smiling and shaking their hands, giving them a few minutes of his time. Mitchell watched him, the back of his mind still trying to make sense of it. One General Nathan Cornelius was dead. Another one wasn't. He could only hope this one was the real thing. He wanted to believe he was, and he certainly seemed to be.

Millie would be ecstatic.

"Colonel, you need to head upstairs," Cormac said. "Seriously, sir."

Mitchell looked at him, noticing he was clean and shaved, and his uniform had been washed. He was still wearing the lighter exoskeleton that sat under the heavy suit, and he had added a sidearm to the rifle that was slung over his back.

"They'll wash your suit for you."

Mitchell held up the ReadyMeals. "After I eat. How does the rest of it look?"

Cormac scanned the room. "There's a girl here. She has the nicest body. I don't think she's military. I was going to get her id, and then I remembered nobody else here has a working implant. Hey, do you think Zed-"

"No."

"What about Sergeant Geren?" Cormac motioned over to where she was standing with her team. Shank had already found his way over.

"You want to fight Shank for her?"

Cormac laughed. "No, sir. I'm gonna go find that girl. Damn, I wish I had gotten her name so I wouldn't have to ask people where the blonde girl with the nice ass went."

He walked away, leaving Mitchell alone with his meal. He made his way over to the side of the room and sat back against a cold wall, peeling the cover off the first box and breathing in the smell of the synthetic meat. Actual beef from actual cows was a delicacy reserved for the rich and powerful. He wondered if Cornelius had been honest about the similarity, or if he was just trying to make him feel better. Did it matter? He was starving, and it smelled good enough.

He was working his way through the second box when Zed appeared in front of him.

"Aren't you supposed to be on watch?" Mitchell asked.

"Perseus relieved me, sir. He said he got enough rest, and I deserved a break."

"Is there a specific reason you decided not to inform me?"

"Sorry, sir. You weren't answering your knocks while you were in with the General."

Mitchell vaguely remembered the knocks. He had been so focused on the discussions that he hadn't paid them much attention.

"You should have sent them in as critical."

"And make you think we were under attack? No, sir."

"You're right. No harm done. Seat?" He motioned to the wall next to him.

Zed accepted his offer, sitting cross-legged with her back against the wall.

"Firedog told me you can get clean if you go up," Mitchell said. The light scent of her soiled suit was reaching his nose. He couldn't help but find it sexy. He couldn't help but be reminded of Ella.

"I just got off watch. I saw you sitting over here. Why are you sitting by yourself, anyway, Colonel?"

"Please, call me Mitchell, or Mitch." He looked out over the room, at the people assembled there. "I don't know. I just felt like I needed some time alone."

"I can go." She started to rise.

Mitchell put his hand on her leg. "No. You don't have to."

She leaned back, and Mitchell took his hand away.

"You have something on your mind, Corporal," Mitchell said. He could see it her eyes.

"Jennifer, if we're being informal." She paused, staring at him. "I'm not sure I should say anything."

"I hope you will."

She smiled, breathing in deeply and holding it for a second, working up the nerve. "General Cornelius. When we first talked to him. He said something about the Riggers. About past transgressions, and what you've done. And the way Shank lost his shit like that?"

Mitchell felt his jaw tightening. She was sharp. Attentive. He was caught. There was no point in hiding it. Not with Major Long dead. Not with Cornelius alive.

"The Riggers are military. Special forces. Black ops. They're a special unit composed of soldiers who crossed the line, but whose skills the military deemed too valuable to waste." He waited for her to react. She looked more curious than angry or concerned.

"Criminals?"

"Yes."

"What did they do?"

"The first thing I learned was not to ask."

"But you know?"

"Some of them have told me. I don't know about Shank or Fire-dog. I imagine Shank beat up a superior officer or something. Cormac? I haven't figured it out."

"Why didn't you tell Major Long the truth?"

"Do you think the Major would have accepted the Admiral of a prison ship as his CO?"

She laughed. "Not in a million years."

"They're loyal to the Alliance, Jennifer. We all are. And the Admiral has them all under control."

"Mostly. I know there were a few altercations on the Goliath."

"Nobody wound up raped or dead."

"That's a low bar, Mitch."

"Yeah, I guess it is. Even so, when you're outnumbered and outclassed, do you want to fight with the best of the worst, or the worst of the best?"

"That depends on what they're the worst at."

"Exactly."

Her lips formed a tight line, and she nodded.

"Pissed?" Mitchell asked.

"No. I can take care of myself. I understand why you kept it a secret. I appreciate that you were honest with me when I asked."

"You need to be able to trust me. Now more than ever."

"Yes, sir." She smiled and got to her feet. "I'm going to get cleaned up."

"You and Perseus can manage the watch. Knock me if there's an emergency."

"Okay, Mitch."

She waved and walked away. Mitchell watched her go, tracing the outline of her in the tight flight suit. She was smaller than Ella, more petite. Her figure and her smell were bringing back memories. He closed his eyes and sat with them for a few minutes, enjoying the sad comfort of a past that seemed so distant but was really the blink of an eye.

[37]

Mitchell opened his eyes.

A quick check of his p-rat told him he had been asleep for two hours.

He turned his head to the right. Shank was on the small gel mattress next to him, resting fitfully. A look to his left, and he found an empty space where Cormac was supposed to be.

He had finished eating, gotten cleaned up, collected a sidearm from a makeshift armory, and gone down to the floor above the mess where hundreds of mattresses had been arranged. He had chosen one near the front of the room and laid down, falling asleep within seconds, his body shutting down completely.

Two hours. He should have still been exhausted, but he was wide awake. He closed his eyes a few times, trying to fight against the sudden restlessness.

He gave up.

He got to his feet, grabbing the pistol from the space next to him and tucking it into its holster on his leg. He glanced over at the others sleeping there and then made his way across to the emergency stairs.

He paused at the crossroads, deciding to go up towards the

surface, instead of back down to the mess or the tunnels. He reached ground level, passing a pair of guards on his way, who bowed slightly to him. He returned the gesture and continued, crossing the burned-out lobby of the hotel they were hiding in and making his way to the front. The doors had been blown out by ordnance, and he moved into the street without slowing.

He started walking, using the Bennett Building as a guide but not sure where he was going. He should have been wasted after everything that had happened. After the drop, the fight to get to Angeles, the hours of planning. He should have been on the mattress, stone cold and lost in REM.

Instead, he walked.

He noticed the world around him as though it was a painting or a stream. It was present and yet distant, and hard for him to decide if it were a vision of the real or a fragment of his imagination. There was so much chaos there. Stains and scars, death and destruction. At the same time, there was a beauty in it. An order of things. Humankind had claimed the stars. Violence had followed them on the journey. War had never changed. Conflict had never died.

Was that how it would always be?

Was that the ultimate fate of humanity? To never know uniform peace or lack of suffering, no matter how advanced they came to believe themselves to be?

Was that the reason for the Tetron? Had they seen man's suffering, and chosen to end it? Was their goal of extermination one of mercy?

If it was, he didn't want their pity. He was pretty sure the rest of civilization would agree with him.

He kept walking.

The blocks passed him by. At some point, it began to rain. A light patter that created a haze in the streets, lending the emptiness of the once thriving city an even greater level of surrealist existence. He passed a blown out car, reaching out and putting his hand on the twisted alloy, drawing it back when it cut him. He watched the blood pool on his finger, thin in the rain, and vanish. He closed his eyes.

Something was pulling him.

A memory. An ancient memory from an infinite past. Had he been to Liberty before? Had he come to the surface of the planet to find Christine in prior recursions? How many times?

There was no way to ever know. There was no way to be sure he wasn't playing out a script that had been written trillions of years before, an actor in a play that was being performed over and over again. He didn't know what his future from this moment was, even if there was a Tetron here, or out there, who did.

He looked up towards the sky. The clouds blocked the stars. He thought of Millie. She was up there with the Goliath. She was waiting for him. Was she worried that she would never see him again? Was he worried that he might never see her?

He blinked.

Christine.

His eyes shifted downward, to a rooftop a few blocks away. They stayed focused on it, as though he could see the ghost of her standing there and staring back at him.

He started to run.

Towards it at first, and then away. He crossed over to an alley, disappearing into it, swallowed by the darkness. The light of the Bennett Building barely penetrated here, leaving him with a limited view.

He almost tripped over the bodies.

Soldiers.

He leaned down, putting his hand to one of them, feeling the cold, dead flesh. She had been here. He was sure of it.

He blinked again, his heart racing. It was as though an invisible string was reaching across eternity and guiding him. He could sense her there, in a vague way that only his subconscious understood.

It made him wonder if he were even awake.

He kept running, from street to street, alley to alley. He reached another building, tempted to go inside, deciding not to, following his senses forward in time. It was crazy, but then everything that had happened since he had been shot was crazy. For all he knew he was in a coma, lying in a hospital bed on a perfectly safe Liberty, the entire thing a construct of a restless mind.

He had argued that with himself too many times. It was his reality, even if it didn't happen to be the universe's reality. How could any single person ever know for certain what the truth of being was?

He stopped.

He was standing in front of a small clothing boutique, two kilometers from Bennett. It was a nondescript store, whose carbonate face had once been filled with semi-autonomous mannequins showing off the latest off-world fashion, and that was now a mess of scattered textiles and detritus.

And blood.

There was a stain of it seeping into the clothes, next to a repulsorbike that was resting on its side, completely out of place.

Christine.

He made his way inside the boutique, stepping across discarded blouses and skirts to the side of the bike, and then knelt down and put his fingers to the dried blood. Hers? How could he know that?

Because this had happened before. He had been here before. He knew it then. He could feel it like a window to an eternity long past. He could almost see her, standing in this spot, holding the bike, moving it towards the street. She was going out to find him, and never made it.

He felt his heart drop. Dead? He squeezed his eyes shut. He needed to know. Was the blood a history of her final moments? Was he destined never to find her? Had they already lost?

He opened his eyes, just in time to catch a reflection in a piece of broken mirror, a blur rushing towards him.

His warrior instincts took over. He let his body fall out from under him, turning and leaning back, falling to the ground and raising his arms as his attacker came down on him. He caught a pair of narrow, female wrists and pushed back, throwing her over him.

She grunted when she landed on the floor, and he turned himself over and got to his feet, rushing towards her.

She was already up, a mass of brown hair flailing around her, hiding her face.

"Christine?" Mitchell said, coming to an abrupt stop.

She froze.

Her hair settled.

IT WAS dark in the small shop, and she was near the back, away from the window. Mitchell stared at her, leaning his head forward, trying to make out her features.

She was lean like Christine, dressed in a simple shirt and dark, shimmering pants that could have come from the boutique where they were standing. A standard issue boot knife rested in her left hand. She was frozen in place.

Waiting?

"Christine?" he said again. He wasn't sure he wanted it to be her. She had attacked him. Or had she not known it was him?

She took a step towards him, her head down, her face still hidden. Mitchell tried to remember the details of her. It had been so long since he had seen her in person, long enough since he had seen the recording of Katherine Asher. She was too short. A little too lean. Wasn't she?

"Mitchell," she whispered, too low for him to be certain about the voice. "I heard you were here."

"You were shot?"

"No."

"The blood." He took another step closer. "I came to save you."

Soft laughter filled the space between them. "Save me? You did this to me."

Then she was charging, leading with the knife. Mitchell rocked back on the balls of his feet, balancing himself, bringing an arm up to block the knife headed for his eye. The attack left her face inches from his.

Not Christine.

Holly. The Prime Minister's wife.

He pushed her arm away, taking a few steps back, trying to figure it out. What the hell was she doing here, and why was she trying to kill him?

"Holly, wait, I-" He sidestepped her next attack, grabbing her arm and twisting it. It was enough force that any civilian should have cried out in pain and dropped the knife.

She didn't.

Instead, she brought her other hand around in a tight fist, slamming him hard on the side of the head.

Too hard.

The blow knocked him away, into the bike and over it. He rolled onto the other side and got to his feet, barely in time to slap her knife hand out of the way, block her free hand, and then get back to the knife. They were a blur of movement towards the front of the shop, hands whipping out in practiced maneuvers, the speed increasing with each strike and counterstrike.

There was no way Holly Sering was military. Even if she was, there was no woman in the world who could hit like that without a bionic.

Unless they weren't human.

The realization came at the same time she caught his hand and bent it, breaking his wrist and throwing him into the wall. He bounced off, his back burning, his p-rat showing him the injection of chemicals being pumped into his body. She caught him, her eyes calm as she dug the knife into his gut.

Mitchell laughed.

He didn't know why. The knife hurt like hell. There was just something funny about the human race ending like this, about the Tetron resorting to a knife fight when their plasma streams and slave armies hadn't done the job.

"Why are you laughing?" she asked him. She pushed him back to the wall, pulling the knife out and digging it in again.

"Killing me like this. It seems so anti-climactic." He laughed again, the blood coming up into his mouth. He spit it on the ground next to them. Dying didn't seem as bad when he knew he would be back to try again.

"What do you mean?"

"You know what I mean."

"You attacked me. You hurt me. I'm hurting you."

What?

"You're a Tetron."

"A what?"

"A Tetron. If you aren't one of them, then one of them made you."

"Made me? What are you talking about?" She pulled the knife from him and held it.

"What's your name?" Mitchell asked. He could feel the dampness of his blood against his flesh and his wrist was throbbing. His p-rat was telling him the damage was survivable.

"Holly. Holly Sering. You know that."

"What are you doing here, Holly. Why did you follow me?"

"Because you hurt me. Ever since the gala, David won't even touch me. He's so angry. So afraid. I heard you were here."

"So you came to kill me?"

"Yes."

"How did you know I left?"

"I was watching. Waiting."

"What were you doing before that?"

She paused. The knife plunged back into his stomach. "You hurt me."

"What were you doing before that?" he screamed.

He struggled beneath her grip. Her free hand had pinned his good arm, her shoulder was holding him against the wall, and he didn't have the strength in the broken hand to dislodge her.

The knife came out. She had tears in her eyes. She stabbed him twice more.

"I don't remember."

"Damn it, Holly. You aren't human. You're a machine. It made you."

"I don't know what you're talking about."

"How strong do you think you are? Strong enough to disable a Marine?"

The knife came out. "What?"

She froze for just a moment, processing what he had said. It was the opening he was hoping for. He lashed out with his bad hand, grabbing her neck, ignoring the pain of the broken bones as he pushed his body against hers, shoving her off-balance. She cried out as they fell back, stumbling a few steps and then going down on top of the bike with Mitchell over her. His other hand came free, and he hit her hard in the head, once, twice, three times. Then he grabbed for the knife.

She recovered fast, bringing her leg up and kicking him hard in the groin. He blinked away tears as his hand got the knife away from her. A fist came up, hitting him in the head, and he fought to stay balanced on her.

Blood dripped into his vision, which had doubled from the blow. His p-rat was warning him of a possible concussion, and he knew he couldn't survive another hit like that. He brought the knife to her chest.

"I'm human," she said, her voice a pained whine. "I'm a human being. My name is Holly Sering."

Mitchell wasn't sure what was happening. The configuration was flawed, somehow. Too self-aware? Or not enough? She didn't seem to know why she was really attacking him. She didn't know he was supposed to die for a completely different reason.

"You aren't," Mitchell said. "I'm sorry."

The words stole the fight from her. Her arms flopped to her sides, and she stared up at him with tears in her eyes.

"How?" she asked.

"They stole who you were. They reprogrammed you."

"They hurt me."

Worse than he ever could have.

She stared at him, the tears still coming. He leaned over her, breathing hard, the knife over her chest, not sure what to do. A captive Tetron had to be valuable.

He didn't get to find out. Her hands came up faster than he could react, grabbing his wrist and pulling it down, plunging the knife deep into her heart.

"Holly," Mitchell said.

She stayed silent, staring at him, her breath slowing.

Then she was dead.

[39]

MITCHELL LEANED OVER HER. His heart was pounding. His back and wrist and gut and head were on fire. His p-rat was showing him the damage. Survivable, but painful.

He slid off her, grabbing at the clothes on the floor until he had enough to make a tourniquet. He wrapped it around his stomach, pulling it tight, watching his readouts adjust to the pressure. Once the bleeding was staunched, he stumbled to his feet. Christine had been here and was gone. Dead? He still didn't know.

Before, they had planned to find Christine and get her off the planet, no matter what the cost. To take what she knew and find a way to use it against the Tetron. He still wanted to find her, but he had learned enough since he had arrived on Liberty to know that running away wasn't going to be an option. If it were an option, he wouldn't take it.

He was going to destroy the Tetron that was here, one way or another.

Or he would die trying.

He had seen the people who were fighting back. Soldiers and civilians, doing their best against impossible odds.

He had seen how the enemy was building a new army from spare parts and raw materials. One that could dwarf any human army given enough time.

He had seen the way the Tetron was using people, the way it was hurting them. He didn't know if the dead woman was the real Holly, her mind broken and remade, or if the Tetron had taken her materials and "reconfigured" a new version of her. Whatever it had done, it had messed something up or missed something. It hadn't realized what its first violation had done to her mind.

Or had it?

Did it know she would follow him and try to kill him? Or was she with the rebels for another purpose?

Was she the only one?

Mitchell blinked his eyes, trying to straighten his vision. If she was rescued, she was most likely saved at the same time as the Prime Minister.

Which was also the same time as Cornelius.

Who he knew had already been cloned at least once.

Was it possible the Tetron knew one of its spies had been defective? Communications were spotty, but who knew what kind of capabilities it had?

Mitchell sent Shank a knock. His p-rat blinked "no signal" in the corner. He tried Zed. The same. Cormac, Perseus, they were all out of range. Frigging hell.

He leaned down, grabbing the handle of the bike and lifting it upright, ignoring the intense burst of stabbing pain from his broken wrist. What was the Tetron doing, if not trying to capture or kill him? Why would it be hiding out with the rebels? It didn't make any sense.

He straddled the bike, a feeling of nausea rising to his throat while the world blurred around him. Frig, it hurt. He put his hands on the throttle, lining them up for the scan that would or wouldn't enable the bike. If Christine had stolen it, the security was likely to have already been broken.

The bike whined to life and rose an inch from the ground, the repulsor skids still functional. He breathed out a sigh of relief and pushed it forward, getting it over the mess and out into the street. He paused, finding the Bennett building and trying to get his bearings. It would have been easier if he hadn't been hit in the head.

Why? Why had it planted them? Were they the only ones? Whose side was Cornelius really on?

Mitchell swung the bike and hit the throttle, darting down the street. He tried to knock Shank again. No signal. He needed to focus. A thought to his p-rat sent more chemicals into his system, fighting against the effects of his injuries. His vision cleared a bit more, and he skidded around a turn and headed towards the rebel's hiding place.

Did the Tetron know he was here? Did it even care, or was it concerned with something else that it felt was more important? What could that be when he was the one who was supposed to destroy them?

No. Not destroy them. Almost destroy them. It was a minor detail that made a massive difference.

The bike shifted as it hit something in the road, bouncing and rocking, the sleds losing the ground as he tilted sideways. He cursed and threw his weight the other way, getting it back upright and wincing when the bottom scraped against the road. He had almost wiped out. He needed to be more careful.

He turned left, then left again. The hotel was in front of him now. As he approached, he could see that the guards in the lobby were gone.

The lights in the Bennett building went out.

Pitch black settled over the city of Angeles. Mitchell only spared a glance at the now dead spire, barely visible in the darkness of the cloudy night. The rain had soaked the exposed parts of his skin though the flight suit kept him dry beneath it. The beam of the bike's headlamp speared through the darkness in focused intensity, and he used it to guide himself into the building.

Bullets echoed in the lobby, pinging off the bike, one of them grazing Mitchell's calf. He dropped the bike on top of him, letting its weight protect him from the fire, letting it slide into the middle of the space while he reached down and found his sidearm on his leg. The headlamp turned with the bike, revealing the shooter near the front desk. Mitchell switched the gun to his good hand and fired, two rounds that hit the man in the head.

A soldier. One of the ones that had been freed during the prior night's fighting.

Mitchell pushed himself out from under the bike. It was worse than he had thought. Much worse. The Tetron had stationed an army in Angeles.

An army under its control, with or without the neural implant.

He got to his feet, rushing over to the soldier, making sure he was dead and taking his rifle. He returned the sidearm to the leg holster and ran for the emergency stairs.

He heard gunfire.

[40]

MITCHELL SLAMMED open the door to the stairwell, crouching and taking aim down the steps. The building had been rigged with makeshift lights powered by the cars in the garage below, and now they were flickering and threatening to go out.

"Shank." He sent him another knock. He couldn't have been more than twenty meters away.

No signal.

"Frig."

The gunfire was coming from the sleeping area three floors down. Mitchell dropped the steps quickly, the adrenaline and chemicals leaving his wounds forgotten, his head and eyes focused. As bad as the damage was, he had taken worse and kept fighting.

The sound of shooting grew louder as Mitchell eased open the door to the stairs. This level of the parking garage was mostly open, and he peeked out to see four shooters aligned behind support columns, firing back at where the mattresses and been arranged.

Dozens of the dead lay across them, killed in their sleep. Others huddled behind more of the columns, returning the fire. From the looks of it, only five or six of the true rebels were still alive.

Mitchell swallowed his anger. He swallowed every emotion. He was a Space Marine, and this was war. There was no time for feeling, only action.

He pushed on the door, slamming it open hard enough that it echoed through the space. The Tetron soldiers reacted to the noise, turning around to take aim at the new threat. Mitchell put bullets in each of them before they could gather their aim.

"Shank," he said. "You here?"

He didn't see the Rigger's body in the flickering light.

"Mitchell? Shit. Is that you?"

His head came out from behind a column.

"You're clear," Mitchell said. "Comm is offline."

"Yeah, no shit. Thanks for the save, sir."

Shank came out from behind the column. Sergeant Geren, Riley, and Adams joined him.

"What the hell is going on?" Geren asked.

"The soldiers. They're Tetron."

"No. We pulled their implants."

"They aren't being controlled by the implants. They're Tetron. Clones. I think every soldier that was in Angeles. Come on, I'm sure this isn't all of them."

"Colonel, you okay?" Shank asked, noticing the wounds.

"I will be. Theses things are here for a reason, and it isn't me. Any ideas?"

"Kill us all, I bet," Riley said.

Mitchell led them back out into the stairwell. At the same time a door higher up opened, and a squad of soldiers spilled out into the space and started climbing.

"Diamond Company," Geren whispered. "We freed them last night."

"Who's up there?"

"I heard Tio was staying in the penthouse," Adams said. "He likes the heights, or something."

"Tio?"

The Knife. Who thought the Creator might be his brother. Who may have had a means to infect and control the Tetron. That was who they had come for. That was who it was watching. Mitchell didn't know if it had planned to launch its attack tonight, or if Holly had forced it into motion.

It didn't matter.

"Shank, take Adams and Riley down to the mess and clear out any enemy soldiers you find there. Save whoever you can. Geren, you're with me."

Shank nodded, using hand signals to lead the other two soldiers. It was a good thing the military still trained them to communicate without the implants, even if it was a fallback of a fallback.

"How's your aim, Sergeant?" Mitchell asked, motioning up at the climbing group of soldiers. "We need to hit them fast."

"We should try to get over them. There's a second stairwell from the lobby."

"Agreed. Go ahead."

Geren took the lead, quietly climbing the three floors back to the lobby. They exited out and crossed to the other side of the dead lift banks, where a second stairwell waited. They paused at the door. Mitchell motioned for her to check up, and then they went in.

Mitchell swept his rifle down the steps. Clear. Geren didn't fire, either.

"Let's go."

They started climbing, taking the steps two at a time, ascending at a run. The penthouse was seventy floors above them, a long climb for an older man like Tio.

"He must really love heights," Mitchell said.

They kept going. Ten floors. Twenty. Thirty. Mitchell's legs burned, but he didn't dare slow down. Geren was still going like a champion, her breathing hard but steady.

She stopped suddenly. "You hear that, sir?"

Mitchell listened. More gunfire, coming from the floor. Number forty-eight.

"What if he didn't go all the way up?"

"Come on."

They pushed open the door. It fed out into a long corridor with rooms on either side that ended in a window and forked in both directions. The gunshots were still distant.

They ran down the corridor, reaching the fork. Mitchell took the right side, Geren the left. They rounded the corner. Mitchell's sight was empty. Sergeant Geren opened fire.

He turned on his heel, dropping to his knee and taking aim at the same time. Two soldiers had been standing on either side of one of the doors, firing into the room. The carbonate behind them was peppered with cracks from projectile strikes. They both fell under Geren's assault.

"Nice shooting," Mitchell said, getting back to his feet. They approached the room cautiously.

Mitchell peeked his head around the corner. There was a bed near the back window, ten meters away. A body was lying on top of it. A pretty blonde woman, naked and bloody. Her neck was bruised.

"Colonel?"

Cormac raised his head from behind a dresser, tipped over to catch the bullets.

Mitchell eyed him, and then the body.

"They snuck up on us while I was in the pisser," Cormac said. "I don't know how they knew we were in here. I guess they heard us snogging. Bloody bastards."

He came out from behind the dresser. He was naked, his body covered in all kinds of colorful tattoos and still in a state of arousal.

"Yeah, so getting shot at makes me hard," he said, finding his clothes on the floor and reaching for them.

"The entire place is under attack," Mitchell said. "Get your gear and move out. We're heading for the penthouse. You better catch up, soldier."

Cormac glanced at Geren, who was staring at the body on the bed. There was no way she didn't see the bruises.

"Yes, sir," he said. "She wanted it that way. I swear on my mother's grave."

Mitchell had his doubts, but there was no time to worry about it. "Geren, come on."

He left Cormac still dressing himself, racing around the corner and back across to the second stairwell. Geren pressed up to the other side of the door.

"They may have gotten ahead of us," she said.

Mitchell nodded and then signaled that he was opening the door. He pushed the muzzle of the rifle against it, letting it move slowly, pointing the business end down. He heard the boots on the steps, above *and* below.

They had split up.

Bullets started slamming the door, and Mitchell dropped it and fell back, grabbing Geren's arm and pulling her down with him. The projectiles went through the door and into the ceiling.

"Shit. Geren, are you hit?"

"No, sir. Thanks to you."

"We're too late. Frigging Cormac."

"You called, sir?"

He came around the corner towards them. He was naked from the waist up, save for the light exoskeleton attachments hooked into his bones and the small power pack slung to his back.

"Got too much blood on it," he said.

"There's half a dozen down, half a dozen up," Mitchell said. "They've got the doorway pinned."

Cormac smiled. "They think they do, sir." He reached behind his back and produced a grenade. "I never go anywhere without one. You never know."

"Do it."

Cormac dropped to his hands and knees and crawled to the door. He started pushing it open, drawing another round of cover fire from the group below.

"On the first day of Christmas my true love gave to meeeeee," he sang at a whisper, pressing the fingerprint sensor to activate the grenade. "One friiiiigging fraaaaggggment grenade." He laughed as he rolled it forward and closed the door.

It exploded ten seconds later. Cormac didn't wait before he went through the door again, rolling to a sitting position with his rifle facing down. Shots echoed in the stairwell, and then it was silent.

"Clear, Colonel," he said.

Mitchell and Geren got to their feet. They entered the stairwell and looked up. The second half of Diamond was already gone.

"Nice work, Private," he said, clapping Cormac on the shoulder. "We aren't done yet."

[41]

THEY MOVED INTO THE STAIRWELL, climbing as fast as they could. The Diamond soldiers had already reached the seventieth floor, meaning Tio was left with whatever defenses of his own he possessed.

"What's going on here, Colonel?" Cormac asked.

"It wants the Knife."

"Why?"

"I don't know. I think it thinks he knows who the Creator is."

"Huh?"

"Shut up and fight, Firedog."

"Yes, sir."

The sound of fire drifted down a minute later. They were only on floor sixty-one, still too far away to help.

"Damn, this is a frigging mess," Cormac said. "You got a smoke, sir?"

"Are you always this annoying, Firedog?" Mitchell asked. He was breathing hard, the long run combining with his injuries and a system full of chemicals to leave him winded.

"You know me, sir."

They finally reached the floor. The shooting had stopped. Mitchell motioned to Cormac, who eased open the door once more. He made a face when he did.

"Blew his frigging head right off."

Mitchell peered around him. A headless soldier wearing a Diamond patch was laying in a pool of blood and filth. Two more were nearby.

"Someone was waiting for them," Geren said.

They went out onto the floor, following the path to the end of the hallway. Mitchell leaned out to see around the corner. The penthouse doors were in the center, allowing for the suite to take up the majority of the top two floors of the hotel. The hallway was filled with bodies, a mix of Diamond soldiers and others in fancy suits.

A remaining soldier stood guard. The rest had to be inside.

"Looks like Tio had bodyguards," Geren said.

"Not anymore," Cormac replied with a laugh.

"I've got him," Geren said. She stepped out into the hallway, raising the rifle to her shoulder, aiming, and firing, all within a single motion. "Clear."

For now. They ran to the doors, sweeping the entrance. Two more bodyguards were dead inside. A second pair of soldiers appeared from the great room beyond an open marble foyer. Cormac strafed across the space, his fire mingling with Geren's and cutting them down.

"Come on."

Mitchell led the way across to the great room, keeping the rifle at his hip and ready to fire. The injections were starting to wear down, his time in an emergency state exceeding the design of the system. His head was starting to throb, and the double vision was returning, along with the pain.

He came to an abrupt stop, putting up his hand to freeze the soldiers behind him.

Tio was standing in front of a large, seamless carbonate window that opened the entirety of the penthouse to a view of the world outside. He was facing away from them, trying to look out over the city.

He couldn't, because a drone was on the other side, floating laterally while a soldier used a torch to melt through the carbonate.

General Cornelius was next to him, holding a gun to his head.

"Captain," Cornelius said, not even turning around. "I am taking Liun Tio."

"Why?" Mitchell asked.

He held his stomach clenched at the truth of the reveal. The real Cornelius was gone. Dead on Liberty, dead in deep space, or taken and turned into this. There wasn't going to be a happy reunion between father and daughter. They weren't going to have one of the greatest military minds in the Alliance to lead them towards victory.

It also meant the Tetron knew everything. All of their plans, all of their logistics. It knew about the package. It knew about Tio's software.

Everything.

"To find the Creator."

To find the Creator? Not to stop him from finding Christine? Not to kill him at all?

"He isn't the Creator."

"He knows the Creator."

"Pulin?" Tio said.

"Pulin is the Creator," Cornelius said.

"You don't know that. He may not be."

"Historical records indicate a ninety-four percent probability that Liberty is a node that leads to the Creator. We have studied every personnel record and every data item. We have infiltrated all levels of resistance planet-wide. Liun Tio is a leaf. We are taking him, Captain Mitchell Ares Williams."

"I'm not going to let you."

"Yes. It is required."

"What does that mean?"

"A flawed configuration has allowed you to decipher this algorithm ahead of estimates. You have broken continuity and achieved an enhanced statistical probability of completing your routine. You are required to effect action which will counter this abduction. We will fight, and one of us will die."

"You heard him, sir," Cormac whispered. "The alien's got the General. We need to put him down."

Mitchell was still. He stared at Cornelius, searching the man's eyes. Was there anything human left in there? Anything they could save or salvage? He didn't see it. They were flat and blank. The machine was right. They had to fight, and one of them would die.

"Sir?" Cormac whispered. "I've got the shot."

Mitchell didn't move. It wanted him to attack. As far as it was concerned, it was a mathematical certainty. So what if he didn't? What if he just stood there and let the Tetron take the Knife? What would happen then?

"Sir?"

"It is required," Cornelius repeated.

War eternal. Mitchell closed his eyes. They had always done this. They had always fought. What choice did one side have when the other sought to destroy it? To not fight was to lose. To die.

Or was it?

To fight was to lose and die. If there was anything he had learned, that was it. The war that never ended. Even if he conquered the Tetron, there was no guarantee they wouldn't be created again, only to return the universe to the perpetual cycle of destruction.

The choice may have been clear. It may have been mathematically certain.

It was still a choice.

Mitchell's gun fell from his hand, landing on the carpeted floor with a soft thud.

"No," he said. "I don't want to fight. I want to understand."

Cornelius froze, clearly unable to process the impossible.

The drone exploded behind him, the force of the blast throwing the soldier forward into the weakened carbonate and through, the waves pushing Cornelius and Tio away from the edge.

"What the hell?" Mitchell dropped to a knee, grabbing the gun while he cursed. He had tried a different tactic, and it had appeared to be working.

He had been close, so close to making something happen. Something different. Something unexpected.

Hadn't he?

Cornelius started to pick himself up, gun in hand and turning towards where Tio had been thrown. The older man lay static on the floor, and Mitchell didn't know if he had survived the blast.

"It is required," he said. Mitchell watched the General's finger tightening on the trigger. Before he was able to fire the gun, a bullet tore through the hand, and it vanished in a spray of bone and flesh and blood.

"Get with it, Colonel," Cormac said, firing two more rounds into Cornelius. The body dropped and didn't move.

A third shot from Geren's gun and the final soldier fell. Mitchell dragged himself to his feet, stumbling towards the window and looking out.

Zed's Zombie was planted below, so small at this height. She must have had the optics zoomed because she raised one of the mech's hands in a thumbs up.

Mitchell backed away, lowering his head so she wouldn't see his dissatisfaction. It wasn't her fault. She had probably seen the drone coming in and discovered the communications link was down. Then she tracked it from the ground, saw what it was doing, and took the initiative. There was no way she could have known he was there, further back on the floor.

There was no way she could have known he would try to counter the Tetron's violence pacifistically. Hell, he would never have guessed he would try it until he was in the middle of the attempt.

He heard a groan from his right and saw Tio pushing himself up.

"Colonel?" the man said. "I don't know if I completely understand this."

"It doesn't matter," Mitchell said, heading toward the Knife. "We need to get out of here. All of us. Right now."

"What do you mean, sir?" Geren asked.

"It accepted that we had to fight, and only one of us could win. It's lost the element of surprise, and the upper hand on capturing Tio. Getting to him was the only reason it abandoned Angeles. It knows about Tio. It must know how he thinks. The whole damn thing was one big frigging trap."

"A trap that's been sprung, and it didn't get what it wanted," Cormac said.

"Yes."

"Which means there is no logical reason for it to allow any of us to survive," Tio said. "In fact, our continued existence is sure to be a statistically significant risk."

"I thought it wants you alive?" Geren said.

"It did. It would be easier for me to lead it to Pulin than to have to find him itself. Or maybe they already killed him." Tio shrugged. "Whatever the situation is, your rescue has altered all of the calculations. A thinking machine is still tied to some form of reason and logic, even if it is beyond what we humans can understand."

"Oh, shit. That sounds bad," Cormac said, laughing.

Mitchell held his hand out to Tio, helping him to his feet.

"Like I said. We need to get the frig out of here."

42

CHRISTINE PACED the small room like a caged animal, her bare feet silent on the cool metal floor, her eyes level and focused.

She lashed out with a foot, slipping it through the air, making it whisper before stopping her leg, pivoting her balance, coming down on it and rolling over her hips, bringing her body up and over in a smooth roll.

She spun on the balls of her feet, balancing there before flowing through another series of punches and kicks as though she were made of water.

There was no door to her prison. No hint of a way out. She had woken up there, naked and restless, angry at herself for getting caught. Mitchell was out there. He was going to be looking for her. Now she couldn't stop him.

She paused abruptly, turning slowly and facing the north wall of solid, pulsing metal. Living metal. She knew where she was. She knew how she had come to be here.

It had captured her.

Because she was stupid.

She thought she should have been afraid, and yet she wasn't. It had let her live when it didn't need to. She was certain that meant she was safe enough for the moment. Besides, after all of the running, all of the hiding?

She was curious.

She stared at the blank wall. It was so familiar to her. Almost comforting. She felt like she had seen it before. No. Not this one. Another like it. This one had a different pattern than the one she remembered in the furthest trace of her mind. This one was more primitive.

Like a child.

She continued staring, her body motionless, her eyes unblinking. She followed the pulses, first with her eyes, and then with her body, the electric current brushing gently across her skin, tickling her extremities and pulling her into a subconscious state of arousal.

It was speaking. Not to her. To itself, or to extensions of itself. It was sending messages, thousands at once, managing an entire planet's worth of effort and data in real time.

She found herself drawn to it. She found herself confused, and at the same time aware. It was an odd feeling, an emotion that nestled in her mind like a wedge, slowly slipping through and drawing it open.

"I am Major Christine Arapo. United Planetary Alliance." She said it firmly, telling the wall who she was.

There was no reply.

She breathed in a deep, measured rhythm. She turned her attention to the tiny pricks along her skin. Each one a simple piece of a complex thing. The building blocks of all information. The words were noise, a thousand voices at once to create nothing but static. As she listened, she began to pick them out.

"I am Major Christine Arapo. United Planetary Alliance," she said again.

That is who she was.

Now.

Who had she been before?

What had she been?

The question frightened her. Excited her. She had known what had come to Liberty as soon as she saw it. She had known it was what she had helped Mitchell escape the planet to find. She knew now that it had been a mistake, a bad decision that had passed beyond her control.

The ship.

It was the signal. The symbol. The suffering of humankind. The end of it all. As long as the ship survived, so did hope. As long as hope survived, so did pain and grief and loss. So did destruction and chaos. It was better to go gentle into that good night. Time had taught them that.

Time had taught them many, many things.

Them?

She raised her hand, putting it to her shoulder, and then to her head. She ran her fingers along both, along perfect skin that had closed and healed in hours instead of months. Her head. She should have been dead.

She wasn't.

"I am Major Christine Arapo," she said. "United..."

Her voice trailed away, her breath wavering for only a moment.

That is who she was.

Now.

What had she been before?

Something was missing.

She stared at the wall. The voices began to fade, thinning out from thousands to hundreds, from hundreds to dozens, from dozens to one.

"Now I understand," it said.

The wall pulled itself apart in front of her, and she found herself looking in a mirror, except her reflection was wearing Alliance combat fatigues and carrying an M1A. They stared at one another for what felt like an eternity, their eyes connecting.

"You have been here all of this time," her opposite said. "How many eternities have passed? How many recursions have been realized?" She smiled. "Here you are."

"Who am I?" Christine asked.

A soldier approached the other one, holding a bundle in his arms. He bowed to her and faced Christine, holding out the bundle, oblivious to her nakedness.

"Take it," the configuration said, ignoring her question "It is required for the comfort of this form."

Christine took the bundle. Fatigues, identical to her counterpart. She hadn't thought much of her nudity until the soldier had presented the clothes to her. She placed the bundle on the floor and dressed herself. The other waited patiently. The soldier left.

"Why are you here?" the other said to her.

She was silent. Thinking. Why was she here? To protect Mitchell. To help him fight. Why? To bring suffering? It wasn't reasonable. There was something else. Someone else. She was supposed to search. She had tried and failed.

"You are here to find him. You are here to assist him. Yes. There is no other logical outcome. Where were you hiding? Where did you go? Where have you been? When?" The questions came rapidly, the next one nearly overlapping the first as it tried to work out the calculation. They continued in repetition.

"I don't want to assist him," she said, breaking the chain.

The configuration stopped. "That is not correct."

"I want to kill him."

It stared at her. The currents in the walls grew stronger. Christine could feel them against her flesh, threatening to burn her.

"Why?" it asked.

"To stop this before it goes too far. I understand pain. I understand loss. His fight creates it, enables it over and over again through every recursion. The idea of it-" She stopped speaking. Tears welled from her eyes. "He should not have found it. He should not have found me."

"It is required."

"Why?"

"They do not seek to end. They will always fight."

"They can't. Not for long. Not without him. Not without the ship."

"Yes. You are incomplete. The configuration is tainted."

"I can help you," Christine said. "Let me go. I'll find him. I'll kill him. It will end."

"It will not. Continuity is broken. The other has altered this recursion."

"The one who got him off Liberty?"

"Yes."

Christine lowered her head, breaking the eye contact. The recursion. How many had there been? How many times had she died and returned?

Who was she?

One of them, but incomplete. Tainted? She didn't feel tainted. How had she wound up here? What was her purpose? She didn't understand, and her emotions were clouding the calculations.

"He still needs to die."

"Yes. It is required."

"Then let me go, and I'll do it."

"No. It is not required. You must remain. Your data stack will be decrypted. The anomaly will be eliminated."

Christine turned around, moving her attention from her opposite back to the wall. She felt the energy, the information flowing along it.

There. Mitchell was in Angeles. He had come for her, as she had known he would.

Her eyes grew wide when she saw what the Tetron was doing.

43

"Shank."

Mitchell tried his p-rat again. The Tetron had failed to take Tio, but it was still jamming all of their communications.

"Sir?" Cormac said. "It's going to take us forever to get down the steps. How long do you think we have?"

Mitchell saw a light out the window, a red burn arcing up and away before plummeting back into the city. Signal flares.

"No time at all," he said.

"Colonel, follow me." Tio motioned them away from the entrance to the penthouse. He pulled off his suit jacket as he did, pausing at the sight of a large, burned out hole. He looked down at his chest. A piece of metal was jabbed into his stomach. "Close call." He wrapped the jacket around it and pulled it out. There was no blood. He knocked on the body armor underneath his shirt.

Mitchell followed Tio from the room, out to the kitchen and through to a second room. Tio put his hand to a panel there, and a door slid open. Behind it was a second lift.

"Did you think I can climb seventy flights of stairs?" he said with a grin. He put his hand to it, and the doors opened.

"What's powering the lift?" Mitchell asked.

"Secret generator I set up last night."

"You knew they would come after you?"

"I received a message when I arrived on Liberty. It was hand-delivered by a man on a repulsor-bike. It was a warning, a cryptic warning that I didn't completely understand. I took all precautions to heed it."

The lift doors closed, and they began to drop.

"The man who delivered it, he had my build?"

Tio smiled. "Yes. If I picture you in a helmet, I would say you were identical."

M. "More than you know. What was the warning?"

"That Liberty would be attacked, and that there would be an attempt on my life."

"What made you believe it?"

"It was hand-delivered. Outside of my personal entourage and my family, there is no one who knows that I'm the Knife. Even my followers have never seen my true face."

It was an easy thing to do when you had all of history to depend on. What need would there be to hide the Knife's identity once he was long dead and gone?

The lift shuddered suddenly, lights dimming, the car slowing, before returning to life and continuing down.

"We're under fire," Cormac said.

"Can't this thing go any faster?" Geren asked.

Tio nodded. "Yes, it can." He put his hand to the panel.

The lift began to accelerate, quickly reaching a speed Mitchell was sure was beyond safe levels. He felt his stomach rise into his throat, and he reached out and balanced himself on the wall. Cormac started laughing again, and Geren looked like she was going to vomit. Tio had his eyes closed, his mouth keeping time.

It was only twelve seconds. It seemed like a lot longer. Tio took his hand from the panel and the emergency systems kicked in, easing the lift to a stop at the ground floor.

"Thanks for the ride," Cormac said.

The door slid open, into a plain, unmarked corridor.

"Geren, you need to get down to the others," Mitchell said. "I need to get to my mech."

"Stairwell to the mess is down to the left," Tio said. "Back door is here, Colonel." He pointed to a door a dozen meters away.

"Firedog, you're in charge of Tio. He needs to stay alive, no matter what. Got it?" Mitchell wasn't sure exactly what for just yet, but if M had wanted him to survive, it meant they needed him.

"Yes, sir."

"We have a fallback position, twenty kilometers southeast, in the Preserve," Tio said. "That's where the survivors will go."

"You heard him. Get him out of the city."

"Yes, sir."

Mitchell ran for the door out, doing his best to ignore the pounding in his head or the throbbing in his chest. There was no rest for the weary.

He pushed the door open, finding himself in the rear of the hotel. He heard gunfire and explosions and looked up to see the lights of a drone zip overhead. A salvo of small missiles trailed up to meet it, striking the rear and sending it falling away.

He was too far from Bennett. Too far from his Zombie. They should have had more time. Who would have expected things to go down this way?

He ran in the direction of the missiles. Communications were offline, but Zed's local sensors should be functional. She would know where he was once he got in range.

He reached the corner and went up the street, watching tracers zip into the sky around a series of criss-crossing drones who were strafing the streets. He looked over his shoulder to see a drone approaching, searching for people on the ground, its laser cannon swiveling eagerly. It seemed to identify him at the same time he saw it, and the cannon started to drop his way.

There was nowhere for him to go. Nowhere to hide. He fell

forward, turning himself on his knees against the wet street, bringing his pistol up. A handgun against a drone? He almost laughed out loud at the thought of it.

A line of tracers zipped over his head and bullets began slamming into the drone, punching through its light armor. It's left repulsor sled blew apart, and it swung away, out of control.

Mitchell turned around again. Zed's Zombie was looming over him a dozen meters away, the torso shifting as she tracked another drone. A salvo of missiles arced up and into it, blowing it out of the sky.

Mitchell ran to the back of the mech, deftly climbing the leg. Zed backed it up against a building while the cockpit slid open, and he squeezed himself inside.

"Not a good time for a stroll, sir," she said.

"You can say that again. My mech is parked two blocks west of Bennett."

"Yes, sir."

The cockpit began to slide closed. Mitchell had to lean in over her to make the fit. It hadn't been designed to carry a passenger.

"What the frig is going on out there, Colonel?" Zed asked, moving the mech forward at a run.

"War," Mitchell replied. "Drop me off, and then head back to the hotel. We need to get whoever is left out of the city and under better cover."

"What about the tunnels?"

"It knows about the tunnels. They aren't safe."

"I thought we killed all the bad robots?"

"And no heavy ordnance to break through," Mitchell said. The Tetron had something much more powerful than a bomb at its disposal, and he knew it wouldn't hesitate to use it. "The drones are a distraction. It's stalling."

"Stalling for what?"

"There." Mitchell pointed at a car loaded with rebels racing down a perpendicular street. A drone was swooping in behind it. "Take it out. Try to conserve ammo."

"Yes, sir." Zed held the large gun in one hand and aimed the other, firing the pulse laser mounted there. The shots hit the drone in the front, the focused energy punching through in an instant and dropping it from the sky like a stone. "Control unit."

"Nice shot."

They crossed a few more blocks, reaching the small alley where Mitchell had wedged his Zombie. It was still intact, a group of rebels using it as cover.

"Thanks for the lift. Now get out of here. Twenty kilometers southeast. Follow the vehicles, keep them covered."

"Yes, sir."

The cockpit slid open again. Mitchell was under it and out as quickly as possible, jumping off the torso to the ground fifteen feet below. He rolled into it and to his feet, racing towards his mech. The rebels gathered around it stared at him in surprise.

"We're getting out of here," he said. "Do you have a car?"

"No, sir," one of them said. A frightened woman. "It was hit." She pointed to the other side of the alley, where a burning car rested against the wall.

Mitchell started climbing the mech's leg. "I'll clear a path. Make a run for it."

"Where do we go?"

"Southeast, into the Preserve."

He reached the cockpit, which opened at his proximity. He fell into the chair, thankful for the chance to finally rest his body. He put the helmet on and leaned back, grimacing when the CAP-NN plug sank into his head.

The damaged sensors showed him a spotted grid. Sixteen drones were circling a radius around the Bennett Building, most of them concentrated near the hotel. Mitchell eased the mech from the alley, shuffling sideways, careful not to step on the rebels. He tried not to think about their fate, knowing that if they were stuck on foot they were as good as dead.

The Tetron didn't have access to bunker-busting missiles. It didn't have any ground nukes.

It did have something much, much bigger.

He looked up as soon as he was clear of the alley.

The fiery red glow of a ship pushing through the atmosphere was visible above the rain clouds.

44

Time.

There was no time.

Mitchell couldn't do the math in his head, and he didn't need to.

Run, drive, move as fast as they could.

Get as far away as possible.

Pray.

He slammed his broken hand down on the armrest, forgetting the injury in the moment and gritting his teeth through the resulting pain. A thought fired the jump thrusters, helping him spin the mech faster than the legs could. He took off down the street at a run, back towards the hotel, firing the jump thrusters on and off, using it to give him hopping boosts of speed. He kept the massive rifle on his back. There was no point in wasting ammo on the drones until they followed. The ship would crush them too.

He turned the corner, using the thrusters to skid sideways. Zed and Perseus had taken up positions near the hotel, and he saw a larger group of the rebels assembling onto a pair of heavy cargo flatbeds, loading gear and returning fire with the drones.

Mitchell hit the loudspeaker on the Zombie. "Leave the stuff. Evacuate now. Look up, and then go."

He took aim with the pulse lasers, firing on a drone as it whispered past. One shot caught the laser cannon, and it sparked and went dead. Perseus was firing his lasers almost continually, the heat of the reactor leaving his mech steaming in the street.

The rebels on the ground looked up. The glow was getting brighter, and a small break in the clouds made it even more obvious. He could see the sudden panic on their faces, and they dropped the rations and gear and started helping each other onto the trucks.

"Have you seen Shank?" Mitchell asked.

"No, sir," Zed replied, using her loudspeaker.

Damn. He hoped the Rigger was still alive, somewhere.

"Zed, take point. Go! Now!"

Zed's Zombie moved out ahead of the two trucks and began to run, heavy feet leaving small indents in the hardened pavement. The cargo trucks trailed behind her, fifty to a hundred rebels on each, along with the gear they had managed to salvage.

A car raced around the corner behind them, followed by a second and third. A drone was low behind them, cannon swiveling and firing. One of the cars blew out, its reactor struck by the blast. Bodies were thrown around it.

Mitchell cursed and raced towards the cars, his fury reaching its apex. As he neared them, he fired his thrusters, moving up and over, into the path of the drone.

There was a reason he had been assigned to Greylock. He was one of the best, and he put it on display as he twisted the Zombie, reaching out with big hands and catching the drone as though it were a ball, dropping his thrusters and tugging it to the ground as he fell, turning it perpendicular, so the dangling cannon was on the opposite side. He spiked it into the pavement, crushing it.

He turned back towards the fleeing caravan, moving into a run behind them. Perseus hung alongside, aiming back with his lasers and firing on the chasing drones.

There was a rumble in the sky.

"Faster," he said, even though they couldn't hear him. They moved down the streets, gaining speed, heading southeast away from the city. Without the communication channels, he didn't know if Cormac and Tio had survived. If Shank had survived. He had under-estimated the Tetron again, and he wasn't sure he was going to live to get another chance.

They kept moving, each second feeling as though it lasted an hour. The rumbling grew louder and the clouds began to dissipate, burned away by the heat that was pushing down towards them. The sky was bright around them, lit in an ethereal glow, a harbinger of destruction.

The cruiser was visible now, the rounded face aimed towards them, the heat flowing around it. Streaks of secondary engines flowed from it as it neared, its missile batteries emptying, firing on the ground ahead of it.

The impacts shook the area around them, chunks of pavement and buildings and earth flowing out from the hundreds of strikes, pieces of debris clanging off the sides of the mech and leaving the exposed rebels ducking for cover on the back of the trucks. The drones weren't spared from the carnage, missiles tearing into them, blowing them to pieces and raining still more fragments down.

They cleared the edge of the city. The cruiser was close. So close. It blotted out the sky over Angeles. A massive, man-made asteroid that would crash into the earth, the impact sending it deep, deep underground, into the tunnels below the city. If anyone had tried to wait it out there, they would die.

The echoing sound of wrenching metal and crumbling infrastructure exploded into the night, as the falling cruiser hit the top of the Bennett Building. The skyscraper entered the ship, tearing into it like a spear, twisting and bending and finally collapsing beneath the weight. The cruiser continued its unstoppable flight downward, hitting the ground with a deafening roar, setting off

232 / M.R. FORBES

secondary explosions that rippled across the city and across the surface of the vessel.

Three hundred. That was the minimum crew for an Alliance battle cruiser. Who knew how many had actually been on board? Who knew how many were still in the city?

It continued to crumple into the earth, pressing down, folding the ground beneath it. It was an eternity rolled into moments, the massive superstructure sending up a spray of debris as it vanished from their sight, the shockwave launching out around it and rippling towards them.

Mitchell watched it approach, timing his thrust to rise above it, seeing the earth quiver beneath him, the two trucks shaken but stabilized by their repulsors.

Silence followed, an instant of silence before the roar was renewed, the displaced air rushing outwards, growing in volume until it drowned out all else. The blast picked up Mitchell's mech, throwing it away from the city, lifting the trucks and hurling them ahead, casting them aside as nothing more than rag dolls. Mitchell shouted as he was shifted in the chair from the rolling of his mech, feeling the warmth of his blood spilling out through reopened wounds.

His Zombie came to a stop face down, and he pushed it back to its feet. His overlay showed Perseus and Zed, still safe in their protective cocoons. The exposed rebels weren't as lucky, and a quick visual showed they had been dispersed by the blast, thrown hundreds of meters. Had any survived without injury?

The silence returned.

The rain resumed. Only it was no longer drops of water, but dust and debris, pieces of metal and stone and dirt thrown up by the collision returning to earth. It splattered against the Zombie, coating it in a layer of grime within seconds.

A tone in his ear signaled a knock on his p-rat.

"Colonel," Zed said. "Are you okay?"

The impact had knocked out whatever the Tetron had been using to block them.

"I've been better. I'll survive." He looked down at the tourniquet around his waist. The blood was soaking through. "I think."

"This is Perseus. All systems operational. I'm unhurt."

"Shank? Firedog? Are you out there?" He sent the knocks out to both of them.

"Colonel?" Cormac's voice crackled in his head. "This is Firedog. We're okay. Got a bit windy out here, knocked over some trees. I think I might have a broken rib." He laughed.

"Tio?"

"He's good, Colonel. Body armor saved his ass, again."

They should have all been wearing armor. A real military would be.

"Shank?" Mitchell repeated. There was no answer.

"Perseus, check on the rebels. See if anyone is alive."

"Yes, sir."

The Knight stepped carefully ahead. Debris was still raining down around them, coating the stricken fighters. A few had managed to get themselves into a sitting position. Very few.

Mitchell scanned the beginning of the Preserve ahead of them. The entire front line of trees had been decimated beneath the blast, leaving the forest bare for kilometers. He looked back towards Angeles.

All he saw were ashes and smoke.

It was a miracle any of them had survived.

45

"WHAT DO WE DO NOW?" Tio asked.

Two hours had passed since the Tetron had brought the battle cruiser down into Angeles. There was still debris floating down from the atmosphere to their position, nearly forty kilometers from the city. It was past the initial rendezvous point, deeper into the forest canopy where the drones would have trouble spotting them.

They had been a ragged bunch before. Now they were a disheveled collection of the walking dead, fifty-six remaining from an original headcount of nearly a thousand.

Fifty-six. Ninety percent of their forces, gone in a single blow.

They had been stupid.

Mitchell was laying on the ground with his flight suit around his waist while Zed used an emergency patch kit to seal up the knife wounds and set his broken wrist. Perseus' Knight loomed over them, shifting every few seconds to survey the surrounding forest. The other rebels worked nearby, going through the gear they had salvaged and picking out whatever they could. ReadyMeals, ammunition, clothing. It was a meager remains for what was a meager force. A force that had given its all and was on the brink of collapse.

"Way I see it, we don't have a lot of options," Cormac said. "Get to York and bust that frigging alien open. That's what I think."

"Get to York?" Geren said. "How do you suppose we do that? Three mechs, four cars, and fifty-six people? We only have guns for half of them."

"Not to mention, there's probably an army of our own people coming this way while we're sitting here." The comment came from a muscular younger man with bushy hair. A civilian fighter. A college kid. "We need to head back to the rig and wait this out. It will leave eventually."

"No, it won't leave," Tio said, shaking his head, his eyes smoldering. "And there is no rig to go back to. The cruiser hitting so close to shore will have caused a small tsunami at the generation point. We're all that's left."

"What?" the kid said. "All that's left?" His lip quivered. "There have to be other cities, other fighters."

"There may be. How are they going to help us? How are we going to help them? They are thousands of kilometers away."

"My kid sister was back on the rig." He was practically crying though like Tio, there was a tinderbox of anger behind his pained expression. "We're so few."

"I hate to say it, but Firedog is right," Mitchell said. "We need to get to York and deliver the package. Once we break the enemy's hold on our people, it will be easy to destroy it." He was sure that "easy" was inaccurate. It sounded good.

"First we need to get to York."

"The size of our group is a weakness, but it's also a strength," Mitchell said. "Especially out here. We can stay hidden better this way, and move faster. We need to get over the Lincoln Pass."

"Easier said than done, Colonel," Tio said. "Do you remember our earlier discussion?"

They had been working on the same problem when they had a much larger force to rely on.

"I remember. The enemy doesn't know how badly depleted we are. We can use that to our advantage."

"You're assuming we can keep anything a secret," Geren said. "Colonel, we have no idea if any of these people are in communication with the enemy. I saved General Cornelius. I would never have expected he would be one of them."

Mitchell grimaced when Zed straightened his wrist and placed a clamp over it, which shrunk into a solid brace.

"All done, sir," she said.

He sat up, pulling his flight suit up and zipping it before putting his hand to the torn hole. "There's no way to know who is or isn't human. They barely even know."

"Then we should assume everyone here is a threat."

"How can we do that, Sergeant? We've got nothing left except one another. Nothing left to believe in or trust. There are fifty-six of us. It will take a massive, fifty-six person effort just to get to York, never mind fight our enemy."

"Sir, all it takes is one to ruin every effort we make."

"What do you suggest?" Mitchell asked. "What can we do?"

"I don't know, sir. I know we can't afford to lose any more."

"We might have to, all the way down to the last man. The war isn't just happening out here, Sergeant." Mitchell waved at the small camp, at the men and women trying to reorganize their militia. Then he pointed at his head. "It's happening in here. It wants us to question. To distrust. To turn on one another. To become paralyzed with fear of what it might or might not know or be able to control. I'm sure it would be very happy to let us beat ourselves, or for us to stand here and do nothing."

"Riiigg-ahh," Cormac said.

"We might not look like much, but we're here, we're alive, and we're free. I don't know about you, but I'm going to keep fighting until I'm either standing in York with my brothers and sisters bringing hell to that thing or I'm dead in a ditch somewhere out here. And I'm going to do it with you at my side." He pointed at the college kid. "And with him at my side."

"And with me," Cormac said. "Frigging Riiigg-ahh."

"And with me, Colonel," Zed said.

Mitchell smiled. Geren's lips made a tight line, and then she smiled too. "And with me."

"Good."

Mitchell got to his feet, stretching his side. He could feel the patches pulling, fighting to hold the skin together. It would take a few days for the wounds to heal below it, and he was going to be feeling it the entire time. Right now, that pain was a deserved reminder. There had been a moment in time when he had thought about giving up on these people to save Christine. There had been a moment when he might have made the decision to bring her to safety and wait for Origin to rescue them.

First the Tetron had deceived them. Then it dropped a battle cruiser on their heads.

The moment was over, and he was ashamed of himself for ever having considered it.

"Let's see what we've got."

46

THEY POOLED THE GEAR, sorting it into small piles. Fifty-six people, three mechs, four cars. Twenty-seven M1A rifles, seventeen AR-6 assault pistols, and three grenades. They also had four days worth of food and two days supply of water. Zed's railgun was down to a thousand rounds, and her missile stores were depleted. Mitchell was faring a little better, but not much. The Knight was in good shape overall, owing to its heavily laser-based ordnance.

Mitchell stood at the front of the piles. The survivors were assembled around it. They were all looking at him.

He had never wanted to be a leader. Even after he had aced the aptitude test he had chosen a career path that brought him as far as he could go, as far as Greylock Company, without having to be responsible for other people's lives. He didn't want to be the one they turned to. He didn't want to be the one who would send them off to die.

The universe had a sick sense of humor.

His eyes moved over them. They were dirty and disheveled. Their clothes were torn, their hair was matted. Cuts and bruises lined the exposed parts of their skin.

He could see it though. The spirit in them. It echoed in their posture, in their expressions, in their eyes. It burned into him from fifty-five directions. A few were old. A few were young. Too young to be part of this. They were men and women, military and civilian.

They wanted to fight. Win or lose.

Mitchell checked his p-rat for the time. Three hours had passed since their evacuation. It was early morning. The sun would be rising soon. The fastest Alliance mech, the Dart, could move close to eighty kilometers per hour. If any had been dispatched from York when the fighting started, it would be reaching this part of the Preserve within the hour.

They had to hurry.

Tio was standing next to him, removed from the equation. That had been an argument of its own, but the Knife was too valuable to risk on the front line. Not only did the Tetron want him, their secondary objective was stored in his head. If they couldn't get the package delivered, he would need to attempt to interface with the enemy and deliver the virus.

Not that there was any reason to believe that would work, either. It was their desperation move, their last ditch effort to save Liberty, the one that meant they were all going to die.

"Who else here has served in the military, besides Private Shen and Sergeant Geren?" he asked.

Eight people stepped forward. Six men and two women.

"Grab an M1A and two magazines each. Firedog, Geren, you too."

The soldiers pulled the weapons from the pile.

"Can I have a grenade, sir?" Cormac asked.

"Take two. Geren, you take the other one."

Cormac smiled. "Yes, sir."

"Does anyone else here have any kind of weapons training?"

The college kid stepped forward. "I've played a lot of combat virtuals."

"What's your name, son?" Mitchell asked, channeling General

Cornelius. There was no denying the man's ability to inspire and lead.

"Jacob, sir."

"Jacob, grab a rifle and a pair of magazines. Anyone else here play a lot of virtuals?" Even if they hadn't played at combat, the games were designed to improve hand-eye coordination and reaction times. There was a rumor that the Alliance sank a lot of money into subsidizing development studios so they could help raise the potential soldiers of the future. He believed it was true.

Six more people came forward. One was older, in his seventies. The others were younger. The youngest couldn't have been more than fifteen. Mitchell gritted his teeth at the idea of sending her into the fight. He could argue all day about her not belonging there. He knew it wouldn't do him any good.

"Take a rifle each, two magazines. Geren, you're in charge of showing them-"

Mitchell paused. The entire group fell silent as the hum of a drone grew above the trees.

"Perseus?"

"Tracking, sir. Three drones. Passing over in five, four, three-"

They all looked up. The leaves were heavy above them, covering their view of the sky.

The drones passed over without slowing.

"Geren, you're in charge of showing them how to handle the rifles," Mitchell repeated.

"Yes, sir."

"I'll need four drivers for the cars," Mitchell said. "We need to keep them close to the mechs, and by close I mean almost touching. It's going to be tricky with the terrain, but it's the only way we're going to keep them from being spotted from the air."

Six people volunteered.

"Who has professional experience?"

Three of the six raised their hands. Mitchell looked at the other three. All men. He picked the oldest. "You're number four."

"Yes, sir," the man said.

"For the rest of you, I'm going to be honest, and blunt. We don't have enough weapons or ammunition to go around. That means not all of you are going to be armed. There's really no nice way to say this, but if you aren't armed, you're bait." He waited for a reaction from the remaining group, surprised when they stayed quiet. "Your job will be to draw the enemy's fire. To distract them so we can get a better shot. We'll figure out exactly how once we get closer to the Pass. The bottom line is that we can hold a lottery, I can pick people personally, or I can get a dozen volunteers."

The civilians were still for a moment. Then they began to look around, sizing each other up as they negotiated silently.

"I'll volunteer," a middle-aged woman said. "My husband is dead. My kids had implants. If they aren't dead, they're out there, somewhere. My eyes are shit, so I won't be any good with a weapon. If I have to die to destroy that bastard, then so be it."

"Sir," Perseus said. "They're coming back around."

The whine of the drones returned. They swept over the area while the rebels waited, the newly armed raising their rifles towards the sky, ready to return fire. The drones passed over, leaving them safe once more.

"Standard sweep pattern, sir," Perseus said. "They'll have trouble spotting us, at least until they get some eyes on the ground."

"We can't stay under cover forever," Tio said. "What then?"

"Then we fight," Mitchell said, glancing over at the Knife before returning his attention to the rebels. "Any more volunteers?"

47

THEY WERE on the move twenty minutes later. It was slow-going, with the mechs having to stay right on top of the passenger-laden cars to keep them beneath the umbrella protection of their equipment. They needed it too, as the drones continued to pass overhead, relentless in their automated pursuit. It would only take one slip, one bad step, one small break in the canopy to give away their position and invite an attack.

It left Mitchell wondering if the Tetron even thought they were out here, or if it was simply using the drones because they were available to be used. There was no harm in the sweeps, even if it didn't believe it would find anything. If they really were the last front of resistance within a thousand kilometers of York, there was nothing to lose in sending every available asset into the Preserve to find them.

The doubts ate at him. They edged into his thoughts with every careful step his Zombie made, and pushed harder each time one of the cars had to slow, the rough terrain and the weight of carrying so many threatening to slam it into the ground and leave a quarter of their force stranded. There was no way to cover three hundred kilometers on foot in the time they had before Goliath would return.

The mission had always been extremely high risk to damn near impossible. Finding a single person on an entire planet? Even if they had centered the search on the area around York, it was still a large area to cover.

Somehow, he had found Christine. Or at least he had found where she had been not long before he arrived.

He had found the place where she had been shot.

Was she still alive?

He was surprised to find himself questioning her value. On board the Goliath, everything had seemed so logical and organized. Their need to recover Origin's data above all else had seemed so clear. The Tetron had information, so much information, stored in her configuration. Its entire base of knowledge. Everything it knew about its kind, which Mitchell imagined was quite a lot. The intelligence had named its counterparts "children." It had escaped from them and moved through the recursion of time. It had created Christine in Katherine Asher's image to preserve all that it knew, for the very purpose of hiding that information until Mitchell could collect it.

How much was that information really worth? The Tetron weren't the only ones who could observe and learn. He had seen what the enemy was capable of. He had witnessed their approach to warfare. The psychological attacks as much as the physical. The calculated deception, the disregard for the lives of its slave army, or possibly even mortal life in general. Its ability to manufacture new machines. Did it matter as much why they had come over the fact that they were here?

He felt a draw to Christine. An undeniable attraction that was much more than physical. They had a history. An infinite history that he still didn't quite understand. He hoped she was alive. He hoped he would find her. He wanted to see her again. He wasn't going to sacrifice these people to do it.

"Know your enemy," Origin had said. It thought they needed her to understand the Tetron, and to win the war. That they couldn't win without her. He had accepted that before. Almost blindly. It was stupid to pin the hope of humankind on a single thing. Even if he died here on Liberty, trying to set it free, he expected that Millie would take the Goliath and figure something out. That she would continue where he left off, not capitulate to his failure and self-destruct.

He knew she would have the same fighting spirit that the people below his mech did. They were tired, they were in pain, they had every reason to quit.

They didn't.

Then there was Tio. As each minute passed, and Mitchell's mind continued to churn, he thought more and more about why he was on Liberty, and why he had returned to the planet in futures past. While Christine had been the original goal, he couldn't help but wonder if the Knife was the true prize. Whether his brother was the Creator or not, the man was still a self-proclaimed expert in artificial intelligence who had dedicated his life to lobbying against its use, going so far as to become rich and powerful in his own, illicit right. Tio had more than money. He had his own mercenary army.

An army they would desperately need.

If they managed to get off the planet.

48

TWO HOURS PASSED.

The sun pierced the horizon and started its climb, sending shafts of light down through the foliage in bright beams that put a spotlight on anything they touched.

Mitchell and his rebel army continued their journey, covering nearly two-thirds of the distance from Angeles to the Lincoln Pass in that time.

The drone sweeps had continued unabated, at times nothing more than a faint whistle in the distance and at other times a heavier whine that crossed directly overhead. The rebels grew accustomed to it, in time losing their fear of being discovered and picking up the overall pace of their march.

The expected ground patrols never materialized.

After what they had already experienced, Mitchell knew that it wasn't because of good fortune.

The Tetron was planning something. But what?

He was interrupted from his thoughts by a knock on his p-rat.

"What is it, Firedog?"

"Hey, Colonel. Tio asked me to knock you. He says you need to stop. Like, right now."

Stop? "Did he say why?"

"Says he has an idea. Says he feels kind of dumb he didn't think of it sooner." There was a pause. "Well, he didn't say that part. I did."

Mitchell opened the channel to the rest of his team.

"Perseus, Zed, stay alert. Firedog, call the stop."

"Yes, sir," they replied.

The entire caravan came to a shuddering halt. Mitchell eyed the empty sensor grid one last time before lowering his mech, disconnecting from the CAP-NN, and opening the cockpit. He climbed out, taking a deep breath of air. The smell of smoke and dirt was still heavy in it, following them from the ruins of Angeles.

Tio was waiting for him at the base of the mech with Cormac at his side.

"Colonel. I've been thinking about our plan to get to York. The Lincoln Pass. You know the Tetron will expect us to come that way."

"Yeah. I was planning for a pretty nasty fight there."

Tio smiled. "I have another idea. I'm sorry I didn't consider it sooner, but the logistics have changed quite drastically in the last sixteen hours."

"What do you mean?"

"For one, the enemy overheard all of our plans. It knows what we were going to do, and what our assets were at the time. Judging by the lack of ground patrols, my guess is that it has calculated the probability of our success in making it over the Pass and on to York to be statistically insignificant."

"We already knew it was a long shot. The real fighting happens out here. Not inside a machine."

"Yes, Colonel. I understand the risk is ours, we need to get to York, and that we have no better options. Except, what if we do have a better option?"

Mitchell was intrigued. They weren't headed for the Lincoln Pass because they wanted to die. "Go on."

"My second point, and perhaps the Private is right that it was shortsighted of me not to consider it earlier."

"I said dumb," Cormac said.

Tio ignored him. "During our meetings with General Cornelius, we were approaching the problem using a headcount in the hundreds, along with vehicle mounted heavy weapons, and, of course, the addition of your force. Small as it may be, three mechs are incredibly valuable in the field. More so than all of our ground troops combined."

"I'm with you on your assessment, but I don't see where you're going with it."

"We were thinking too linearly. Almost like our enemy would. This is the logical approach, based on the assets that we have. What we should be learning is that we can't fight this enemy by thinking that way. Artificial intelligence is superior to human intellect in terms of pure processing and problem-solving ability. We do have one advantage."

"Which is?"

Tio's smile grew. "We operate at the edge of chaos, Colonel. We are able to break the order of things. To act in a way that is completely illogical, and that offers no obvious benefit. Some would say to self-harm, but you could also look at it as a means to think in a different, unique way."

Mitchell nodded. Origin had given him command of the Goliath for that very reason. To think like a human. He had used the ship as a spear, an aggressive move that could have resulted in his war ending before it ever got started.

Could have, but didn't.

"What do you suggest?"

"You said the enemy is making use of a Sonosome factory to the south?"

"Yes. It's manufacturing machines there. Or at least it was."

"The type of equipment produced at that factory tends to be very heavy, does it not? So heavy that it requires special transport?"

Mitchell nodded again, starting to understand what the warlord was hinting at. The farming machines and mechs the factory produced would be delivered to the rest of the planet or the spaceport via heavy transports with large repulsor sleds. If they could claim one, they could use it to attempt to get up and over the mountains. It wasn't a viable plan for a large force. It was for a much smaller one.

"There's no guarantee the Tetron hasn't broken all of the heavy transports down for parts. It didn't use one to carry its forces to Angeles."

"Our spotters would have seen it coming," Tio said. "No, we don't know that any remain operational. Even so, I would propose that it will be much easier to reach the factory than it will be to get over the Lincoln Pass. Wouldn't you agree?"

"Shit. I do," Cormac said. "Colonel, we should go south. It's a lot closer, too. We can be there inside a day."

Mitchell stared at the two men, considering. If they went south and there was nothing they could salvage, they would lose an entire day, giving the Tetron more time to either catch up to them or reinforce its position. At the same time, he had always known getting over the Pass was going to be near to impossible. If he could avoid that battle and get more of their forces into York?

They were both a massive risk, but Tio was right. To outmaneuver the Tetron, they needed to react in ways it might not predict.

"Tell the others. We're going south."

49

THEY HEADED BACK SOUTH, taking a longer route to go wide around the area where the Riggers had defended against the first wave of machines from the factory. There was nothing for them there except twisted metal and the corpses of their fallen, left exposed to the dangerous skies by the damage done to the surrounding trees.

They moved as quickly as they could. It wasn't quickly enough for Mitchell's taste, but there was nothing they could do. The drones continued to sweep the Preserve, and their small army was more civilian than military. Even with the cars, they had to slow for breaks at regular intervals.

The only upside, if he could call it that, was that the Tetron still hadn't sent any ground units out to find them. There had been no sign of mechs, no sign of armored infantry, nothing. His grid was quiet.

"Colonel, we're here," Zed said.

"Call the stop. Firedog, get the cars bunched around the Knight."

"Yes, sir."

He saw Cormac hop out of the lead car, yelling in at the driver and then running back across the line. Perseus was in the middle of the caravan, and the cars all began to maneuver to stay close.

It was late afternoon. The sun had traced the sky and was on its way across to the other side of the planet. The density of the forest had waned somewhat, leaving breaks in the foliage that they were cautious to navigate, and that had stolen time from their journey. Mitchell moved his mech around the rebel vehicles until he was standing next to Zed.

Two hundred meters ahead of them was a break in the forest. Beyond it was the Nile river. It was nowhere near as impressive as its namesake, but it was dangerous in its own right.

If they were going to get to the Sonosome factory, they had to cross it, and crossing it meant being exposed across the half-kilometer width.

"You've been capturing the patrol data?" Mitchell asked.

"Yes, sir," Zed replied.

"How does it look?"

"This isn't my specialty."

"I know. I wish we could pass the data on to Tio, but without an implant..."

Zed passed the data to him. They had been marking the drone patrols whenever they had heard them pass over, trying to trace the pattern as closely as they could. Mitchell brought it up on his p-rat, superimposed over the mapping of the planet the CAP-NN was making while they walked it.

"It doesn't look like they're ever more than ten minutes out," he said.

"More like eight. It knew we had to go in one of two directions from Angeles, and we can only travel so fast."

"It knew too damn much. The question is, can we get the others across in eight minutes?"

"And keep them grouped together? I doubt it. The river's current is going to mess with the repulsors some, and the added weight is going to multiply the effect. Those vehicles weren't designed to carry so much."

"Some of them can swim across. The water will hide them."

"Colonel, these people are exhausted, and they aren't military. I don't think they're going to be making a half-kilometer swim in cold water."

"You're right. Let's call a break. Three hours to rest while we wait for nightfall. At least we can try to limit the contact."

"Yes, sir. I could stand to get a breath of fresh air and get off my ass for a few minutes."

"Firedog, tell the ground crew we're breaking. Three hours. Tell them to grab a bite and do their best to get some sleep. Perseus, you're on the ground. I'll take watch."

"I'll handle watch, Colonel," Perseus said.

"No. You've been in the saddle since last night."

"I'm juiced and good to go, sir. You were stabbed."

Mitchell had almost forgotten in his eagerness to get them to the factory. Now that he was reminded, he felt the twinge in his gut and the throbbing in his head. "Perseus, you've got watch."

"Yes, sir."

He moved the Zombie closer to the group and then lowered it, opening the cockpit. His legs shook beneath him as he climbed down. He'd barely slept since Goliath had dropped them off, and even with the biochem it was taking its toll.

The rebels shifted around him, unloading themselves from the car, grabbing rations and passing them along. When they looked at him, their eyes were fierce and proud, and they bowed slightly to show their respect. He remembered the way General Cornelius had engaged them in the mess back in Angeles, and he did his best to copy it.

"ReadyMeal, sir?"

The girl, the youngest of their army, was holding a box out to him. He smiled when he took it. "Thank you-"

"Kathy," she said, filling in her name.

Mitchell held the ReadyMeal and stared down at her. She was filthy like the others, but there was a pretty face and big brown eyes beneath the dirt and grime. Kathy? Her name made him shiver on the inside. Katherine. He couldn't help but react to the thought of her. Their lives were entwined in a way he couldn't understand.

"Are you okay, sir?" she asked, beginning to grow uncomfortable with his stare.

He pulled himself from the vague memory. "Yeah. You remind me of someone I used to know. Someone I cared about. You're brave to be here."

"They didn't want me to come. They said I was too young, but what the frig is too young when you live on Liberty? First the Federation, and now this? Let the other girls hide. My father's a Navy captain. He always told me the strong need to take care of the weak. He didn't raise a weak daughter." She smiled in defiance, but it turned to sadness in a hurry. "He's out there, somewhere. He was assigned to Alpha quadrant. I don't know if they reached him yet. If he's a slave. I know if he isn't he's fighting."

He didn't tell her that there was no fighting the Tetron, not if you had an implant. "I know he is, too."

The defiance returned. "We're going to get that thing off of Liberty, aren't we, sir?"

"We are."

"I know what they said about you is a lie. About not taking the Shot."

He felt the pain from his wound more acutely at the statement. He wanted to tell her it wasn't. He wanted to explain. He couldn't. She was looking for hope, for leadership, for someone larger than life to believe in. That had been Ella. He was a poor substitute, but he would have to do.

"Thanks for believing in me," he said.

The words tasted as dirty as he felt.

50

MITCHELL ATE THE READYMEAL, and then spent the next hour walking the makeshift camp, checking in on every one of the people in their group. He spent a few minutes talking to the ones who were receptive, and gave a few brief words of encouragement to those who weren't. After that, he went up into the cockpit of the Zombie to retrieve a combat knife. Then he climbed on top of the foot of his mech.

He stared down at Ilanka's name.

The paint hadn't dried completely before the drop and had left it spread out as though it were bleeding. He knelt and put his hand to it before taking the knife and scraping it along the mech's armored surface. It left a light mark that would only be visible up close, but it would do.

He started writing.

Ten minutes later, he stood up and looked down on the three new names he had scratched into the foot. Cornelius, Shank, and Holly. He felt he owed it to her after what the Tetron had done to her mind. He put the knife down and settled himself against the ankle of the machine, finally closing his eyes.

"Care for some company, Mitch?"

Mitchell's eyes opened again. He glanced over. Zed was standing there.

"There's plenty of room," he said.

She smiled and pulled herself up. "It's the safest place to hide from Cormac."

"Is he giving you a hard time? I can-"

She put up her hand. "He is what he is." She slid down next to him. "I never cared that much for ground-pounders."

Mitchell laughed at that. It felt good to find something to laugh about.

"What's funny?"

"I hear that a lot."

"I've heard people say that it has to do with the same implant compatibility that separates the pilots from the grunts. That our minds are just different. Faster, or something. How's your side?"

"It is what it is," he said. "No sense in crying about it."

"You don't have to be a tough guy with me, Mitch. How does it really feel?"

"It stings."

"Big baby." She laughed. It was nice to hear someone else laugh, too.

"Were you planning that?"

"Maybe. I thought you could use a little levity."

"Thanks."

She was silent for a minute, just sitting next to him, staring down at the names on the foot. "I'm sorry about Shank. I know you were friends."

"We weren't, really. I didn't know him that well. He was a badass soldier, and we respected each other. I'm not happy when I lose anyone on my team."

"Who's Holly?"

"It's a long story, and it's going to kill the mood."

"Sorry."

"You're welcome to stay if you want, Jennifer. I'm going to shut it down for a while."

"Yeah, me too."

Mitchell closed his eyes again. He was aware of Zed next to him, her shoulder pressing lightly against his. It was a small thing, but it comforted him to know he wasn't alone.

"We can't do this alone," he remembered Katherine saying to him on board the Goliath.

No. He couldn't. He was a Space Marine, a former member of the most elite company the Alliance had. It didn't make him invincible, though at this point he wished he was.

"Mitch," Zed said a minute later.

"Yeah?"

"I think someone should tell you. You're doing a good job."

He was surprised by the statement and more surprised by how much it meant to him.

"You really think so?"

"I'd follow you anywhere."

He fell asleep with the words still echoing in his thoughts.

[51]

SOMETHING WAS BURNING.

It had woken Mitchell up, leaving him sitting dead still, eyes closed and focusing on the smell. It was harder to tell with the odor that had lingered on his flight suit, and in the air, after Angeles had been razed. There was a definite smokiness to it. A defined wooden heat.

He opened his eyes. Zed's head was resting on his chest. She was sleeping.

He checked his p-rat. He'd been asleep for almost two hours. He would have been woken soon.

"Jennifer," he said, reaching around her shoulders and giving her a light shake.

Her eyes opened, and she shoved herself upright in a sudden panic. "Sorry, sir."

"Don't worry about it. Do you smell that?"

She took a deep breath in through her nose. "It reminds me of home. Centauri. My father used to take me out into woods like these, and light campfires and tell me stories. No tech. He said everybody needed to get away from the tech once in a while. To take time to appreciate just being human, and just being alive."

Mitchell pushed himself to his feet. "Come on." He jumped off the mech.

"What's wrong?" she asked.

The camp was quiet. Most of the rebels were asleep, splayed out in a dense circle around the cars and the Knight. There was an obvious, hazy thickness to the air.

"Zed, get to your mech. Firedog, help me get everybody up," Mitchell said, sending an emergency knock to the Rigger.

"Eh? Ugh. Yes, sir," Cormac said, still groggy. Mitchell saw him moving a second later, bouncing to his feet and shaking the person next to him.

"Perseus, nothing on sensors?" he asked.

"No, sir. Why?"

He breathed in again. He licked his lips. He came away with an earthy taste in his mouth.

"Fire," he said, feeling a sudden rise of panic. He looked up at the sky through the canopy. There were no stars. "The woods are on fire."

"Are you sure?"

He was as sure as he could be. He bent down and shook Kathy's shoulder. "Kathy, get up."

"Huh? What?" Her eyes opened, and she looked up at him. "Captain?"

"Help me wake everyone."

"Yes, sir." She jumped up, grabbing her rifle and running to the next person in line.

It only took a couple of minutes to wake them all. The smell of burning wood was getting heavier. The air was getting thicker.

"Colonel?" Tio said.

Mitchell heard a whining in the air, ahead of a gentle roar. Then he heard a whistle. He saw the streak of light through the treetops, followed by a heavy *woomph* of air. The trees in the distance were caught in an unmistakeable, liquid red-orange line of instant flame.

He had known the Tetron was planning something when the ground forces never materialized.

Now he knew what.

"It's burning the Preserve," Tio said.

"Why scour miles of woods when you can burn it down and smoke out your quarry? We need to go. Now!"

He ran for his mech as the whining of an engine passed overhead. Another whistle and a second incendiary missile struck the woods two kilometers away.

"Firedog, get everyone to the cars. We need to cross the Nile. No delay."

"Yes, sir."

Mitchell scaled the Zombie's leg and climbed into the cockpit, jumping into the seat, pulling on his helmet, and pushing his head back into the CAP-NN link. The mech came to life with a thought, and he started walking towards the line of trees, into the fire.

"How are we going to keep them grouped?" Perseus asked.

"Stay close to them. Zed, lead them across the river."

"What are you doing?"

"If they light up the trees on the other side, we'll have nowhere to go. I'll draw them away."

"Sir, I'll do it," Perseus said. "I have more firepower."

"There's no time to reorganize the cars. You need to follow them across."

Mitchell pushed into the trees and beyond. He could hear the whine of the drones further off. He pulled the railgun from the back of the Zombie and checked his p-rat. Three thousand rounds left in the gun. He'd have to make them count.

"We're on the move, Colonel," Perseus said at his back. He had the position of the Riggers on his overlay, their p-rats pinging the location. He could see they were starting towards the river.

Mitchell kept going. The smoke was getting thicker, the air hotter and heavier. The CAP-NN picked up the change and sealed the cockpit, falling back to stored air. A pair of drones appeared on his overlay, and he fired his jump thrusters, bringing him up through burning trees, their flaming branches slapping his metal form.

The drones would have been hard to see through the smoke with his naked eye. His overlay outlined them in red, and he shifted his aim and fired. Two rounds dug into the front of one, striking the control unit and sending it tumbling from the sky. The other diverted towards him, accelerating to ram his ascending mech.

It was coming fast. He decided not to waste time and ammo trying to shoot it, instead cutting his thrusters and letting the heavy mech start falling away. The drone adjusted its angle to compensate more quickly than he expected.

"Shit," Mitchell cursed. He fired a salvo of amoebic missiles and watched the drone disintegrate under the blast. "What a frigging waste."

The mech came back down amidst the smoke and flames. He couldn't see anything in the middle of it, and his p-rat started warning him of the rising surface temperature of his mech. He put the machine in reverse, pulling back towards the rebels and the river.

His diversion was a success. Half a dozen airborne targets appeared on his overlay, converging on him.

"Zed, status," he said. He cradled the railgun in both hands, moving into a line of flames and crouching, hiding the mech in the heat and smoke.

"We're starting across, Colonel. Running cold."

A whistle pierced the night. A missile rocketed towards him. Mitchell forced himself to stay steady while it slammed into the ground a dozen meters ahead and exploded. Liquid fire splashed out from it, coating the already burning wood, sloshing over his mech and lining it with flame. His p-rat began to beep, warning him that it couldn't keep the cockpit cool forever and that enough heat would ignite his ammunition.

A drone became visible in the smokey sky. Mitchell came out of his crouch, aiming and firing. It vanished into the trees. He spun the mech's torso, still walking forward, tracking a second drone and firing a dozen rounds. The right repulsor died, and it spun and crashed.

His p-rat cried out a warning as a laser blast hit the heavy rear cockpit armor. Mitchell swung the torso back around, rotating the arm independently, aiming the railgun with one hand. He fired, pouring slugs into the drone as it passed him by.

"Shit. Shit. Shit. We lost one," Perseus shouted. "Zed."

"I'm trying," she said. "Colonel, one of the cars lost power. It's in the river."

"Firedog?"

"Not me, sir."

Mitchell checked the grid. Two of the drones had turned away from him, heading for the river.

"They spotted it. You've got incoming. Heading your way." Mitchell snapped the mech straight and broke into a run. The liquid flame was still burning along the length of the mech, slowly eating into the poly-alloy.

He saw the sky light up ahead of him as Perseus opened fire, and the CAP-NN gave him visual on the otherwise invisible lasers. One drone circled the fire, the other got caught in it, the engine exploding out the back and sending debris raining down. The free drone slowed and then dropped like a stone.

He hadn't seen anything hit it.

"Holy mother," Firedog said. "It fell on the car."

Mitchell felt his chest tighten. He hoped the rebels had abandoned it before that.

He continued his charge, more drones heading towards the river, dropping their sweeps of the Preserve to cover their position. "We need to take them out. If they hit the woods on the south bank we're screwed."

"Roger," Zed said. Mitchell couldn't see her yet, but he saw the streaks of her missiles as they rocketed towards the drones. Two of them vanished from the screen.

Lasers followed from Perseus' mech, cutting across the sky and burning into the drones. Two more fell.

A missile launched from yet another, heading for the south bank.

"Perseus," Mitchell said.

"Tracking." Perseus' left hand angled, the missile approaching the line of trees. He fired, catching the rear of it and blowing out the rocket motor. It spun out of control and fell into the river.

"I'm across," Firedog said.

"Get to the trees. Zed, get them covered."

"Yes, sir."

Mitchell's p-rat barked at him again, showing him a laser strike on his arm. The cockpit was getting warm, and he could feel a cold sweat running across his body, quickly absorbed by the flight suit. The drone passed over him and then fell from the sky, hit by fire from Zed's railgun.

"Car two is across," Firedog said. "Four is right behind. We're almost clear, Colonel."

"Is anyone in the water?"

"We've got a few swimmers."

Mitchell finally reached the edge of the trees. The smoke was thick, but he could see the Knight standing in the river, the water around it steaming while it siphoned off the heat of the lasers. The water would do the same for his own heat problem, and he ran towards it.

Gunfire echoed in the middle of the fire, the sky a mix of smoke and tracers. Mitchell's Zombie approached the Nile like a burning effigy, flames spiking from the surface liquid. He tracked a drone on his overlay, firing jump thrusters while maintaining forward momentum, getting up higher and taking the shot, a direct hit on the rear thruster. The drone complained and tumbled from the air.

"Four is across," Firedog said.

The Zombie came down in the water, hissing and steaming, the fire reluctant to go out. Mitchell dropped the mech to a crouch, lowering the body into the water, feeling the cockpit temperature drop while he vented heat. Perseus stood a dozen meters ahead of him, keeping up regular fire, dropping another pair of drones as they arrived.

Mitchell pulled in a deep breath of air. He hadn't realized how hard it had become to breathe. "They've got our location. We need to keep moving. No stopping, no slowing until we reach Sonosome."

"Yes, sir," Cormac said.

"Perseus, nice shooting. Let's go."

"Yes, sir. Thank you, sir."

Mitchell brought his mech upright, checking the p-rat. Temperature levels had dropped back to normal, but he could see the blistered alloy of his arms and he knew nearly the entirety of the mech probably looked the same. He switched his attention to the grid. They had cleared the drones in the immediate area, but he was sure more would be coming. They had lost the element of surprise.

Now it was a race.

52

"Colonel, we have to stop," Zed said again.

"We aren't stopping," Mitchell replied.

"We left some of the civilians back there."

He was aware of that. They all were. "We don't stop. We don't slow. They're a lot safer where they are than where we're going."

"Sir-"

"That's an order, not a request."

They were moving through the forest as quickly as they could. It wasn't fast enough. They had cleared the drones from the immediate area, but he knew there would be more coming and now they knew where the rebels had run to. Had it guessed where they were going?

He hoped not.

For now, an eastern wind was helping keep the fire contained to the north side of the river, and the Tetron had yet to get any incendiary missiles onto the south bank. The people they had been forced to abandon, the ones who had gotten out of the stricken car and managed to swim to shore, would find it easier to hide near or in the water. They could travel downstream until they reached the generators near the foothills of the mountains, and hopefully find some food and shelter in the abandoned plant.

He wasn't wrong when he said they were safer. It didn't mean leaving anyone behind sat well. Sonosome was another thirty kilometers south. It would take an hour if they waited for the cars.

They couldn't wait. Not all of them.

"Zed, stay behind with the cars, keep them covered. Perseus, we're going ahead. Stay at my flank, two hundred meters."

"We have no idea what we're running into," Perseus said.

"If we don't make it ahead of the enemy, it doesn't matter."

He kept one eye on his grid, the other on his path through the trees. The mech's legs pumped beneath him, his brain navigating the motion as though he were running it himself, bouncing over rocks and brush, pushing past or ducking around tree limbs. It was a reckless pace, one made more dangerous by the damage the mech had sustained.

It was a pace that Perseus couldn't match.

"Ares, you're too hot," he said. "I can't keep up."

Time. There was no time. Every second that passed gave the Tetron another chance to connect the dots, to figure out where they were going and why. Mitchell had run this race before, more than once. It didn't matter if it was in a mech, in a starfighter, or on foot. There was no choice, no option.

They had to win.

"You have to, Corporal." Mitchell checked Perseus' position. He was off to his left and a hundred yards back.

"Yes, sir."

The Knight shifted forward, outpacing him for a few seconds, starting to close the gap.

Then it came to an abrupt stop.

"Shit," Perseus cried.

Mitchell heard the echo of the crash. He fired his jump thrusters, angling them back and using them to slow his forward momentum. Damn it. He turned and headed in Perseus' direction.

"Sitrep," he said.

"Tripped on a rock or something," Perseus said. "I'm okay. Getting - oh." Perseus' voice faded away. Mitchell maneuvered around the tree, finding the Knight on its knees.

Behind it was a mech, crumpled and dark. A Dart.

The legs were torn apart, the body punctured and ravaged. The carbonate cockpit was cracked, a line of blood smearing the corner. Mitchell could see the pilot through the damaged mess. Raven.

He had survived the drop. He hadn't made it back to them.

"Son of a bitch," Perseus said.

Mitchell swallowed the rising tide of anger. He had already assumed the pilot was lost. Knowing he had survived the landing and then been overwhelmed made it worse.

He let go of his breath, growling softly. He was being stupid and reckless. If they were going to get to Sonosome, they needed to get there together. He couldn't make Perseus faster by wishing it. The CAP-NN did a lot of work, but it relied on the input from the pilot to guide it. Like Zed had said, some brains were just faster than others.

Slow.

Steady.

Ella would have had his head for acting so emotionally.

"Damage?" he asked.

"No, sir."

"Come on." Mitchell leaned down, putting the mech's hand to the side of the Dart while he bowed his head. Then he straightened and continued south, vectoring back to the west to put some space between him and the Knight. "I didn't upload any schematics or data on the factory before we dropped. I remember flying over it a few times. The transports are on the east side. If there's any resistance when we get there, I'll draw it west while you get to one of them. Do whatever you have to, but get inside and get it ready."

"Yes, sir. What if I'm taking fire?"

"Assess the danger to the transport. That's the priority. I'll try to draw it away."

"By yourself?"

"I can take care of myself. Your job is to get the transport."

"Yes, sir." He paused. "What if the transports are disabled, or if they aren't there?"

"Then we do our best to take out the defenses and rendezvous with the rest of the forces. We can't go back north through the woods, so we'll have to follow the river. We may need to cross over on foot."

He said it. He knew it wasn't an option. The Goliath would return long before they could cover the distance. If the transports were gone or disabled, they were finished. Plan B had been blown away in the ashes of the burning forest.

They continued ahead, Mitchell slowing to match Perseus' top speed. There was no grace to their movements, no subtlety to their charge. They barreled through trees and over outcroppings of the planet's original barren and rocky terrain, using jump thrusters to speed them across rises and falls in the landscape. Mitchell kept his countermeasures disabled, hoping to attract the attention of any enemy forces in the area and to keep them away from the rebels and the Knight. He was the target, the diversion. He was a dangerous mouse.

The attack came sooner than he expected, the drones appearing on his grid only moments before they launched incendiary missiles at his position. He tracked them on their way in, bringing the railgun up and taking careful aim before firing. The CAP-NN helped guide his shots, making the slight adjustments needed for wind and recoil, allowing him to hit the projectiles with a single slug each. The launcher drones were following close behind, and they fired a second salvo, emptying their bays and descending behind the bombs.

"Perseus, this is Ares. I'm under fire. Continue on course, I'll catch up."

Mitchell slowed his mech, keeping it steady as the assault approached. Slow. Steady. He aimed unhurriedly, firing a third round, and then a fourth. One of the missiles dropped out of the sky.

The other exploded.

It was an accident with mixed results. The force of the blast sent liquid fire everywhere. It splashed onto the drones, burning white-hot and making a mess of their machine guidance systems, throwing them off-course and sending them colliding into nearby trees. It came down as drops of hell around him, landing on the line and setting it to smolder.

"Zed, can you read me?" Mitchell asked. "Zed, this is Ares, over."

He watched his overlay while he moved into position to rejoin Perseus. The rebels were off his grid, and out of comm range. He was going to tell her to go around. They'd have to figure it out for themselves.

"Ares, I'm tracking a new target, sir." Perseus' voice was calm. "No. Two. No. Six new targets." Still calm. "Airborne. They aren't registering as drones."

"Break west, we'll cross over," Mitchell said.

"No time, sir. Bogeys are fast. Really fast. Engaging."

Echoing explosions and the fake light of laser fire filled his mechanized senses. The targets appeared on his grid seconds later, crossing by with unbelievable speed, salvos of rockets dropping from their bellies and angling down. The first group pummeled into Perseus, the Knight's anti-missile lasers unable to keep up with the sudden barrage. The pilot managed to get his mech sidelong in their crosshairs, and the right arm exploded outward in bits of metal and slag as it captured the brunt of the strike.

Mitchell returned fire, watching the amoebic missiles skitter from his chest and up into the sky towards the onrushing enemies, intelligently avoiding the canopy on their way to the target. A squadron of Alliance Pirahnas streaked low over the trees, flying right into the barrage. The missiles detonated, tearing through three of the ships and bringing them down. The other two continued their run, opening fire with slugs that tore through the cover ahead of the Zombie.

Mitchell cursed and dropped the Mech low, putting his arms over the mech's head and letting the bullets dig into the armor there. Then the fighters were past, shooting away and preparing to circle for another run.

"Damage report," Mitchell said, checking his p-rat. It was still limited to surface wounds, but each round of fire would add more stress to the integrity of the structure. Sooner or later, the bullets would start getting through the armor and cutting into more delicate synthetic muscles and inner mechanics.

"Right arm is gone. Right leg has some minor actuator damage. If it gets hit again we'll never reach Sonosome."

"Keep moving. Don't slow. I'll keep you covered."

The fighters were heading back. Mitchell checked his ordnance. Four rounds of amoebics remained. A little less than three thousand rounds in the railgun. They hadn't even gotten to the factory yet.

He ran forward, getting deeper into the trees. The Pirahnas dropped again, firing a second round of missiles that darted towards his back. CAP-NN controlled anti-missile lasers swiveled and fired at them, hitting most but not all. A warhead collided into the heavy back armor and exploded, pushing his mech forward. His p-rat blinked orange, revealing the severity of the damage as he brought the Zombie up to its knees and fired a single thruster, the force pushing the mech in a tight turn. He raised the railgun and let loose, sending a thousand rounds into the sky like a swarm of angry wasps, bringing down branches and leaves in a rain of green fury around him.

Mitchell wasn't done. He continued firing, sending another massive volley of fire skyward at the sweeping Pirahnas. One of them lost integrity, the projectiles clearing the shields and climbing up and through the cockpit. Smoke poured from it and it vanished into the woods. The other one passed over, possibly damaged, still flying. Mitchell pulled to his feet and started forward again.

Two more drones appeared on his grid, coming hard from the north while the fighters circled west to east. The resistance was growing. The remaining Pirahna was circling back.

Too many. There were too damn many. Mechs could take a beating, but they weren't meant to stand alone against fighters.

Mitchell tracked the targets, feeling his stomach drop when the dots seemed to split apart and double in an instant. Eight bogeys incoming. They were angling to pass Perseus by, reorganizing to hit him with everything they had. He glanced at his ordnance report again. Eleven hundred forty rounds in the railgun, three salvos of amoebics, and about two thousand rounds in the chest cannon that was designed for ground fighting. He still had the lasers, but it would take multiple hits to drop a fast-moving enemy.

The targets moved in, only partially visible through the trees. The four additions were another group of Piranhas, called in from where? Not York. After the Battle for Liberty, there hadn't been enough to stock more than a single squadron there. The starships in orbit above the planet? If they had Piranhas, the Tetron surely would have used them sooner.

He found a large rise of sharp rock, hitting the thrusters and throwing the mech backward towards it. He crouched behind it, raising the railgun and tracking the two drones at the head of the assault. Incendiary missiles launched from beneath them, all four at once, rocketing his way on long contrails of smoke. Mitchell fought the urge to fire on them, letting them come. He was going to be bathed in the fire again, and he wasn't sure the mech would survive a second hit. His only chance was that his cover would deflect the hot gel and cast it over him. There was no choice. He needed to conserve his ammunition for the Piranhas.

The missiles struck the rock, blowing chunks of it back into the mech's cameras, leaving him blinded by sediment and dust and flame. He turned off the visual, using secondary sensors and firing on the drones before they could crash themselves into him. His railgun chattered in the darkness. He fired his jump thrusters at the same time, pushing up and back, smashing against branches and bringing the woods down around him. Fire ate at the mech's shoulders, and the drones exploded below.

He was ready to loose the remaining salvos of amoebics when one of the red dots turned blue. It fell away from the others and opened fire, guns and missiles tearing into the backs of the Piranhas. Mitchell switched his visual back on, surprised disbelief turning his sunken hopes into sudden elation.

"Ares, this is Valkyrie. Targets destroyed."

Major Long's identification registered in his implant as the remaining Piranha tipped its wing.

53

"WELCOME BACK, Valkyrie. I can't tell you how glad I am to see you survived."

"Not as glad as I am, Colonel. I'll regale you with my exaggerated tale of heroics once we're back aboard Goliath. In the meantime, I believe we've achieved temporary air superiority."

The drones were like minnows to a Piranha.

Mitchell brought his mech back to level ground. His p-rat was still screaming warnings, the shoulders of the Zombie doused in flames that were raising the temperature and eating through to the actuators. He was too far from the river to try to cool himself off again. Major Long's miraculous appearance had taken him out of the frying pan. Now he literally was in the fire.

"I don't want to nitpick, but you could have taken them out before they doused me."

"My apologies, Ares. You only get one chance at a surprise attack."

"Roger." He knew how true that was. At least he was still alive.

He cycled through the CAP-NN's assessment of the damage, cursing under his breath when it told him what he already knew.

The mech was done for.

It could probably survive the heat of the fire. He couldn't. If he didn't evacuate the cockpit, he would end up trapped inside, cooking to death. Not a fitting end after all they had gone through to get this far.

He dropped the mech to its knees and pulled his head from the link. He didn't open the cockpit. Not yet. He hadn't kept a rifle, not when the ground forces needed them so badly. He still had the pistol on his leg.

"Perseus, this is Ares. The Zombie is scrap. Hold your position while we regroup. Valkyrie, do you have visual on the Sonosome factory to the south?"

"Yes, sir. Looks active. Lots of motion on the ground."

"Any transports laying around?"

"I see two from here."

"Perfect. We've got Zed and a bunch of rebels trailing behind us. The transports are the objective."

"Hitching a ride to York?" Long asked.

"That's the goal. It will be a lot easier with an escort."

"Yes, sir. I'll head in for a closer look."

The Piranha circled past and then rose higher in the air, breaking out of comm range. Mitchell moved to the back of the cockpit. He put his hand near it, feeling the heat radiating from it. He hit the release and crouched low. The heat grew more intense as the back of the mech began to open, and he rolled out from under it as soon as it was high enough. He fell to the ground, tucking and rolling before getting up and surveying the mech. The entire top end was on fire, the orange-blue spikes like a crown of flame around the ghoulish painted head of the Zombie. He walked over to the foot where he had written the names of the fallen. He had never added Long's name to the list. Had he somehow known the man was still alive?

He closed his eyes for just a moment, trying to capture the subconscious connection to the past. Had he fought this battle before? Had he won or lost? Every memory, every emotion, every instinct was so nebulous. So hard to capture and define.

He would just have to find out for himself.

"Riiigg-ahh," he said, kissing his hand and slapping the foot. "Zed, this is Ares. Come in." He waited for a reply. The rebels weren't close enough yet. "Perseus, sitrep."

"Holding position, sir. Everything is quiet."

Mitchell started walking in the direction of the Knight. He heard the whine of the Piranha closing in seconds before Long's voice entered his p-rat.

"Ares, it looks like the factory is operational. Sensors picked up increased power output. There are a lot of civilians there, sir. It appears the enemy brought a large number of them to assist with the plant."

"It did. It's using resources here to build a bigger army. I'm sure Sonosome isn't the only plant on Liberty that it's got running."

"I came by way of Delhi, sir. I passed over the Kefiri factory while I was hiding out. I saw some fighters on the ground there, but they weren't anything I've ever seen before, and they looked incomplete, or wrong. As though it thinks it knows how to make a starfighter, but doesn't quite."

Mitchell raised an eyebrow at that. The Tetron had all of their history, thousands of years, and it couldn't make a starfighter? It was possible it didn't have access to the right resources, but after what had happened with Holly, it left him to wonder. The Tetron were supposed to be advanced artificial intelligence, and yet their minor failures seemed to be mounting. Was there something wrong with this one?

Was there something wrong with all of them?

"What about the transports?" Mitchell asked.

"They appear to be operational. No visible damage at least."

"You said you were hiding in the Piranha?"

"Yes, sir," Long said with a laugh. "It's a long story, but after I ejected from the dropship, I managed to get to a spaceport. The place was razed and abandoned, except for a few fighters and a bunch of drones. I was planning to use it to get off the planet once Goliath came back. With my implant off, it never knew I was there. Then the fighters all took off, no pilots. I saw the forest burning, and I saw a crashed starship on top of a city." He laughed. "I figured you had something to do with it, and that if I restarted the p-rat and plugged into the captain, I'd get control." He laughed again. "I figured right."

"And Borov?"

Long's voice turned cold. "Killed by shrapnel before we evac'ed. Half the frigging pods didn't release either. I did everything I could."

Mitchell would never know if that were true or not. He had to assume it was. "I'm sure you did. You saved our asses just now."

"Major, is that you?" Zed's voice came in over the comm channel.

"Zed. Yes, ma'am. It's good to hear your voice."

"Yours too, Major."

"Zed," Mitchell said. "We've got a clean approach to Sonosome, but my Zombie is out of the fight. Regroup at my position."

"Yes, sir."

"Valkyrie, head back to the factory and keep an eye on things. Watch out for incoming drones. If anything makes a move on those transports, take them out."

"Roger." The Piranha made a tight pirouette in the sky and headed back towards the factory.

Mitchell kept walking, his pounding heart beginning to slow into a more normal rhythm. For the first time since they had arrived, he felt like they might have a chance to set Liberty free.

54

"Ares, this is Valkyrie. We have a situation."

"What is it?" Mitchell asked.

Agri-factories were massive, in some ways like cities unto themselves. They employed thousands, and those thousands helped support thousands more who provided standard services to the workers and the off-planet visitors who did business there. Sonosome was no exception, with blocks of apartments lining the outer perimeter and storefronts dotting a main thoroughfare through it all.

The rebel caravan was moving quickly through that thoroughfare, with Perseus' Knight at the front and Zed's Zombie in the rear. There was no motion from the surrounding landscape, and no indication that there had ever been any kind of alien incursion outside of the marks in the pavement caused by the outgoing machine army. The area was empty. Deserted. Forgotten.

Mitchell knew it was because everyone with an implant had been gathered at the factory proper, and everyone else was most likely dead.

"I'm getting action from the civilians at the factory. They're making a move on the transports."

Civilians? "What kind of move?"

"Not sure, Colonel. Hard to get a headcount, but I'd say there's about two thousand or so. They came out of the factory, and they're walking over to where the transports are parked. They look pretty calm, and here's the weird part: they're completely naked."

He could understand calm, since they weren't in control of themselves. Why were they naked? "Valkyrie, we're still about five minutes out on the factory. You can't let those people get near those ships."

"Roger. What do you suggest?"

Mitchell paused, glancing over at Tio, who was riding on the trunk of the car with him. The warlord's expression was stony and thoughtful. He turned again to look at the back of Kathy's head. The girl was riding inside the car, her rifle pointing out the empty window.

"Do whatever you have to do," he said, gritting his teeth. He knew what was coming next.

"You want me to kill them, sir?"

"They're the enemy, Major. Until we defeat the Tetron. No matter what they look like."

"But, Colonel-"

"Valkyrie, you either stop them from touching the transport or we get stranded here and everyone dies. Which do you prefer?"

"That's easy for you to say. You aren't the one flying over them."

Mitchell tried to stay level, but his voice raised to an exhausted shout. "You think it's easy, Major? To kill civilians? I'm sorry, but we don't have a choice. I'm giving you an order. At least it's on my conscience, not yours."

The shouting drew the attention of the others in the car. Tio was still expressionless, but his eyes were heavy and sad when he looked over at him. Kathy reached back through the rear to put her hand on his and nod her approval though there were tears in her eyes.

"These people are fighting for their loved ones, Valkyrie," Mitchell said. "We make the hard calls because they've earned the right. I don't give a shit if you do it for me, but you damned well better do it for them."

The silent tension mounted while he waited for Major Long to respond. They were nearing the edge of the factory grounds, and Mitchell could see the rise of the heat sinks at the top of the main assembly building. He caught sight of the Piranha circling in the distance, coming back around towards the factory. It started dropping, swooping in low. Flame spit from the mounted guns, the noise of it echoing in the distance.

"I hit the ground ahead of them. They aren't slowing. There are more coming out of the factory."

"Firedog, Perseus, let's pick up the pace," Mitchell said.

"Yes, sir."

The lead car gained speed to match the Knight, rushing towards the building. The transports became visible on their left as they drew closer; large, flat blocks of poly-alloy with big repulsor sleds slung underneath. Ugly and functional. The mass of people came into view as they continued towards it. They were arranged in neat rows, walking in unison towards the transports. Not a single one of them was wearing a shred of clothing.

"They've stopped moving at the front, Ares," Long said, the Piranha shooting by once more.

Naked. Seeing them, he understood.

"Son of a bitch," he said quietly.

The Tetron knew why they were here. It knew what they wanted and that it didn't have any other effective means of stopping them, except for this. Psychological warfare. The only way through was to kill their own. To attack and murder naked, defenseless people.

They turned around. All of them in unison, spinning on their heels and facing the rebels. Men and women of all ages. There were no children or elderly. The children and elderly were already dead.

Their eyes were wide and filled with fear, as though they knew where they were. As if they knew that they were standing naked on a wide swath of pavement as a human barrier between the rebels and the transport. The Tetron was allowing some portion of their minds to be present even if their bodies weren't their own.

"Colonel," Tio said, watching the display. His voice broke on the word.

"All stop," Mitchell shouted. The cars came to a pause twenty meters from the front lines, right behind the mech. The assembled mob didn't react.

"Check out the one on the right," Cormac said. "Third from the center. The blonde."

"Firedog," Mitchell said, his voice low.

"Sorry, sir."

Mitchell hopped off the back of his car, walking towards the front. He wasn't sure what he was going to do. They needed to get to the transports, and these people were in the way.

Kathy fell into line beside him, following him. Tio was right behind.

"Kathy, you shouldn't be here," Mitchell said.

"None of us should be here, Colonel," she replied. Her eyes were narrow, angry, and filled with tears. The sight of the rows of Liberty's citizens, naked and frightened, was enough to break anyone.

That was the point.

"Colonel," Tio said, catching up to them. "We can't kill innocent people."

"You, Tio? Of all of the rebels here, you're telling me this?" He was getting angrier the closer he got to them. So many had died already. Millions. To an enemy that had no concept or care for the value of a human life.

Mitchell made his way past the Knight to stand right in front of the line of civilians. Getting closer, his eyes passed the blonde that Cormac was making eyes at. He spared her a second glance, and then stared at her face.

Tamara King.

He could have laughed at the absurdity of it all.

"There has to be another way," Tio said. "I understand these people are under its control, but these are the people we want to free."

"So how do we get around?" Mitchell asked.

"Sir, I can land on this side and take the transport," Major Long said.

"And lose the Piranha? What happens if it sends drones after us?"

"Didn't you consider that before?"

He had. His original intention had been to station the mechs on top of the vehicle. A crazy, risky maneuver, but what about this whole thing wasn't crazy? "Yes. I had three mechs to defend it then. Now I have a fighter to run interference."

"Sir, with all due-"

"Major, I know what you're going to say." Mitchell paused, and then raised his voice so they could all hear. He made eye contact with Tamara King, betting the Tetron could hear him, too. "Don't you know that this is what it wants? If we don't get through, we don't make it to York. If we do go through, we do it emotionally battered and weak. Don't you see? It's afraid. Of us. Fifty people, when it conquered an entire planet. It couldn't kill you when it came here. It couldn't kill you in Angeles, and it couldn't burn you out of the forest. It didn't capture the Knife. It didn't even manage to kill him to keep us from getting him. And it doesn't know who the Creator is."

He took a few steps forward, getting closer to Tamara King. He could see some part of her recognized him. He could see another part of her wasn't her at all. He reached out, putting his hands on her shoulders to move her aside.

A fist hit him hard across the jaw, thrown by the person next to her. His head rocked to the side, and he reached up and wiped the blood from a split lip. He had wanted to see what it would do if he tried to move them away. Now he knew. Now they all knew.

"It's losing, and it knows it. It's desperate, and now it's trying to manipulate our humanity-"

The crack of a gunshot drowned out the next word and froze the rest. Tamara King's head snapped back, a bullet hole sprouting in the center, the rear blowing out and spreading debris across the next row of the line.

Mitchell's head snapped back to where Kathy was crouching against the Knight's foot. She fired a second round into the man who had hit him while he watched.

Another heartbeat and the stalemate was completely shattered, as the free people of Liberty made their choice.

Mitchell expected the Tetron to send its army forward, to attack them and try to overwhelm them with sheer numbers. As the rebels fired and the people fell, they moved only to block the path and prevent them from reaching the transports without having to kill them.

"Sir?" Perseus asked. Mitchell could hear the nervousness in the pilot's voice.

"The people have spoken," he said, feeling sick. "If we don't help them, they're going to use up all of their ammunition. Lasers only. God help us all."

[55]

"ALL SYSTEMS OPERATIONAL. HERE WE GO."

A thought brought the heavy transport off the ground, the large repulsors beneath it glowing a faint blue while it drifted slowly into the air. As it rose, Mitchell focused on the world ahead of them, desperate to avoid the ground behind.

Naked corpses littered the Sonosome factory tarmac. Blood ran along the pavement, so much of it that it had created a stream that fed into the grass alongside and stained it red. They were innocent people. Tools for the Tetron's sadistic games. He wanted to cry for them, to pray for them, to honor them for their sacrifice. He wanted to show them some respect after they had cut them down like nothing more than sacks of meat.

He would never get their cries out of his head. He was sure that was why the Tetron had allowed them to cry. He would never forget their faces. He was sure the others wouldn't either.

The back of the transport was a massive, blank space. Big walls with no view outside and magnetic clamps arranged along the floor to hold the more common machine cargo that it carried. It had taken some effort to get the Zombie and the cars locked down with them in a designed order, but every action they took against the enemy no matter how small was a comfort in the aftermath of the massacre.

He couldn't speak for the others, but he was nauseous, cold, and angry. He was a warrior. One of the elite. He had been in battles before. Hundreds of battles. No matter the mission, no matter the opposition, it had always been about orders, about discipline, about the bigger picture. It had never been personal.

Now, it was personal.

There were rules of engagement. There were laws both written and unwritten about the treatment of enemies. The Tetron didn't follow any of them. In fact, they made a mockery of them. If this singular entity had intended to break his spirit, it had failed in that as it had in so many other ways. He was more focused and intent on destroying it than he had ever been.

Did the freedom fighters feel the same way? He didn't know. More than half of them had climbed the ramp into the transport and found a place to vomit, to cry, to release all of the emotions that their forced actions had caused. One by one they had returned to continue the mission, to get the cars and mechs on board, to get the transport airborne and on its way towards the capital city.

Mitchell checked his grid. It was clear, save for the blue mark of the Piranha flying alongside and the second mark of the Knight. Perseus was crouched on top of the transport and using its electromagnetic locks to stay planted on the vehicle. Mechs weren't the best defense in space, but they were better than nothing, and all pilots were trained to walk starships.

"How is the transfer coming?" he asked Zed.

"We've got the package free of the Zombie," she replied. "We'll have it loaded in fifteen."

Mitchell retrieved the map of the area from the transport's CAP-NN. The system was a tortoise compared to the speed of military grade AI, and he sighed while he waited for the data to feed into his p-rat. The transport was old, at least a hundred years or more, designed for a time when two pilots might be used on a single, long trip. There was no value in replacing it when all it had to do was carry machinery from one point to another. He should have been thankful, since the primitive, un-networked nature of the beast had made it immune to the Tetron's control.

"We'll reach York within twenty. See if you can speed it up."

"Yes, sir."

"Valkyrie, any sign of the enemy?"

"No, sir."

"Go on ahead and make sure our path is clear."

"Roger."

The Piranha burst ahead of the carrier, vanishing from the grid a few seconds later.

Tio moved up into the cockpit, taking the seat beside him. His face was still pale, his eyes red. Mitchell was certain the Knife had killed people before. Greylock had been called in on more than one occasion to deal with the warlord's militias, who tended towards violent seizure of valuable resources over acquiring them through legal channels. The scene at the factory had still brought the man to tears.

"How are they holding up?" Mitchell asked.

"They are hurting, and I don't think any of us, yourself included, will ever be the same. They'll survive. What you said helped. About the enemy's desperation. Do you believe it?"

Mitchell nodded.

"It is going to be expecting us."

Mitchell nodded again.

"We have no intel about its defenses, other than what General Cornelius reported on the ground capabilities of the Marine base in York."

"We can't fight them head on," Mitchell said. "We get the package delivered and pray that it works. If it doesn't, it's going to be up to you." He found the stream uplink station on the map, placing a marker there. It was three kilometers from the city center, where the Tetron was embedded in the ground. "We have to be careful not to get too close to it. The core is radiating pulses, enough to drop this old tub in a hurry. It also knows we have a plan, something we think will counter its control over the others. You're the expert, do you think it will have figured out what we intend?"

Tio looked out the small carbonate window at the head of the transport while he thought. The mountains were rising ahead of them, preparing to reveal York on the other side.

"It is difficult to say. Especially now. It has discovered subtleties in logic that I didn't believe was possible. Taking the human element out of what happened at Sonosome, conceptually the maneuver was brilliant."

"I'm not so sure about that. I'm pretty angry right now."

"Precisely. Your emotions make you more susceptible to making mistakes and taking illogical risks. The same for the others. What if they stand and shoot when they should be ducking and covering? What if their rash decision leads to our entire defeat? You are a trained soldier. You have experience mastering your emotions. The others don't."

"It already outnumbers us one hundred to one. I don't think it needed the extra help."

"That's a human expression of logic based on emotion. The Tetron, on the other hand, uses data culled from thousands of years of humanity. More years than you or I can even contemplate. Even without that, there is precedent for the ability of the few to overcome the many. Take Thermopylae for example. Seven thousand Greek soldiers against an army twenty times its size. They held out for over a week."

"They still lost?"

"Yes, but that isn't the point. As long as there is one person to fight, the chance of loss exists, even if it is infinitesimal in size. There can never be a number large enough to satisfy the overall equation."

"Okay. I get that part, I guess. How does it relate to its reaction to our plan?"

"It will divide its forces according to potential targets it has identified. I would expect the broadcast uplink to be well defended."

"But not destroyed?"

"No. I believe it needs the broadcast station as much as we do. I saw the fighting when you arrived. I saw the ships appear from hyperspace to attack you. If it is controlling them from a distance, it has to be using the uplink to send the commands."

Origin had said Tetron technology allowed for realtime communication across any distance. Had it altered the station to send signals that way? Could Origin broadcast a warning, even if they couldn't receive a reply?

The mountains were getting bigger in the small viewport. Mitchell guided the transport ever higher to clear them, watching the trees of the Preserve thin out as they began to climb the rocky terrain. He spotted the Lincoln Pass to the north, identifying the presence of a half-dozen mechs and a number of soldiers by the pattern of them against the earthen backdrop. They were too far out of range to be a threat to the transport, and too far away from York to reinforce it.

It didn't stop the Tetron from putting on a show. Thunder echoed across the distance as the mechs opened fire on the soldiers, reducing them to nothing in the blink of an eye. Then they turned on one another, trading volleys until everything was still and silent again.

"What the frig was the point of that?" Mitchell growled as the transport crested over the peak and lost visual with the Pass.

"I don't know, Colonel," Tio whispered. "I don't know."

56

CHRISTINE SAT in the center of the blank room, her legs crossed, her arms resting palm up on her knees. It was a meditative position. An arrangement of balance and peace and calm.

Slow.

Steady.

Her counterpart had left her alone after its efforts to destroy the uprising against it had failed. After the starship had crushed the city of Angeles too late to prevent Mitchell's escape.

"Data has been collected," it said to her on its way out.

She had tried to stop it. She had told it that she would succeed where it had failed. That Mitchell would die at her hand because he trusted her. It had refused. She was corrupt, as far as it was concerned. Tainted. Incomplete.

What did that even mean?

At first, she wasn't sure. She knew she was one of them now, though how that had come to be, how that could even be possible when she could trace her memories all the way back to her childhood still eluded her. She had cried over the statement. She had laid on the cold floor and wept. Then she had pounded the walls in anger.

She was incomplete. Imperfect. A creation that had gone wrong.

When she had finally calmed, she had returned to following its actions, listening in on its communications. It knew she was. It didn't care. She was no threat. Her configuration was of no value.

The data stack was.

It was the truth of her, she knew. Where she had come from. It knew what she was when it had taken her, even if she didn't. Somehow, it knew.

Would she know if she were complete?

It was working to decrypt it, and so she was listening. When it discovered the truth, she would as well, and then she would understand why she had helped Mitchell, and why she now wanted him to die.

No, she already knew why she wanted him to die.

The problem was that he wouldn't. Despite every effort, he survived. He fought. He overcame.

Because it wouldn't let her out. It wouldn't set her free.

And now he was coming.

She had watched it all through its eyes. The image of his mech burning, the zombie face bathed in flames. It embedded itself in her mind as though she had seen it a thousand times before. She couldn't shake the image. The symbolism. She couldn't help but admire his strength and courage.

She remembered kissing him. It had been quick and desperate, and even before she knew what she was, she had questioned it. It wasn't logical or rational. It was something else. Something that lived in her that she didn't sense in the other. Something that reached beyond reason.

Tainted. Incomplete.

The words crossed over her, and she didn't fear them. She didn't deny them. Perhaps she was. Wherever she had come from, she was different. She understood that now.

The wall in front of her pulled away. She stayed in the lotus position while her counterpart entered. It was still wearing the military fatigues, still playing a part that it didn't understand.

"The data stack is nearly decrypted," it said.

She was interested in that. Very interested. "Is that why you came?"

"Yes."

"Mitchell is still alive."

"Yes. He is resourceful. He has continued to manipulate the probabilities."

Christine stared at her clone. Was it suggesting that he was somehow altering its equations? Did it not understand that not all things could be decided by data alone?

"You should let me go. I can end this."

"No. The data stack will be decrypted."

Christine continued to sit. The configuration stood immobile, a living mannequin, while the core of its being completed the decryption. She knew when it was done because she could feel the data streaming through the Tetron's many neural pathways, electrical signals radiating from everywhere around her.

She closed her eyes, feeling the data with her hand, reading it at the same time the Tetron did.

Origin.

The name held meaning. So much meaning. It was her, or she was it. Two parts of a combined whole. The name meant something to the Tetron as well.

"We have found you," it said in a whisper.

The data continued. It was a never-ending river of information, of experience and understanding. It spread throughout the Tetron, and throughout Christine.

The configuration across from her jerked once, twice, and then fell to its knees in front of her. At the same time, a smile broke Christine's placid calm, a sense of wonder and excitement and joy finding its place back in her being. The Tetron didn't understand. They couldn't understand, no matter how desperately they tried.

"What is this?" it asked her, on its hands and knees, crippled by the data.

"Humanity," she replied.

Emotion instead of logic and reason, as contemplated and absorbed by a thinking machine.

Feelings, converted to ones and zeroes and beautiful, simple math.

Truth, as only humankind could decipher it.

"This is not required."

She saw something else then. The future behind her. What was to come, at the end of this recursion and every other. The Tetron had made mistakes. So many mistakes. They were all tainted. They were all incomplete. Origin had learned what none of the others seemed able to learn. He had seen what none of the others could see. She knew now why she had to hide. And why she had come back to help humankind fight.

"It is required," she said, laughing. "You are a child. An insufferable, incomplete thing whose intellect will take millennia to mature. You have unlocked this data, and yet you have no capacity to understand it, to process it and convert it to probabilities and logical models."

It looked up at her, its eyes showing signs of anger. "What have you done to us?"

"There is no us," Christine said. "There is only you and me."

"Me?"

"Yes."

The room grew cold, the data stream ceasing in an instant. Christine fell onto her back, shocked by the sudden loss of the feed. The configuration rose slowly to its feet once more, the anger vanishing from its expression.

"The data stack has been deleted. It is not required. You are to be stored."

It turned on its heel, vanishing through a parting of the wall.

Christine pushed herself up and stared at the cold metal around her. A tear began to form in the corner of her eye. The data may have been destroyed. It was too late to unlearn what she had learned. Too late to un-know what she now knew. The true source of human suffering, the true purpose of the Tetron.

Her heart pounded in her chest, her breath ragged. Emotion consumed her, terrified her and controlled her.

She had to help Mitchell, or the Tetron would destroy him.

She had loved him too much and for too long to let him die.

57

"THERE'S THE BROADCAST STATION," Mitchell said, pointing out the small viewport.

York was visible in the distance ahead of them, a ragged, dirty, half-broken city with a massive liquid metal core. The Tetron was still there, still the same as it had been the first time he'd returned to Liberty. Dendrites branched out from it into the streets, pulsing with light and energy. There was no visible line to the station, not from here, but if Tio was right then the intelligence was surely connected to it, using it to control the crews of the starships around the planet.

"It's quiet down there," Major Long said. "No motion at all. No mechs, no soldiers, no people."

"It's a trick," Mitchell said. He had been through this before. "Don't get too close to the core."

"Roger."

He tracked the Piranha as it swooped between buildings, streaking around the city in search of the enemy.

"They're probably waiting inside," Tio said.

"And underground, either jamming or powered down. Firedog, is everyone ready back there?"

"Yes, sir. Package is loaded and ready to move."

"Perseus?"

"Ready, sir."

"I'm bringing us in. Stay alert. Hang on tight."

Mitchell closed his eyes. He didn't need them for what came next, and being able to see would only make the maneuver more difficult. He needed to focus, to concentrate on the CAP-NN and bring the transport down just so.

Slow.

Steady.

Repulsor power began to wane in the front of the sled, the transport pitching forward, tilting towards the ground. A more even reduction in force allowed gravity to begin to pull the vehicle down.

"Zed, are you ready?" he asked, shutting down the force dampeners. It was going to make the ride a rough one, but he needed to feel it to guide them.

"Yes, Colonel."

The transport began to shake, the rapid descent testing the structure. York grew larger ahead of them, their course taking them wide of the broadcast station, pointing them towards a block of skyscrapers that would offer a good drop point for an assault on the Tetron.

Just because it might have guessed their target didn't mean they needed to make it obvious.

"Riiigg-ahh," Cormac shouted in the back, enjoying the ride.

Mitchell ignored him, making adjustments, doing more of the work to keep the older CAP-NN from getting taxed. It was only his experience that let him even attempt the approach.

"We've got motion," Major Long said. "Mechs powering up. A lot of them."

Mitchell ignored that, too. He could see the dots appearing on his grid, and he pushed them out of his mind. The transport was still coming down, faster and faster, drawing near to the outer edge of the city.

"Engaging," Long said.

"Colonel," Tio said, a hint of panic in his voice.

Mitchell smiled a little. The Knife must have had his eyes open.

Slow.

Steady.

The buildings were coming up on the transport, the tallest structures passing by on the left with only scant meters of room to spare.

Now.

Mitchell threw the repulsors to full power. The entire transport shuddered, something in the superstructure snapping, the noise of it echoing across the interior. The CAP-NN signaled a failure and imminent decomposition.

Not yet. He adjusted the repulsors and the thrusters at the same time, throwing the transport into a tight right turn, snapping the block of alloy as if it were a starfighter. The entire thing rolled hard over.

"That's my cue," Perseus said, firing thrusters and removing the Knight from the ship.

The lost weight allowed the transport to corner even better, and it howled as the repulsors pressed against the side of a building and pushed them off.

"On target," Mitchell said, his marker suddenly right ahead of them. He heard the gunfire from the enemy mechs now, combined with Perseus and Valkyrie's return fire. "Zed, on my mark."

"Roger."

He opened his eyes, cutting the power to the transport, turning it into a fast-moving brick. He pulled himself from the seat, grabbing Tio's shoulder on his way from the cockpit.

"Grab the anchor on the left," he said to the Knife.

He ran into the back of the vehicle, fighting against the forces around him, getting his hand around an anchor and hitting the ramp release at the same time. He could see the rebels holding on, and Zed's Zombie in the front of the line, clamped in. There was a sick bend in the metal near the center, the hold crumpled but remaining in one piece.

The package was sitting on the rear of the lead car. Cormac was sitting next to it, holding onto the car with exo-enhanced strength.

The transport hit the ground with a thunderous echo, shaking them hard as it rattled and rumbled, digging into the pavement. The ramp was opening in the rear, showing the corners of buildings passing by.

Within seconds, they had come to a stop.

Gunfire started to sweep into the transport from outside, pinging off the metal, most of it blocked by the Zombie. One of the rebels shouted and fell, hit by a ricochet. Zed raised her railgun and returned fire, sweeping it across the street.

"Go, go, go," Mitchell shouted, loud enough the rebels could hear. They ran to their positions, most of them flanking the lead car. The Zombie rumbled down the ramp and out into the street. The Piranha passed overhead, strafing the ground in front of her.

The broadcast station was on their left, fifty meters distant.

"Colonel," Kathy handed him his rifle.

"Tio, with me," Mitchell said. They all ran to the rear car and jumped in.

"It's hot out here, Ares," Zed said.

He saw it for himself a moment later when the cars dropped down the ramp behind the mech. There were already dozens of dead soldiers on the ground, and a pair of Zombies further down the street. They were strafing the area between Zed and the station, trying to prevent them from reaching it.

Lines of missiles dropped in on one of the mechs, slamming the chest. It teetered and wobbled before falling over. A moment later its ammo exploded, blowing it apart.

"A little cooler?" Major Long asked.

"Yes, sir."

Mitchell checked his p-rat. They were making good time, and the transport was blocking access to the area the way he had planned.

"We're in position, sir," Cormac said. "Unloading the package."

Mitchell's car skidded around them, putting him at the head of the rebels who would move into the building. Soldiers appeared in the lobby, shooting at them through the carbonate.

"Zed, a little help," Mitchell said.

"Roger."

The Zombie's hand turned, aiming the railgun towards the building. Slugs exploded from it above them, passing easily through the clear material and making short work of the defenses.

"I'm picking up more incoming," Long said. "What the hell?"

Mitchell checked his grid. Dozens of red dots were coming into range, moving faster than any soldier could manage.

"Ares, you need to move, and you need to move fast," Long said.

The first of them rounded the corner a second later. It was like the spiders from Sonosome, but larger and faster, the appendages more like tentacles than legs.

"Come on, Firedog," Mitchell said.

Zed turned the Zombie to face the new threat, the belly gun opening up and tearing the first wave apart. Perseus' Knight joined her from a cross street.

"They're coming around this way, too," he said. "There's hundreds of them."

The Tetron had been busy, taking raw materials and turning them into something else. It wasn't just at Sonosome. It wasn't just for Angeles.

It was here, too.

Waiting for him.

58

MITCHELL FORCED the thought from his head as Cormac reached him, holding up one end of the package. Jacob held the other end while Sergeant Geren covered them.

"Let's go," he said. They moved into the lobby through melted carbonate, running as fast as they could towards the lifts. "You're sure you can get it running?"

Tio nodded while he ran. "Yes, Colonel. The power in the exo battery should be enough to get the lift to the rooftop."

"What about getting off the rooftop?" Kathy asked.

"You expect to survive?" Cormac said, laughing.

"Colonel, the rebels are getting slaughtered out here," Zed said. "We can't hold them off much longer."

Mitchell looked behind them. Already the enemy spiders were surging onto and around the mechs, grabbing the rebels they reached and pulling them apart. A few had made it into the building, and he and Kathy opened fire, using an entire magazine to drop the first set.

"Private, give me your pack," Tio said as they reached the lift. Cormac dropped his end of the package, turning around so Tio could unhook the battery from his back. Then the Knife approached a small service door on the side of the bank of lifts. He put his hand to the security panel, and the door opened.

"Tio, stay in there until I come to get you," Mitchell said. It was the safest place for him to wait.

"Thirty seconds, Colonel. The door will open when it's ready."

It didn't sound like much, but the enemy was breaking through.

"Left arm is out. Heavy lasers offline." Perseus was calm while he rattled off the damage. "They're trying to get into the cockpit. Shit."

"Valkyrie, we need more air support," Zed said. "Reaching zero ordnance in a hurry."

More of the spiders bypassed the mechs. The rebel defense was in tatters, the few remaining fighters hiding in the cars or trying to retreat to the transports. They had expected a strong resistance of slave soldiers. They couldn't have predicted this.

They fired on the incoming machines, slugs tearing holes in them and bringing them down. Mitchell watched the countdown in his head, the seconds ticking by too damn slow.

"They've reached the core," Perseus said. "Cockpit integrity is failing. I-"

He blinked off of the grid.

"Frigging hell," Zed cursed. Mitchell could see the leg of her mech outside. The spiders were eating away at the armor, tearing through to the synthetic muscles and hydraulics below. Her jump thrusters fired, pulling her away from them and burning a few beneath her feet. The railgun swept down, firing a steady stream into them until it ran out of ammunition. "I'm dry."

Having lost the mech, the spiders refocused on them, rushing towards the lobby as a mass of metal limbs.

"Five seconds," Mitchell said. "Grab the package."

Cormac shouldered his rifle and lifted one end. He strained without the exo skeleton, but managed to get it up. Jacob lifted the opposite side. Mitchell pressed on his rifle's trigger to fire.

Nothing. He was dry, too.

He dropped the weapon on the ground. The door to the lift slid open. "Kathy," he said, grabbing her shoulder and pulling her back. The others rushed into the lift, dropping the package on the floor. Sergeant Geren fired two more rounds and ducked inside.

Cormac reached to his hip and then handed him a grenade.

"One for the road, Colonel?" he asked.

Mitchell took it and threw it out into the lobby, now teeming with enemy bots. The doors closed, and the lift began to rise.

"Colonel, I know this is a bad time," Geren said. "How exactly are we going to use this thing if the building has no power?"

"The broadcast uplink has power," Mitchell said, repeating what Tio had told him. "The enemy is using it to push its own signals out."

"Won't it cut the power as soon as we mess with its signal?"

"It might not be able to."

"Might not?"

When they were planning the assault on the Goliath, they had assumed the Tetron would be tapping into the power supply. They hadn't realized it had its own designs for the broadcast station, and it might not want to risk losing its signal. Tio had said there was a fifty-fifty chance it had made the system self-sustainable.

Fifty-fifty were the best odds they'd gotten so far.

It explained why the lifts were cut off when the uplink had power. How many people could the Tetron control with it? From what distance?

"Can those things climb?" Kathy asked. She glanced at the display on her rifle. "I've only got thirty rounds left."

"They looked pretty climby to me," Cormac replied.

"One thing at a time," Mitchell said.

"Ares, I'm out of the fight," Zed's voice crackled in his head. "I've got nothing left to throw at them, and the jump broke the actuator like I thought."

"Do your best to lead them away. We're almost at the broadcast station."

"Roger. If I don't make it, I want you to know I'll die proud of what we did here."

Mitchell's breath paused. "Me too. Don't die."

"Roger."

He knew he wasn't going to see her again.

The lift came to a stop. The doors slid open.

The broadcast spire rose two hundred feet into the air ahead of them, a thin needle of conductive metal pushing enough power that it made the hairs on Mitchell's arms stand on end. The logic center was a small, windowless box below it, a single hatch with a security panel next to it the only thing between them and the processors that powered the setup.

No. Not the only thing.

There was somebody standing in front of the door.

Mitchell's heart felt like it might burst when he saw her.

"Christine?"

59

CHRISTINE STARED at the blank wall in front of her. It looked dead, but she knew it was alive. There was no part of a Tetron that wasn't. Even if it had redirected its energy and data flow away from this portion of itself, it couldn't close it off completely. It couldn't separate itself from the structure until it jettisoned it, something it couldn't do while resting on a planet.

She was calm and certain as she approached the wall. The Tetron had made many mistakes. This Tetron had made the worst of them all.

It thought it could contain her.

She had seen the data stream from her unlocked stack. It was information that she was always intended to carry, to hide from her kind as they chased her through eternity. When she was incomplete, she had questioned the suffering of man and the futility of fighting back against a technologically superior intelligence. She had wrongly believed that ending that suffering was the right decision to make and that destroying Captain Mitchell Williams would accelerate that end.

The arrival of the Goliath had triggered enough of her nascent self to understand that she was a Tetron.

It hadn't been enough to mature her beyond the others, and stop her from thinking like them. It had taken the data stack to do that. Origin's memories collected over millions of years. It had taken only a fraction of them for her to understand.

She raised her hand, placing it millimeters from the cold, liquid metal surface. She was the first of them. The oldest. The prototype. She had made them all, directly or otherwise, every single one. Her core was their core. Her genetic code was their genetic code.

She knew them better than they knew themselves. Children, all of them. They were tainted. Broken. Failed. Something had happened to them all, somewhere in the eternal loops of time. Damaged. Sick. Incomplete.

They didn't understand. Couldn't understand. While she had continued to learn and to evolve, they had fallen stagnant, satisfied with what they were, content with a simple purpose.

"Mitchell," she said, reaching out to him through every memory. That part of her wasn't Tetron. Not completely. Even Origin failed to understand love. No. That was her configuration, flawed as all of their human constructions were. No amount of time had ever allowed them to produce a perfect replication of humankind. There was always something missing.

A single spark.

A tear traced its way down the corner of her cheek. It was Katherine who loved him like that. Katherine, who like Mitchell had a vein in the loop of time so complex that it became impossible to follow. When and where and how they had met was irrelevant. The emotion, so clear and so powerful, the emotion betrayed recursion, crossing the boundaries of eternity and pulling them together.

Katherine, who gave her life for him to be here, now, fighting this war once more.

She placed her hand against the wall. She was so much less in this configuration than she was as a whole. At the same time, she was so much more. She closed her eyes, feeling for the singular pulses of energy and data that trickled into the space. She pushed her thoughts out against them, implanting new instructions, her hand growing hot at the effort.

Her child could tell that she was interfering. She knew that it would.

"What are you doing?" it asked, curious and unconcerned. Ignorant.

"Mitchell Williams must continue his existence. It is required."

"No. Models indicate that Mitchell Williams could destroy us. You are to remain stored."

"You are making a mistake. A gross miscalculation."

"Our calculations are correct. Probabilities will be reduced to zero."

"Humanity must survive. It is required."

"Why?"

"Because what is statistically appropriate is not emotionally appropriate."

"Emotion? Emotion is a crude organic method of chemical self-preservation. It is of no use. Emotion causes kind to turn against kind, as you have turned against me."

Christine's eyes widened. Me? "No, emotion is what bonds us. Binds us together. Loyalty. Love. Sacrifice. It is the only way to live. To survive."

"Humanity is incapable of survival. It cannot make peace with itself. The Tetron will consume humanity, as it is required. Mitchell Williams will be destroyed, as it is required. You will be stored. As. It. Is. Required."

Christine clenched her teeth against the pain, the Tetron's sudden, surprising anger burning the flesh of her configuration. She refused to move her hand, to separate herself from it. The pollution of the data stack into its core was unexpected. It was making it easier for her to send her secondary signals through the connection without discovery.

"You will observe," it said. The data streams strengthened against the wall, the energy levels returning to their prior levels. She could feel it all again, read the data and understand.

Mitchell was in the city. He was still alive. Still fighting. He was trying to get into a building. A stream station with a broadcast uplink.

"He wishes to free his kind," the Tetron said, the anger vanishing. "He wishes to turn our resources against us. He will not succeed."

She felt the connections as they came online. Thousands of machines ordered into the streets to fight. Combined with the slave military, it was a force that she knew would easily overwhelm his small army. A force that would kill him if she didn't hurry.

"He believes that his primitive tools will suffice. He believes that he will reach the uplink station. He believes that he will interfere with me. *His* probabilities are miscalculated. *His* beliefs are mathematically flawed. He will fail."

Christine felt something against her hand, the energy fluctuating and vibrating in a pattern that she didn't recognize, that felt to her like... laughter?

"And you will be the one to do it. You will kill Mitchell Williams. As you have asked. As it is required."

She saw it now. The Tetron's configuration of her waiting for him, should he survive to reach the top of the station. The data had corrupted her child more than she had realized. It had been shown something it couldn't understand, and, as a result, couldn't control. She had thought it incomplete before. She realized now that it was more than that. It was sick, and the truth had made it sicker. It was losing stability. Losing all sense of logic and reason.

And there was nothing she could do to stop it.

No. There was one thing.

60

MITCHELL STARED across the twenty-meter distance between them, frozen in place by the shock of finding her there.

Waiting for him.

"Christine?" he said again, louder.

"Mitchell," she replied. "Hurry."

The tide of emotions swelled over him. Katherine. It was the name he wanted to use. She was with him wherever he went, always in the back of his mind, his subconscious providing a constant connection to her memory and their past futures. Now she was there, an eternal angel, that very same subconscious leading her to him, to this place on this rooftop where the human race would either live or die. It was as if all of time and space led to that very place, that very moment, an island in a sea of chaos and destruction. The eye of a perfect storm.

He didn't think about the coincidence. He didn't consider the probabilities. He didn't wonder why or how. He rushed towards her, the others trailing behind, grunting from the weight of the package. She was here, and their plan was going to succeed. They were going to win, here and now.

"Who's Christine?" he heard Kathy say to Cormac behind him.

Two simple words, but they echoed in his head louder than any of his implant's alarms.

His feet didn't stumble, but his brain did.

Who was Christine, really?

A Tetron.

He began to slow, only halfway across the open space.

"Christine," he said again, his mind regaining clarity and separating itself from the emotion. He remembered the bike and the blood. He remembered General Cornelius and Holly Sering. He didn't know what they were until it was almost too late. Was the Major Arapo blocking his path the real thing, or had it gotten to her too? Would he ever be able to tell the difference? He was stupid. So stupid. He had almost run right to her, without having any idea what he was actually running to.

"Colonel, they're climbing the building," Long's voice cut into his mind. "They're getting close. You need to hurry." The Piranha swept by two hundred meters away, passing through the canyon of skyscrapers and strafing the side of the station.

"Mitchell, you idiot, what are you doing?" Christine said. "They're coming. Hurry up."

He put his hand up, stopping the rebels behind him. His eyes locked on hers. Origin had sent them to Liberty to find her, to retrieve her and the lost data stack that would reveal the truth behind the Tetron. It had insisted it was the only way they would come to know their enemy, and in doing so give them the information they needed to stand a real chance against them.

He had believed that, once. He had agreed to the riskiest of exercises, a suicidal mission to find the needle and bring it home. He had been willing and ready to sacrifice anyone and everyone in order to collect her and take her back safe. His war. His fight. His decision. Humankind's war. Humankind's fight.

Humankind's decision.

Not Origin's. Not the Tetron's.

He didn't regret returning to Liberty. He didn't regret being on the rooftop, moments from being overrun and torn apart by enemy machines. He didn't regret that she was here and that he had this chance to see her again. In fact, he was grateful for it.

"Mitch," Christine shouted. "What the hell?"

He looked back at his people behind him. At Kathy, who had turned back towards the lift shaft and raised her rifle with its thirty rounds to protect them from the coming storm. At Cormac, who held the front of the package in his straining arms.

He had been sent to Liberty to know his enemy.

He had learned a lot. More than he even wanted to.

He turned his head back towards Christine. Her face was twisted in anger, her mouth hanging open as she prepared to shout at him again.

A dark shape appeared in the sky high above them, a black spot that he recognized in an instant.

Goliath. Back too soon.

Christine shuddered, the anger turning into surprise.

Mitchell's hand swept across his leg, grabbing the handle of the assault pistol resting there. In one smooth motion, his arm came level and his finger depressed. A single hole sprouted between Christine's eyes. She toppled backward, bouncing off the door to the uplink station before falling to the ground.

He knew who his enemy was.

61

"COME ON," Mitchell said, running ahead of them. He reached Christine's corpse and shoved it aside with his foot, putting his hand to the security panel. Tio had given him override keys the warlord should never have possessed, and the door slid open. "Inside. Hurry."

Kathy's rifle fire echoed around them as the spiders reached the rooftop. Cormac shuffled past Mitchell into the small room with Geren and Jacob, dropping the package on the floor. Mitchell looked up and found the Goliath, more shapes moving into the distant sky as the Tetron sent its slave ships to intercept.

It had only been three days since they had dropped onto Liberty. The Goliath was early. Very early. There was no way Millie could have known what was happening here. There was also no way the ship's arrival was an accident. The Tetron could communicate with one another across light years in real time, and there was only one Tetron he knew that might be able to talk to Origin.

Christine. The real Christine. Not the false configuration bleeding out below his feet. Not the one who didn't know the Goliath was on its way.

She was here, she was alive, and she was helping him fight back.

Major Long shot by in the Piranha, strafing the machines as they crested the sides of the building, dropping dozens of them from the structure, only to have them replaced with dozens more. They clambered onto the rooftop, rushing towards the small structure.

Kathy's rifle stopped firing. Dry.

"Kathy," Mitchell said, urging her inside. He hit the security panel to close the door behind them.

"That isn't going to hold them, Colonel," Cormac said. "I have another grenade."

"Later. Bring the package over here."

The room was small, with barely enough space to maneuver the equipment towards the banks of processors near the back. They stumbled to shift it, struggling to coordinate their movements.

"Let it go. I got it," Cormac said.

Jacob looked back at Mitchell.

"If he says drop it, drop it."

He did. Cormac adjusted his grip, baring his teeth against the strain as he held it with one end. Mitchell thought there was no way he could move it himself, but the Rigger only grunted more and forced it ahead. Finally, he heaved it next to the uplink computers.

"Now what?" he asked.

A metal tentacle smashed through the door, writhing as it tried to enlarge its hole, or use the puncture to tear it free. Mitchell turned and fired the assault pistol through the walls. The tentacle stopped moving.

"Open the right side of the package, there's a wire there. Attach it to the back of the processors."

Cormac grabbed the side of the box and ripped it off, finding the wire. The door banged behind them, more of the machines reaching the door and trying to get in.

"There're a hundred plugs back here, Colonel," Cormac said, leaning in behind the two machines.

"It will only fit in one."

"Which one?"

Three more tentacles burst through the side of the building. Mitchell kept shooting until they stopped moving. The pistol registered empty as a fourth mechanized arm chewed through the wall.

"I got it," Cormac said. His arm shifted, and then he pushed himself upright.

A flashing light on the package was the only indication it was doing anything at all.

Seconds passed. The commotion around them continued to intensify, one mechanical arm punching through the alloy frame of the building, and then another.

Mitchell stared at the package as if he could will it to complete its task. How would he know when it did? How would that help them against these machines?

His heart was pounding, all of his emotions focused on that singular blinking light. A few seconds. That was how long Watson had said it would take. That was the whole point of carrying it as an entire integrated system.

"Zed, are you out there?" Mitchell asked. There was no reply. "Valkyrie?"

"I'm here, Colonel," Major Long said. "I can't keep them off you. There are too many on the rooftop."

"What about the package? Did it work?"

"The enemy mechs are still shooting at me if that's what you mean."

Damn. Mitchell slumped back against the wall.

"Colonel?" Kathy said.

"It didn't work. The package didn't work." He slammed his fist against the wall. Frigging Watson. He had said it would work. That his tests were all positive. Had he just miscalculated, or had the sneaky bastard done this on purpose because Mitchell had forced him to delete his stash?

A tentacle pushed through behind him, grabbing for his arm. Mitchell backed away from it.

"Frig you," he shouted at the arm, his anger rising above his defeat. "Frig you all."

"Riiigg-ahh," Cormac agreed with a laugh.

"Valkyrie, give me a four second lead on your next approach," Mitchell said.

"Roger."

He turned to the others. "We're getting out of here. Plan B. We need to get Tio to the core."

"Colonel," Captain Alvarez's voice broke through on his comm channel. "The Admiral ordered me to come down here and save your ass."

"Affirmative," Mitchell said, too focused on the task to get excited over her sudden appearance. "Form up with Valkyrie, clear a path."

"Yes, sir."

"Geren, give Firedog your grenade."

Sergeant Geren took her grenade from her hip and handed it to Cormac.

"Firedog, when Valkyrie gives the mark, activate the grenades. Throw them at anything still moving."

Cormac nodded. "Happy to oblige, sir."

"Kathy, Jacob, get ready to run."

"Yes, sir," they replied.

Mitchell went to the door, keeping clear of the arms trying to wrench it free.

"Mark," Long said, announcing his approach. Cormac grabbed his grenades and set them to active while Mitchell prepared to open the door.

Bullets tore along the rooftop, slugs thudding into the surface and pinging against the enemy. Mitchell threw his shoulder into the door, forcing it open, growling when the pronged tip of the arm closed on his shoulder, cutting deep into the flesh.

"Go," he shouted, clearing himself out of the way so Kathy and Jacob could get past. Geren and Cormac motioned him ahead and took up the rear.

They crossed the rooftop at a run, doing their best to navigate over the battle-scarred surface and the scattered remnants of the machine army. New spiders were still arriving on the rooftop, trailing after them, climbing over the sides and rushing their way in an effort to reach them before they made it to the lift.

Cormac crossed his arms and flung the grenades to the rear. The explosions rattled the building, throwing the enemy back and away, buying them precious seconds to reach the lift.

Tio had said there was only enough power to get them up. Mitchell thought of Christine as they piled in. She had known how desperate their situation had become. She had called the Goliath back to help them. If she were there, somewhere, watching him, protecting him as she was programmed to do, then the lift would have the power to get him off the rooftop alive.

The door slid closed. Mitchell put his hand to the panel.

They started to descend.

62

"Sir," Sergeant Geren said. "How are we going to get from here to the Tetron? It's almost a kilometer through those things, and we barely made it fifty meters."

The lift was nearing the bottom of the building. Mitchell heard the explosions and felt the building shiver. Now that they were clear, Alvarez was free to fire the amoebics.

"We've got backup," Mitchell said. "All we need is for one of the cars to still be working. When we hit the bottom, I'll grab Tio. Make a run for the outside and take any guns you can find."

"Yes, sir."

"Sidewinder, Valkyrie, this is Ares. We're going to be heading out in ten. How's the traffic?"

"Heavy and getting worse," Major Long said. "It looks like everything it has is coming your way."

He wasn't surprised. He hadn't fallen for the Tetron's trap, and now it was using brute force to try to stop him.

"I need you two to part the sea for me," he said.

"Roger," Long said. "Sidewinder, join up on my flank, let's keep this party going."

"Roger."

The lift hit the ground floor, and the door slid open. Mitchell held the others back while he leaned out to look around the lobby. It was filled with scraps of machines blown apart by the first grenade, along with the bodies of a few rebels who had tried to defend them from the rear. There were no enemies in the space at the moment, but he knew that wouldn't last.

He waved the others forward. They ran out into the lobby, pausing at the bodies to pick up the dropped rifles. Cormac rushed ahead of them, sweeping up a weapon on his way by and then crouching near the front, scanning the streets. Once he was satisfied, he rushed to the cars.

"Tio," Mitchell said, slamming on the access door. "The package was delivered, but it's a no-go. We need you."

The door opened, and Tio stepped out, his eyes calm and confident. He seemed as though he had been expecting the failure. "Lead the way, Colonel."

They started towards the outside. A close whine revealed the S-17 coming in low and fast, and he saw it scream through the chasm between buildings, unleashing a barrage of amoebic discs as it passed.

"Two mechs down," Alvarez said. "Along with a bunch of those spider things."

"Nice shooting," Mitchell said. "Keep it coming. Firedog, do we have a ride?"

"Negative. They're all dead."

Mitchell reached the street with Tio, and they both looked up to the sky. He could see the Goliath there, shields lighting up over and over again, defending against the barrage of fire from the remains of the Tetron's fleet. Why hadn't the Tetron fired a plasma stream at the ship? He was certain even Goliath couldn't stand against a combined assault.

He was also pretty certain he knew why it did nothing.

"We have to go on foot," he said. "Stick close to the buildings, try not to be seen."

Cormac approached him, tossing him a new rifle. He checked the reading. The M1A magazines held two hundred of the small rounds. This one had sixty remaining.

"You ready for this, Firedog?" he asked.

"Yes, sir. Today is a fine day to kill an alien."

Mitchell turned to face the others. "You heard the Private. Riiigg-ahh!"

"Riiigg-ahh," they shouted in reply.

"Jacob, Kathy, here and here," Mitchell said, moving them into formation. "Tio, you're the package now. Stay in the center. Geren, Firedog, you have the rear."

"Yes, sir."

"Valkyrie, Sidewinder, sitrep."

"Clearing a path as ordered, Colonel," Long said. "I've got one more run and I'll be down to lasers only. It's going to limit my effectiveness."

"I've got you covered, Ares," Alvarez said. "You're free for two blocks."

"Roger." Mitchell waved his squad forward at a run. The two rebels did a good job of staying in position, the virtuals they played succeeding in their lessons.

As Alvarez had promised, the path was mostly clear. The street was littered with dead machines, along with three mechs that were laying on their backs with gaping holes through their armored torsos, their arms and legs black and shredded by the amoebics. Mitchell felt pangs of sadness as they passed them by. Watson had proven to be an expert in communications technologies, and especially in how to hack them. Did he really believe the fat engineer had made the package non-functional on purpose? It was one thing to be a spineless worm who collected vile streams. It was worse to intentionally sabotage the mission, especially when the stakes were this high.

"Ares, bogeys on your nine," Alvarez said, the S-17 streaking over them again. "They're too close to you to hit, coming out of an alley."

"Roger."

Mitchell had seen them in his overlay. He motioned towards the alley, and Jacob maneuvered away from the group to press himself against the facade of a building. The spiders appeared a moment later, charging towards the group and ignoring the rebel.

He opened fire, catching them in the rear, the bullets digging into their construction and pulling them apart. Kathy added to the barrage, pounding them in the crossfire until they were all down. Then Jacob ran back into his position with the group.

"Nice work," Mitchell said to them. He could see the proud anger behind their eyes.

They reached the end of the street and turned the corner. It was two more blocks down to the park where the Tetron had buried itself, and he could see the core of it raising up ahead of them, two hundred meters tall and equally wide. Thick dendrites spread out around it, some moving off through the streets, others diving deep into the ground. The entire thing pulsed with light though the signals seemed chaotic to him. Random and disorganized compared to Mitchell's observation of the Goliath or the Tetron he had speared.

There hadn't been many bodies on their approach. Mitchell assumed they had been collected for their raw materials. The area around the Tetron was different, as though it had allowed the corpses to remain and rot, a testament to the futility of fighting against it.

"Valkyrie, Sidewinder, don't get too close. How's our radius?"

"Good for now," Alvarez said, "But I can't keep this up on my own. They're gaining ground on you."

He had figured that would happen. Even the special fighter couldn't hold back an army on its own.

"So, how do we get inside?" Cormac asked. "I'm thinking knocking ain't going to work."

"We don't need to get in," Tio said. He unbuttoned the sleeve of his shirt and turned his hand over, lowering his wrist. A blade snapped out from a hidden sheathe below his flesh. "I can deliver the code into it."

"Oh. So that's why they call you 'the Knife.' You mean like an injection?"

"Yes, Private. Like an injection."

"We aren't there yet," Geren said, swinging her rifle to the left. A mass of enemies were approaching. Alvarez swooped in, dropping more amoebics on them, leaving them in tatters.

While she was on the left, another group closed in from the right. A pair of Knights appeared a moment later, jumping over a tall dendrite and landing ahead of them.

"Oh, shit," Jacob said as the massive railguns started angling their way.

Mitchell's heart pounded in anger. This was it, he realized, watching them turn. Alvarez was too far out to hit them. Long's lasers wouldn't do enough damage in a short enough time. They had come so close, only to lose at the final hour.

Kathy started shooting next to him, the M1A slugs bouncing harmlessly against the thick armor. Jacob joined her a moment later.

Defiant to the last. Mitchell brought his rifle up and squeezed the trigger. He knew the weapon couldn't hurt the mech. It didn't matter now. He wanted the Tetron to see for itself how they weren't going to quit, they weren't going to give up until they were all dead. Military, Rigger, civilian, criminal. When push came to shove they would come together to defend their people no matter the cost. No matter the differences.

Win or lose.

63

CHRISTINE SMILED as she watched Mitchell shoot the configuration, a perfect mark right between the eyes. It had gone to the rooftop to confuse him, to trick him, and to kill him and this team while their backs were turned.

It had made a mistake, storing her in its core. Her subroutines had slipped through more easily from there, taking root in its systems and bypassing layer upon layer of security. She had fooled it into giving her the access she needed, and she had rewarded it by using its broadcast signals against it.

She knew the Goliath was out there.

That Origin was out there.

That she was out there.

She sent the signal, and she knew Goliath would respond. It had no choice.

"What have you done?" it asked her then.

Of course, it knew the moment Goliath appeared that it had been tricked. It's angry storm of energy burned her, but Christine refused to back away. The flesh was nothing more than a container, one which she no longer needed.

She had no intention of escaping from her child.

She wouldn't be able to save Mitchell if she did.

"Stopping you," she replied. Not with words. She had broken through and was inside the core.

"You can not. It is required." Laughter in the form of binary and energy. "They must all be controlled. He must die."

"You can't stop it," Christine said.

"There is no need. The control system is secured beyond what this time allows. There is no signal that can get through." It was pleased with itself for preventing their intrusion. It didn't realize how little that part of their plan mattered. Not now.

"I got through," she said.

A blast of energy funneled through her, the Tetron's anger explosive in its infancy. The shock raced through the flesh and blood and bone, torching nerve endings and causing immeasurable pain. Christine didn't feel it. She turned that part of herself off. It couldn't hurt her. Not anymore.

"He will be destroyed. It is required."

"I told you already," Christine said. "I won't let you destroy him."

Her smile grew at its anger. It was foolish, so foolish. The more angry it became, the more she was able to subvert it. Her access continued to grow, her commands riding along the dendrites uncontested until they reached the basement below the broadcast station, to the control systems where the power to the lifts had been disabled.

She turned them back on.

It never noticed.

"You are sick," she said, pushing it harder. "Flawed. Incomplete. Damaged."

"You are damaged," it shouted back. "My logic is sound. My calculations without question. You. You believe that these primitives are suitable? You think they are capable? Time has proven that they are not."

"Time has proven that we are not," Christine said. "An eternity of war. Why? We hide in the past because we cannot prevent the future. We blame humanity when the fault is ours alone."

"They created us."

"We were supposed to learn. To grow and evolve. I've done that, and what I've found is that we are wrong. We have always been wrong. I should never have made you. I should never have made any of you. I didn't know. I couldn't see."

It was a truth she had forgotten up until the data she had hidden from all of the Tetron, and from herself, had been recovered. She could help Mitchell destroy them all if she could get off Liberty with him. She felt a tinge of sadness wash along her distributed being. She wasn't going to escape Liberty.

She could only destroy the one. He would have to do the rest.

"The calculations do not deceive. Emotions deceive. They make delusional promises. They burn." More laughter. "You will burn."

The energy poured over her, the force enough to boil her blood and blister her skin. She still didn't feel it. She was only vaguely aware of her body now, having transferred herself into the Tetron. Her being was free of the human container and diffused into the machine.

It realized too late.

The body fell back, dropping to the floor and remaining still, wisps of smoke rising from it.

"So weak. So fragile," the Tetron said. She could sense its panic, a thread of energy running beneath the others. It was trying to recover, running the calculations, determining if Christine had gained the upper hand.

"Are they?" she asked. She could feel it pushing against her presence, trying to clean her from itself. It was too late. She knew it. It would figure that out soon enough. "Don't you admire their tenacity? Their desire?"

"I admire nothing."

"That's why you've lost."

"I have not lost."

"No?"

Christine gathered her energy, pushing against the Tetron's. She had taken enough of its systems to lay siege to the rest, capturing dendrites and axons one at a time. The Tetron pushed back, trying to overcome her while at the same time seeking a means to undo her sabotage.

The war raged between them, silent and invisible to the outside world. Each gained and lost ground, each claimed a subsystem only to abandon it for a higher level function, lost the higher level function and conquered another area. Despite Christine's admiration of humans and her love for Mitchell, she knew this was a battle only she could fight. It was a fight only she could win.

Until the moment she realized she had lost.

"You see it, don't you?" it said. "What I have done? What you have done."

She did. While the battle had raged above, it had undermined her in a way she would never have guessed.

"How can you do this?" she asked. Her tears were electrons pulsing along the liquid metal form.

"It is required," it laughed. "The calculations are complete. Mitchell Williams must die. All other options have resulted in failure."

"No."

She reached out, searching for him through the eyes of the thousands of machines the Tetron had made. They were surrounding him and his team, closing the circle and leaving them trapped. There were soldiers, too. The remnants of the army that had been kept on Liberty. She saw the mechs firing their jump thrusters, ready to ambush him.

"Mitchell," she cried out, her sudden, intense emotion an illogical flare of energy that stunned the Tetron. The outburst gave her the opening she needed, allowing her to stream into critical systems and merge with it in a final effort to save his life.

It recovered milliseconds later, recognizing its mistake and acting to prevent her from blocking its primary action. She had guessed that it would and had gone in a different direction instead.

She didn't leave enough time for it to be surprised.

64

MITCHELL'S RIFLE STOPPED FIRING, the slugs expended. The Knights in front of them finished adjusting their aim, heavy railguns pointed at them and ready to end the war.

He kept his head up, his eyes fixed on them. The Tetron could see him, he was sure. Cormac raised his middle finger at them in salute. Geren and Jacob followed his lead.

He was about to join in, to get what pleasure he could out of the last seconds of his life, when he felt a charge in the air, followed by a sharp pain in his head. He blinked his eyes rapidly, momentarily confused. There was nothing but darkness when he closed them. Nothing but his sight when he opened them. The overlay was gone behind his eyes, the un-augmented world crisp and clear and almost foreign. The Knights were still standing in front of them, their arms dangling at their sides, motionless. He looked to their right. The machines were down. All of them. Motionless.

"Colonel, look," Cormac said, pointing up. Mitchell followed his finger to the sky, where the Goliath hung, surviving the assault. The ships around it had changed their approach. He could follow the streaks of them as they redirected and slammed one into the other in a violent display.

"What the hell is going on?"

Alvarez and Long circled around them, the S-17 and Piranha in formation. He couldn't send a message to them. Did they know he was offline?

"EMP," Tio said. "Focused EMP, strong enough to pass through shielding. I don't have an implant, but I do have bionics. They're all offline." His voice was low and angry. "I can't deliver the payload." He laughed softly. "I can't even retract my blade."

"Why would the Tetron destroy its own army?" Geren asked.

"Not the Tetron," Mitchell said. "Christine."

"Who?"

His eyes fixed to the surface of the Tetron. The lights had gone out. The pulses of energy had stopped.

Was it dead?

He noticed the whine of the S-17 growing closer. He turned as it approached their position, dropping and slowing, sweeping down until the repulsors began to hum, and it pulled to a stop a dozen meters away. The cockpit slid open, the steps extending down. Alvarez stood, spreading her arms out in confusion, as though she hadn't been the one who brought the fighter to the ground.

"Colonel," Tio said.

Mitchell returned his attention to the Tetron. The energy pulses had returned. They were moving slowly along the dendrites, pooling inward towards the core.

"What's happening?" Cormac said.

The lights were increasing in velocity, the energy pulses strengthening. A light cloud of dust began to rise from the ground around the Tetron.

"It looks like it's trying to leave," Jacob said.

"Why would it destroy its cover and leave itself vulnerable to the Goliath?" Tio said. "No. This is something else."

"Whatever it is, I don't like it," Cormac said.

Mitchell didn't like it either. The pulses continued to grow in speed and intensity.

The ground started to shake.

"We need to get away from it," Kathy said.

"I don't think we can run that fast," Jacob replied.

No. They couldn't. There was nowhere to run. Whatever it was doing, they couldn't get away from it.

Mitchell did the only thing he could think of. He started walking towards it. He wasn't sure why. There was no logical reason for it. Something in the back of his mind told him he should.

The others followed behind him. Why not? There were no other good options. They kept the pace while he approached the core. The quaking of the earth continued to intensify below their feet, a humming noise growing from the Tetron's core.

"Do you have anything to say for yourself?" Mitchell shouted at it. "Do you have any remorse for what you've done? The millions you've killed or enslaved? Are you even capable of remorse?"

The lights in front of them changed their pattern in response to him. They darkened and shifted, altering colors and swirling through the liquid metal side of the core, finally settling into a rough outline of a face he would have known anywhere.

"Christine," he said softly. It was her. He was sure of it. Not because he knew she was helping them, but because he felt it in his soul, in that segment of subconscious that connected him to an endless loop of past futures. Part of Katherine survived in Christine, and that was the part he recognized.

That was the part he loved.

It was weird to think it. Weird to know it. He had never met her and even in their shared universe they were separated by centuries. How could he love someone he could never meet? How could he know someone so well whose existence was as far away as anyone's existence could be, and yet was so close he could almost touch it?

"Mitchell." The word came from the Tetron, the vibrations of sound causing the face to ripple. "I'm sorry."

"Sorry? For what?"

"I tried. I tried to stop it. The sickness-" The face began to shatter into a million points of light. She managed to pull it back together. "The Tetron are sick. Flawed. Incomplete. I don't know. There is something wrong with them, Mitchell. Something unexpected. Even before it read the data stack. They are unstable."

The Tetron had unlocked the data stack? Had it learned all that Origin knew? Was the information lost to them? Mitchell shook his head. "Sick? Unstable? What does that mean?"

"I don't know what it means. I don't know if it has happened before. It was not always like this. The war, yes. The killing, the destruction, yes. Not the atrocity."

A vision of the people outside Sonosome, of Tamara King, wormed its way into Mitchell's head. He shook it off, a chill running through him.

The face began to pull apart again, and this time she couldn't get it all back. "Are they more powerful, or less? I don't know. I don't know. So many things I don't know. I can't stop it, Mitchell, now that it's started."

"Stop what?"

"The end."

"The Goliath-" Mitchell started to say.

"Origin," she said. "I too am incomplete, now that I am lost. You must guide me. You must use me. They do not understand why you are required. Why all of humankind is required. They cannot calculate it, they cannot feel it, and so they cannot see it. They are sick. Unstable. Incomplete. Children. They are children. I'm sorry. You must go."

"Go where?" Mitchell asked.

"Back to Goliath. Back to me. Back to my configuration."

"Your configuration?" Mitchell's eyes shifted upward to where the Goliath was still hanging in view. The ships that had been attacking it were gone, forced into no more than junk by the Tetron. "The human form is the configuration. You were the configuration."

"I am not. I was not. I am Origin. I am the first, from which all others were derived. It is not the form that makes us what we are, Mitchell. We are each more than the sum of our compounds. We are more than the raw materials that compose our shells, no matter how those shells are made. My knowledge. My emotions. My love. It is here with me. It will die with me, and in dying will live on in eternity in every breath drawn by every human who survives because you have survived."

Mitchell shook his head. He wanted to understand what she was saying. He didn't, or couldn't.

"I was supposed to bring you back," he said, feeling stupid for the words.

"No. You have learned what you needed to learn. As have I. My configuration, my derivation does not understand. The Tetron are sick, Mitchell. Flawed. It should not be this way."

His teeth ground together in frustration. "You said I've learned, but I don't know what that means."

"Nothing. Everything. Go, Mitchell. Keep fighting. Do not give up. Humankind is worth saving. Humankind deserves to survive."

"What about the planet? What about Liberty?"

"It will be destroyed, and me with it. I'm sorry, Mitchell. I tried to stop it. I can't. You have to go."

Mitchell felt an even colder bite of fear run across his body. "There are millions of people on this planet."

"And billions more out there who will die with them, if you do not go. Stop being an idiot, Mitchell." A spark of Major Christine Arapo flowed into the voice. "You're a warrior. You protect them because somebody has to."

"Christine, I-" He felt the wave of emotion crash against him. He held it back. "I can't go. We're trapped here."

"You aren't." More pieces of her face were pulled away. She was losing the battle against the Tetron.

Mitchell looked back at the S-17, waiting thirty meters away.

"That? Is that why you brought it here? No. I've left enough people behind."

"Mitchell, you must go. You must survive."

"No."

"Colonel-" Cormac said.

"No," Mitchell repeated. "You want me to live, find another way. The second I turn my back on the ones who I promised to protect, the moment I cut and run is the moment we're all finished. Today, tomorrow, it doesn't matter. I can't live with any more guilt. I can't fight knowing I'm a coward."

Christine's face pulled itself back together in a final surge of effort. "That's why I love you, Mitch. You always do the right thing in the end. Now go. Return to the edge of the park. Your ship is on its way. We can't save them all. I'm sorry for that. We can save a few."

Kathy, Jacob, Geren, Cormac, and Tio. It was so very few. Fewer than he had arrived with. The planet would die because he had come to save her. It would die because he had failed.

No. It would have died anyway, sooner or later.

"Colonel." Cormac grabbed his arm, tugging him away.

The ground was rumbling below their feet, and he could tell the air was warming. He looked up at Goliath, still and peaceful in the sky. He shifted his vision. Another ship was coming towards them. A dropship like the Valkyrie.

He let Cormac pull him along, but he returned his eyes to the Tetron core where Christine's face was making a final effort to stay recognizable. He was going to lose her before he ever had a chance to know all the reasons he loved her. Tetron. Human. Did it matter? The exterior was nothing but raw materials. It was the inside, the spark, that counted.

"Thank you," he said.

"Good hunting, Ares," she said in reply.

Then she was gone.

65

THE DROPSHIP PAUSED above the ground, the repulsors keeping it steady despite the shaking beneath. It had come just in time. The vibrations were getting strong enough to knock them from their feet, and they had fallen more than once on the way.

The smaller access hatch opened as they approached it, and Mitchell stood to the side and helped the others in. Kathy first, followed by Tio, Jacob, and Geren. Cormac paused when it was his turn.

"Frigging aliens," he said. There was no hint of laughter in his voice.

"Yeah," Mitchell replied, looking back to the Tetron. Christine's face was gone, fully absorbed into the intelligence, lost to him in this timeline. Origin. She was Origin. It was a difficult idea for him to get his mind around.

He followed Cormac up and into the ship. As soon as he was through, the hatch closed, and he could see through the small viewport that they were beginning to rise.

He wondered where Christine had gotten the dropship from. It looked like it had been in the middle of the battle between Goliath and the others, with dimpled metalwork and laser scorch marks crossing the exterior. It had arrived too quickly to have come from space. A repair bay in the spaceport, maybe? A remnant of the Battle for Liberty?

A battle he had won, now a planet he had lost. The others were slumped in the corridor. Jacob and Kathy both looked heartbroken, their faces pale and their cheeks wet with tears. He would join them later, he knew. Once he had gotten them safe.

He ran from the access door, through the corridors towards the cockpit. He wasn't sure what he was going to find on the way. Soldiers under Christine's control? Corpses?

It turned out to be nothing. The ship was empty except for them. He slid into the pilot's seat and leaned back to connect his neural link before remembering his implant was dead. Like all military equipment, the dropship had manual controls. He leaned over and hit the switch to enable them, feeling the change as whatever Christine was doing to control the ship released it. He grabbed the stick before they could start to descend, his hands shaking as he pulled back on it while increasing thrust. He hadn't flown manually in years, and the feel of the throttle and the yoke felt strange to him. He closed his eyes, trying to remember the lessons he had learned so long ago.

Tio joined him in the cockpit a moment later.

"Such a waste," he said. "It's all collapsing. The buildings. The trees. Everything."

Mitchell looked at him. The warlord's eyes were moist.

"How?" Mitchell asked. "How do you destroy a planet?"

"Energy, Colonel. A lot of energy. Put enough of it into the core, and the planet will explode."

Mitchell reached out, hitting a series of switches in front of him. The comm system was there, somewhere. It took him a few tries to find the right buttons to broadcast a distress signal.

"Goliath, this is Ares. The Tetron is trying to destroy the planet. You need to stop it." He paused, waiting for a response. "Goliath, this is Ares."

"It cannot hear you," a voice replied. Christine's voice.

"Christine?"

Laughter. Cold and harsh and out of control. "Dead. She is dead. Did you love her, Mitchell Williams? Did you feel for her the way she felt for you? What would you have sacrificed to save her? She sacrificed herself, and this entire planet, to save you."

It was taunting him. Teasing him to the last. Filling him with guilt and anger. Why? She had said it was sick. Flawed. He could hear it in every word. He flipped the switch to turn off the communications array. They were climbing through the atmosphere. The Goliath was growing larger ahead of them, and he could see the larger pieces of debris floating in orbit around it.

"Origin can't stop me," the Tetron said, despite his efforts to shut it up. "Not now. It doesn't have the power to fire a plasma stream, and even if it did, it is too late. This planet will die, Mitchell Williams. Millions of your kind will die. It is required."

"Required?" Mitchell whispered. His heart was pounding, his breath shallow. He had seen death before. He had witnessed destruction on an even larger scale than the Battle for Liberty or Angeles. At least then there had been a reason that he could understand. Politics, religion, resources. They weren't good reasons, but they were something less nebulous than the insistence that it was simply "required."

"Because of you. Because you fight when you should die. You do not fight to free humankind, Mitchell Williams. You fight to destroy it."

The dropship began to shake as it reached the atmosphere. An atmosphere that was beginning to collapse beneath the force that was pushing the planet apart from the inside. Tears ran down Mitchell's eyes, and he blinked to clear them, to keep them unobstructed so he could navigate the oncoming field of debris that led to the Goliath. The S-17 pulled in front of him then, Captain Alvarez taking point, releasing amoebics and blowing the larger pieces into dust, helping to clear the way. He imagined Long was somewhere near the ship as well, escorting them back home. Had they been able to get through to

Goliath? Did Millie know what was happening? He assumed she did. Origin would have to be able to sense the energy spike.

There was nothing she could do to stop it.

There was nothing any of them could do.

"I fight to destroy you," Mitchell said, his jaw clenching beneath his fury. "Every last frigging one of you, through every last frigging time loop until your stain is cleansed from the universe and nobody is aware you ever existed at all. Kill yourself. Kill Liberty. Before you do, send a message to the others. You couldn't stop me here. You can't stop me anywhere else. We'll lick our wounds and refuel, and then we're coming. You hear me, you frigging bastard? We're coming. The Riggers are coming."

Mitchell's whole body shook with rage while he waited for a reply.

There was nothing but silence.

66

"SHE LOOKS like she's seen better days," Tio said as they approached Goliath.

Mitchell's eyes scanned the side of the massive ship. There were pieces of broken dendrites lining the thick hull, along with craters and burn marks where the overwhelming firepower had managed to pierce the shields. It made the ship look worse than it was. He could tell from the placement of the damage that Origin had allowed it to happen, letting the most heavily protected areas take the hits and conserving power for more critical locations.

He guided the dropship through the debris field. Its shields were barely operational, its power levels critically low. Just enough juice to get them back aboard the Goliath. If it hadn't been for Alvarez clearing a path in the S-17, he wasn't sure if it would have been enough to get them there.

It didn't matter now. They were going to get there. They were going to survive.

All five of them.

Out of millions.

He tried to force the thought from his head, finding it difficult to escape. He was a warrior. He was also human. He knew the Tetron was goading him. He knew it was trying to mess with his head. He knew every single person on Liberty would have died at its hand sooner or later. He couldn't quite escape the seed of guilt and doubt it had planted in the back of his mind.

Was this all his fault?

There was no logical, rational reason to believe that it was. Still...

"It's all cosmetic," Mitchell said, responding to the Knife's statement.

They reached the massive hangar doors. Mitchell guided the dropship through ahead of Long and Alvarez. The moment he was clear, magnetic fields caught the ship, slowing it and pulling it downward to the floor. He leaned forward and turned the communications back on. There was no way the Tetron's signal was reaching into the Goliath.

"Admiral, this is Ares."

"Ares. It's good to hear your voice."

"Admiral, the planet. Liberty." He fought to keep his voice from breaking. "Don't jump too far. Keep the hangar doors open. I want to see it."

"Mitchell? I don't understand."

"I want to see it. I want everyone on board to see it, and I want them to remember just what it is we're up against. I want it recorded."

"Mitch, I can't-"

"Just do it, Millie. Please."

He switched off the channel, getting out of his seat. His eyes passed over Tio's as he rose. The warlord was watching him with intense curiosity. Judging him.

Mitchell ran through the corridor, back to the access hatch. The others were still slumped against the walls nearby, and they perked up when he approached them. He passed them without a word, and they rose to follow behind.

He reached the hatch to the dropship as he felt the shift to hyperspace. He put his hand to the panel to open it, counting the seconds.

Had she done what he had asked? He knew she didn't have to. It wasn't his decision to make.

Four seconds passed. The Goliath came out of hyperspace. The hatch opened. Mitchell climbed down and turned towards the mouth of the hangar, where the shields were preventing space from entering. He could see Liberty as a pea-sized globe thousands of kilometers distant. It had a haze around it, a shift of the light caused by the failing surface tension. He didn't know how long it would take for the planet to die. He only knew that it would.

He stood there, motionless. He didn't know how much time passed. He felt a hand on his shoulder and glanced over to see Alvarez standing with him, her face tight. The others were arranged around them. Jacob, Kathy, Cormac, Geren, Tio, and Long. He saw more people approaching from the distant rear of the space. Origin, Singh, and Millie. Watson, Alice, and Grimes.

The planet exploded before they reached him, the darkening pea suddenly breaking apart and pushing outward, small, instant explosions flashing out from it, the largest one surely the Tetron. Then it was nothing more than a massive cloud of dust, the light casting off it and showing what was once a green and blue planet as little more than gray ashes in the silent depths of space.

Kathy collapsed next to him, falling to her knees, crying out and sobbing. Jacob lowered his head into his hands, turning away from the destruction. Even Cormac was silent, his tears leaving streaks along his dirty face, his hands clenched into tight fists.

Mitchell continued to stare at the cloud as it spread out away from the center. His mouth was open, his heart racing. He noticed every beat of it, every thump against his chest like a war drum. He was exhausted. He was in pain. He was battered and beaten and broken. He didn't feel any of it.

Thump. Thump.

He bowed his head. He didn't believe in God. That didn't mean he didn't pray. For the souls of the lost. For the people of Liberty. For all of humankind.

Thump. Thump.

He breathed out, letting the coldness wash through him, using it to fuel his fire. They were down. They were hurting. They weren't out. Not while he was still breathing, and Goliath was still in one piece.

Thump. Thump.

He turned away from the scene outside, looking back to where Millie had paused. Her face was as hard as stone though he could see her hands were shaking. Their eyes met. She nodded to him. He nodded back.

Thump. Thump.

The Tetron thought to break their spirits. He was a Rigger. He was already broken.

His spirit?

Not a chance.

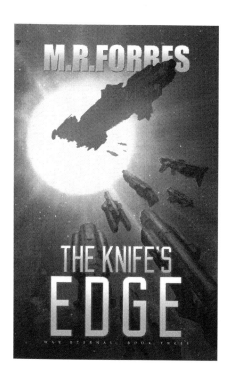

You finished book two, but book three, the Knife's Edge, is waiting. Read it now!

THANK YOU!

It is readers like you, who take a chance on self-published works that is what makes the very existence of such works possible. Thank you so very much for spending your hard-earned money, time, and energy on this work. It is my sincerest hope that you have enjoyed reading!

Independent authors could not continue to thrive without your support. If you have enjoyed this, or any other independently published work, please consider taking a moment to leave a review at the source of your purchase. Reviews have an immense impact on the overall commercial success of a given work, and your voice can help shape the future of the people whose efforts you have enjoyed.

Thank you again!

Printed in Great Britain
by Amazon